"About that kiss last

Max leaned forward curiou what it's always like to kiss you?"

"I wouldn't know. I've never kissed myself."

"*Something* happened when you kissed me, Lissa."

"You mean the earth moved under your feet?" she joked.

He frowned across the table at her. "I'm serious."

She really wished he would drop the line of questioning, but she sensed there wasn't a chance in hell he would do that. Instead she asked a shade shortly, "Describe *something.*"

"It was like my imagination went crazy. I saw all kinds of images and felt all kinds of feelings. But it all happened in, like, a millisecond."

She swore under her breath. Did he have a gift of his own, then? "Has anyone ever told you you're an empath?"

He leaned back hard in his chair. "I have some experience in watching other people's body language. But that doesn't make me some kind of psychic."

He said the word as if it was filthy. A momentary knife of pain twisted in her gut.

* * *

Be sure to check out the next books in this exciting new miniseries, Code: Warrior SEALs: Meet these fierce warriors, who take on the most dangerous secret missions around the world!

* * *

If you're on Twitter, tell us what you think of Harlequin Romantic Suspense! #harlequinromsuspense

Dear Reader,

It seems fitting that, ten years after Hurricane Katrina, you and I should return to New Orleans for a steamy story of intrigue, magic and love. In the next installment of my Code: Warrior SEALs series, the team receives some unexpected help from Eve Hankova's older brother, Max, and from the strange and wonderful fortune teller he meets while performing surveillance on her shop. The Warrior SEAL net is tightening around the shadowy Russian spy running a mob ring in New Orleans, and their foe is more dangerous than ever as they close in on learning his true identity.

I've long been fascinated by the role of intuition in special operations situations. Soldiers rely heavily on gut feelings to warn them of unseen danger and approaching threats. But exactly how far will a warrior trust not only his own intuition, but the intuition of a woman who may be working for the enemy?

Let's find out as Max and Lissa run for their lives and run for love...

Happy reading!

Cindy

HER SECRET SPY

Cindy Dees

HARLEQUIN® ROMANTIC SUSPENSE

Recycling programs
for this product may
not exist in your area.

ISBN-13: 978-0-373-27980-7

Her Secret Spy

Copyright © 2016 by Cynthia Dees

All rights reserved. Except for use in any review, the reproduction or
utilization of this work in whole or in part in any form by any electronic,
mechanical or other means, now known or hereafter invented, including
xerography, photocopying and recording, or in any information storage
or retrieval system, is forbidden without the written permission of the
publisher, Harlequin Enterprises Limited, 225 Duncan Mill Road,
Don Mills, Ontario M3B 3K9, Canada.

This is a work of fiction. Names, characters, places and incidents are
either the product of the author's imagination or are used fictitiously,
and any resemblance to actual persons, living or dead, business
establishments, events or locales is entirely coincidental.

This edition published by arrangement with Harlequin Books S.A.

For questions and comments about the quality of this book,
please contact us at CustomerService@Harlequin.com.

® and ™ are trademarks of Harlequin Enterprises Limited or its
corporate affiliates. Trademarks indicated with ® are registered in the
United States Patent and Trademark Office, the Canadian Intellectual
Property Office and in other countries.

Printed in U.S.A.

www.Harlequin.com

New York Times and *USA TODAY* bestselling author **Cindy Dees** started flying airplanes while sitting in her dad's lap at the age of three and got a pilot's license before she got a driver's license. At age fifteen, she dropped out of high school and left the horse farm in Michigan, where she grew up, to attend the University of Michigan. After earning a degree in Russian and East European Studies, she joined the US Air Force and became the youngest female pilot in its history. She flew supersonic jets, VIP airlift and the C-5 Galaxy, the world's largest airplane. During her military career, she traveled to forty countries on five continents, was detained by the KGB and East German secret police, got shot at, flew in the first Gulf War, and amassed a lifetime's worth of war stories.

Her hobbies include medieval reenacting, professional Middle Eastern dancing and Japanese gardening.

This RITA® Award-winning author's first book was published in 2002 and since then she has published more than twenty-five bestselling and award-winning novels. She loves to hear from readers and can be contacted at www.cindydees.com.

Books by Cindy Dees

Harlequin Romantic Suspense

Flash of Death
Deadly Sight
A Billionaire's Redemption
High-Stakes Bachelor

Code: Warrior SEALs

Undercover with a SEAL
Her Secret Spy

HQN Books

Close Pursuit
Hot Intent

Visit Cindy's Author Profile page
at Harlequin.com for more titles!

This book is for all the brave and resilient residents of southern Louisiana and Mississippi who survived and bounced back from the devastation wrought by Hurricane Katrina. You remind us all of the best of the human spirit. Let the good times roll!

Chapter 1

Lissa Clearmont looked around her aunt Callista's shop—her shop now—torn between both affection and dismay. The purple string lights hanging all around the ceiling cast a spooky light on the eclectic inventory of Callista's Curiosities of the Magical and Macabre. An inventory that was hers to replenish and grow now, ideally by embracing the inner weirdo she'd spent years doing her best to deny.

Until last month her world had been thoroughly cleaned out of both the magical and the macabre. But then her peculiar aunt called to announce that she'd had a vision and was going to die any day. And, oh, by the way, she'd willed everything she owned, including her wacky store in New Orleans, to her favorite niece.

She hadn't taken Auntie Callista seriously at first, but the woman had been adamant that the end was near and she had to get her affairs in order immediately. The curiosity shop was infamous within the Clearmont clan, which was populated by generations of rational, logical, scientific souls who saw anything having to with the unexplained, prophetic, occult—or heaven forbid, magic—to be rubbish of the first water. The family grudgingly gave Callista credit for managing to sell her crystals, tarot cards, talismans, spells and palm readings to a gullible public and making what was, by all accounts, a decent living at it. But their patience for her eccentricities ended there.

Lissa, named loosely after her aunt, had been the only family member to take Callista's startling announcement of her forthcoming demise seriously. She'd questioned her aunt in alarm over any diagnoses or heretofore unknown health issues, and Callista had responded firmly that she was in the bloom of fine health. Nonetheless, the spirits had spoken, and she was about to die. Of course, Callista had snorted at the mere mention of visiting a traditional medical doctor.

If only her aunt had been more specific about how she'd expected to die and why. Maybe then Lissa wouldn't have this nagging feeling that something was very wrong with the circumstances of Callista's abrupt death two days after that phone call.

Frustrated, Lissa turned off the bronze lamp by the antique cash register, pausing for a moment to admire the deep rose silk shade with its beaded fringe and black lace edging. It was a pretty little thing in spite of its uselessness at actually emitting light. She trailed her fingertips wistfully through the cool fringe.

Sometimes she felt like the little lamp. Pretty and useless. The only thing in life she was good at was the one thing she was determined to leave behind in this cross-country move to New Orleans. Not that her parents hadn't tried to suppress her talent for years before now. In fact, they'd done everything in their power shy of trying to pray it away to eliminate her gift for seeing past and future events, and, worse, seeing into people's souls.

She'd kept the shop open late tonight for a coven of witches who'd come in to buy supplies for an upcoming Imbolc ritual. The holiday coincided with a full moon this year, and they were planning to throw a big shindig to celebrate the conjunction. The group couldn't agree quickly on anything, and they'd lingered a full hour after her usual closing time at seven o'clock. She barely had time to rush out and grab some cat food for Mr. Jackson, Callista's entirely cliché black cat, before the convenience store two blocks away closed for the night.

The women had just left in a joyous cluster, taking with them their noise and laughter and leaving her alone. Worse, night had fallen while the customers browsed the shop. To say that the store turned creepy after dark would be like saying the sun was hot. She peered into the dim corners and to the back of dark shelves in an effort to find the source of her unease. Yet again, she failed to spot whatever it was that made her so blasted nervous. It was as if she was being watched by some foreign, and possibly malevolent, force.

Shuddering a little, she wrapped herself in her favorite vintage wool coat, locked the iron grillwork over the glass door behind her and hurried away from the store into the bowels of the night. It was a sorry thing when a dark, deserted street in a dodgy neighborhood in a sometimes violent city felt safer to her than her own

store did. Aunt Callista would have told her to do some
sort of exorcism or cleaning ritual to the curiosity shop
and see if she could improve the place's vibe. A white
sage smudge probably wouldn't be enough. No, a full
spell, complete with a ritual circle, libations, candles—

*Stop whispering into my brain, Aunt Callista! You're
gone. I'll make my own decisions.* She didn't do that
kind of woo-woo stuff anymore. Immersing herself in
the mystical world had cost her too much. Brought her
too much pain. No more. Henceforth, she would live
life as a normal, mundane human being.

A warning vibrated somewhere in the back of her
mind, and she scoffed at it. *Nope.* She didn't pay attention to baseless intuitions and vibes anymore. She
could handle life entirely on her own. The powers that
be could just get over it.

Something big slammed into her from behind as a
hand slapped over her mouth, yanking her back against
what turned out to be a powerful body. "Don't fight.
Don't make a sound, or else I'll mess you up right here."

Son of a— Stupid warning intuition had to go and be
right, didn't it? But then panic and terror rolled through
her, and all else disappeared in the face of certainty that
this man was intent on doing something terrible to her.

The voice vibrated with malice. Urgency. Accent:
local. Smell: cigarette smoke and cheap strip club. This
assailant clearly planned to harm her or worse.

His plan roared through her mind, projected so
loudly he might as well have spoken the words. He
was going to drag her into an abandoned space—big,
open, drafty like a warehouse of some kind—tear off
her clothes, beat her up, cow her into submission and

then do unspeakable things to her before finally stran-
gling her.

She fought then. For her life. With all the violence
and desperation her five-foot-two frame could muster.
Which wasn't enough, of course. But she gave it her best
shot. Her attacker merely tightened his arms around her
in a vise that crushed her ribs and made breathing nigh
unto impossible, and then he waited out the expendi-
ture of her remaining oxygen. This obviously wasn't
the first time the man had done this.

An image of another girl's face, bloody, scared and
pleading for her life, flashed into Lissa's head. She
froze, arrested momentarily by the image, memoriz-
ing the face carefully.

Lifting her slight frame mostly off her feet, the man
dragged her backward toward an alley even darker than
the street they currently wrestled on. If only he would
take his hand away from her mouth and nose and let her
draw a proper breath. Then she could scream. Or fight
some more. Or do *something* to save herself.

She felt herself dropping into a state of shock. This
must be what it was like to be a gazelle in the mo-
ments after a lioness caught its neck in her mighty jaws
and crunched into it. Paralysis first and then blessedly
numbing shock. The gazelle wouldn't even be aware of
its bleeding muscles being ripped away by razor-sharp
teeth, its living organs being torn from its warm belly.
There would be just the shock. The blessed, detached,
distant awareness of encroaching death. Warmth. Quiet.
Calm. She was going to die, if not right now, then soon,
at this man's hands.

Vague regret at having never been in love—the real
thing, with all-consuming need, soaring heights of ec-

stasy, a melding of minds and souls, and, of course, really great sex—passed over her. She was too young to die. And she sincerely wished it didn't have to be like this.

But maybe it was fated. She'd been conceived in violence, after all. Maybe that meant she had to leave this life the same way. Was this some cosmic evening out of the scales? Had she never been meant to be born? Was that why the universe saw fit to take her out like this? Or was it some wrong she'd committed in her own life coming back to haunt—

Something big and fast flew at her from the side. More shadow than man. But big. Fully as big as her attacker. A second attacker? *Oh, Lord.* Were they going to gang-rape her?

Her first attacker grunted as the newcomer barreled into him and Lissa, knocking all of them into a pile on the ground. She rolled clear of the melee of flailing limbs as the two men struggled to untangle themselves.

She scrambled to her hands and knees, sucking air into her oxygen-starved lungs gratefully. *Must get up.* Run away while they still tried to gain their feet. She must fly like the wind—

But no wind could outrun the wave of psychic power that rolled over her as she panted on the sidewalk. It was as if a great floodgate had swung open and a massive flood of energy clobbered her. The scale of it was staggering. It made the rest of her life look as though she'd been sipping at a trickle of psychic power from a leaky faucet. But this. This was unbelievable. Time had no boundaries; her vision had no limits. Knowledge of all things was right there, hers for the taking.

Something hot and wet and smelling of iron splattered

her face, jolting her out of the vision and banging the floodgates of time and power shut. In front of her nose, a fist connected with her attacker's jaw again. Hard. With a smack of flesh on flesh that spoke of violent intent. *Wait. What?* The new man had just slugged his partner in crime? Maybe *not* his partner in crime?

Very belatedly she realized the two men were fighting. The second man was rescuing her! *Well, then. That changes things.* She pushed to her feet, balled up her fists, waited for an opening…and dived into the fray.

Max mentally groaned as the woman he'd just rescued leaped into the fracas in a misguided attempt to help him. He could kill this punk here and now if he wanted to, but he was trying hard to keep the guy alive so the police could have a chat with him. The attack on the woman had been too practiced, too perfect, for some amateur lowlife looking to score drug money. This guy was a professional stalker of women.

The woman, however, had different ideas. She seemed hell-bent on killing the bastard and was punching and kicking with all her strength. Although, on second thought, she was probably too tiny to do the guy any serious damage. And it was undoubtedly therapeutic for her to kick the hell out of the punk for scaring her like that.

The stalker finally rolled into a fetal ball with his arms over his head to protect himself from the woman's fury, which was prodigious now that she wasn't on the verge of dying.

Max rolled away and pressed to his feet, panting. He jerked his leather bomber jacket back into place and dusted off his jeans, which were torn at one knee. Dammit, he liked these jeans.

"Okay, lady," he said drily. "That's enough, or else the cops will charge you with assault when they get here instead of that jackass."

The woman looked up at him, confused. As if she was just now registering what her feet and fists were doing. "Oh. Oh! Right." She stumbled back and commenced shaking so hard he could see it from where he stood.

The attacker made a move to jump to his feet and take off, but Max put a hand on the back of the guy's neck and shoved him down to the ground with casual strength. "You stay right there, or I'll break your neck." The punk lurched one more time, and Max increased the pressure. "For real, man. I'll kill you. Right here. Right now. No compunction."

The punk subsided.

For good measure, Max went down to one knee, kneeling on the spot between the guy's shoulder blades and no doubt pressing the stalker's cheek painfully into the gravel-strewn sidewalk. He glanced up at the woman. "Ma'am, if you'd be so kind as to call nine-one-one. Tell them to send the nearest cruiser. Then tell them to call Detective Bastien LeBlanc and pass the message that Max could use a hand."

"Is that your name?" the woman asked in a shaky voice close to tears. "Max?"

"Please make the call, ma'am."

"What is it?"

"What is what? You mean my name?" he echoed blankly. That was a good question. He'd been living under that other name, not his own, for so long, he almost didn't remember his real name anymore. Not that he had any great fondness for either his real name or his real life. All of it had turned out to be a lie of epic proportions. And he was so caught in this new lie, so deeply ensnared in its tangles, he couldn't breathe, let alone move.

"Max," he mumbled. "Call me Max."

"Max what?"

Damn, she was persistent. "Smith," he muttered under his breath.

In what little light there was in this crappy corner of town, he made out a faint frown puckering her brow. The sort of frown that said a person didn't believe what she was hearing and was trying to understand why the speaker would lie to her. An urge to tell her the truth, to tell her his real name, bubbled up from somewhere deep in his gut.

But thankfully a siren's wail sounded just then, and the woman looked away, relief painted in every sweet line of her face. She was a little thing. She looked like Mary Poppins in that old-fashioned wool coat and those funny curved-heel granny shoes. Her hair was curly, and about half of it remained in a bun at the back of her neck. The rest fell around her face in a wild, sexy riot of curls that fit her face massively better than the old lady attire did.

A police car careened around the corner, and in the glare of the headlights he saw the woman's curls were dark, dark red. Almost maroon. And she was young, midtwenties maybe. Which he supposed wasn't *that* young. It was just the age of his younger sister, who would forever and always be his baby sister, even when she turned old and gray.

Like his sister, the woman trembling in front of him was beautiful in an old-fashioned way. Her skin was porcelain, her lips rosy and full, her eyes huge and dark. Her beauty was soft.

Under any other circumstances but these, he would have registered this woman as ridiculously attractive, walked away from her and then obsessed about her for weeks afterward, kicking himself for not talking to her or at least getting her name and phone number.

It wasn't that he'd never successfully put the moves on a hot female. But he'd been undercover for so long that he was starting to worry about forgetting how to come on to women at all.

He could not see her figure under that ridiculous coat, but even swathed in heavy wool, she was slight in stature. She hadn't fought like an athlete. And then there'd been that horrifying moment when she'd started to go into shock. She'd gone limp in her captor's arms like prey in the jaws of death.

He hadn't intended to leave his surveillance post. He'd been prepared to let her get robbed, maybe even roughed up a little. But when that bastard had started to drag her away—and, worse, she'd appeared to go catatonic—he'd had no choice but to leave his hidey-hole and act.

She might be the target of his op, but that op did not include watching the damned subject die. He needed her contacts. Her connection to the top leadership of the group he'd spent all these months infiltrating.

It was a huge breach of security protocol to blow his cover like this, to come into direct contact with the person he was supposed to be watching. But what choice did he have? He couldn't stand by and let that jerk drag her off and do his worst to her. Swearing to himself, he pasted on the bland expression of a casual passerby who was just grateful to have been in the right place at the right time to lend a hand to a lady in distress.

The cops collected the assailant, who was now looking quite a bit worse for wear. He watched carefully to make sure they didn't mess up Mirandizing and cuffing the perp.

As a police officer stuffed the assailant in the back of a squad car, Max straightened and turned to check on the woman. He lurched as something light plastered itself against his chest. It was her. *Oh, God, sobbing.*

"I got to you as fast as I could," he muttered unwillingly. "I'm sorry it wasn't sooner."

Reluctantly his arms came up around her, and, swear to God, she *snuggled* against him. The strangest feeling washed over him as this tiny female burrowed closer against his chest as if he were a combination furnace and Second Coming. It made him feel protective. Possessive. Needed. What the hell was *that* all about?

Lord knew, other people had needed him his whole life. His father after the divorce devastated him. His mother after the car accident paralyzed her. His baby sister after their mother died and left him alone to raise her. But never had any of that made him feel like this. Like he could climb a mountain or conquer an army single-handedly.

The woman's shaking lessened as he held her, and eventually a policeman peeled her off his chest to take a brief statement from her about what had happened. She gave her name, Lissa Clearmont, but, of course, he already knew it.

He already knew lots of things about her. Like what

time she opened the bedroom blinds in the morning to greet the sun. That she practiced yoga almost every day. That she didn't like being in the store alone after dark. Which electric company and telephone company the shop used. What brand of laundry soap the owner preferred. After all, he was very good at his job.

He was intrigued when she begged off coming down to the police station immediately to make a report, saying that she had something pressing to do before she talked to them again. What was more important than putting away the bastard who'd tried to assault her and possibly kill her? There'd been something about the way the assailant had attacked Lissa that smacked of a psychopath and not a regular, garden-variety mugger.

Another police car pulled up, this one unmarked except for a magnetic siren stuck to the driver's side roof. Bastien LeBlanc, a friend of his sister and her fiancé, piled out of the car. He looked as if he'd been pulled out of an undercover mission, too. Or maybe he'd been at a strip club down in the French Quarter using all those bad-boy good looks to get lucky. He stopped to speak briefly with the arresting officers and then made his way over to Max.

"Hey, bro. What up?" the New Orleans cop and former navy SEAL asked him.

"That guy—" he pointed at the perp in the cop car "—mugged that woman—" he pointed at Lissa "—a few minutes ago."

"Lemme guess. You dived in and saved the day. Dude's looking a little rough around the edges. Street name's Julio G. He's a notorious gangster. We've been working on taking him down for a couple of years. Problem is, his flunkies keep taking the fall for him and he keeps slipping out of our net. But not tonight, methinks. Make sure the NOPD doesn't get blamed for busting him up like that, eh? We wouldn't want him to get off on yet another technicality."

Max grimaced. "The girl did most of the visible damage after I took the bastard down. I thought it might be good for her to work out a little of her fear on him before we called you guys."

Bastien grinned. "I'm beginning to see why my future brother-in-law called you an ice-cold motherfu—"

"Yeah, yeah," Max interrupted. "Listen. I need a favor."

"Name it. The district attorney's going to be thrilled that we finally got Julio G. dead to rights. We think he's top dog in one of the more violent gangs in the area. Not only did you take him down, but you gift wrapped him for the police. No way is he passing off these charges on to one of his boys. We owe you one."

"I need my name kept out of the police report. In fact, I need all mention of my being involved with this incident sanitized out of the official record."

"You don't want any credit at all for catching this slimeball?"

"Nope. None. I was never here."

Bastien grinned again. "I dunno. The way that pretty little lady's lookin' at you, I might rethink that 'never been here' thing. She's one sweet piece of—"

"And that'll be enough out of you," Max interrupted.

Bastien frowned. "The woman's testimony ought to be enough to put Julio away. But if it's not looking good at trial, I'm gonna have to give your name to the DA and let him call you to testify. We can't let this guy slip out of our grasp. He's seriously bad news."

Max nodded reluctantly. "Understood." This was the paradox of being undercover and going after bad guys. It became a trade-off of blowing one's cover versus putting away the scumbags one encountered along the way. At what point was it worth blowing two years' worth of undercover work to put away one guy?

"Do me a favor in return, bro," Bastien said.

"What's that?" he asked cautiously.

"See to it Ms. Clearmont gets home safely. She's refusing to come down to the station until tomorrow to make her statement, and I'd hate for one of that bottom-feeder's buddies to find her overnight and take it upon himself to silence her before she can press charges. Given the gang he affiliates with, he's got some downright unfriendly associates."

"You protect her. That's your job."

Bastien shrugged. "She's refusing any police protection. Insists on you being the one to take her home."

Max rolled his eyes. It wasn't as if he could say no to that. *Dammit.* "Fine. I'll follow her to her place."

"You'll do more than that if I'm keeping your name off the report. You hold her hand and tuck her into bed. She's had one hell of a scare, and the way she tells it, she's got no family or friends in town to take care of her."

"Why me?" he protested. "I'm on an op and she stumbled into the middle of it…" He left out the part where she *was* the op.

Bastien threw him a withering look that said he'd thought better of Max than to abandon a lady in need. Max huffed. "All right already. I'll walk her home and make sure she's safe overnight."

"You'll stay with her?"

Max frowned. "If she'll let me. And if not, I'll spend the night outside her place and keep an eye on her. She'll be safe."

"Promise?"

"Yes, Bastien. I've got her back."

The cop stared at him intently for a moment and then nodded, accepting his word. "All right. I got me a date to get back to, then. Can't keep the ladies of New Orleans waiting for all this hotness."

Max rolled his eyes as the cop strolled away; then he turned his attention back to the problem at hand. Rather, the damsel in distress at hand. *Dammit.* He really didn't need to pull babysitting duty when he should be out hunting bad guys. Or maybe *being* the bad guy would be more accurate.

A soft hand touched his sleeve, and he reacted violently, spinning to face Lissa, who pulled back sharply at his abrupt move. He carefully stilled his entire body and pitched his voice to calming tones. "The police asked if I'd mind walking you home. Would that be all right with you, or would that frighten you?"

"Why on earth would that frighten me? You saved me. You're my knight in shining armor."

Oh, God. He was so *not* a good guy. Were it not for some random creep attacking her, he'd be the one scaring her. He would be the one stalking her without her knowledge, the one peering in her windows with a telescope, the one bugging her house and cloning her computer and cell phone. He would be the one putting that haunted expression in her big dark eyes.

He shoved a distracted hand through his short hair. "Look. I'm going to be honest with you. The police have asked me to keep an eye on you tonight since you won't accept their protection. Does that freak you out?"

"No freakage. But I hate to impose on you. Keep you from your family…?"

She left it hanging as a question. "No family," he replied shortly.

"Job? Pet? Girlfriend?"

"None of the above. Correction, I have a job, but I work for myself. Set my own hours."

"Perfect! You can stay at my place. We'll make a party out of it."

Did she have to sound so damned tickled about having a slumber party with him? There was no way he was spending the night in her apartment with her. He might be a cad, but he wasn't that giant a cad. "I think the police have pretty much wrapped up here. We can go soon. Where do you live?" As if he didn't know already. *Ha.*

"I live over the curiosity shop down the block. But I was on my way to the store. I'm out of food. And Mr. Jackson—well, he's not patient about missing supper."

He frowned. He'd seen no evidence of a man of any kind in her life. He glanced down to verify that her ring finger was naked. It was. "You have a boyfriend?"

She blinked up at him rather owlishly. "What?" A look of dawning comprehension. "Oh! You mean Mr. Jackson?" Gay laughter. "I'll introduce you two when we get home. He's gonna love you. C'mon. I need tuna fish and mayonnaise. He loves my homemade tuna salad and asked after it this morning."

Something deflated inside Max. Had he actually been a little attracted to her? Hell, how could he not be? She was fascinating in a strange kind of way. The woman had an eccentric style that had nothing to do with regular conventions of society or fashion. A hint of…death…clung to her. Or at least a knowing of it. And yet, within that overriding impression of darkness, a discordant note of happiness was audible. It was entirely at odds with her darker self.

Either that, or the long months undercover had finally gotten to him, and he was losing his marbles. He did a quick mental craziness check. Nope. It wasn't him. There was something special about her, something alluring, that called to him. Hell, tempted him. This was the way he felt when he found a lost art masterpiece. The discovery brought out the greedy poet inside him.

Or maybe his reaction to her stemmed from the fact that he'd just saved her life. *Yeah, that must be it.* That had to be why he felt so protective all of a sudden. He was a lot of things, but compassionate was not one of them. And yet here he was, walking his own personal damsel in distress home.

Frowning, he fell in beside her as she strode off down the street. For a woman who'd just been attacked and nearly killed, she'd recovered her mojo damned fast. Either that or she was a fine actress.

"Are you okay?" he asked, blatantly throwing out a trial balloon to gauge her mood and mind-set.

"Why wouldn't I be? You're here now."

Well, hell. It kinda made a guy want to puff out his chest and put a little swagger in his step. He glanced down at her and caught her staring sidelong up at him. Their gazes met, and something crackled between them. He could almost see the energy forming a complete circuit between them. *Sheesh.* His imagination was working overtime tonight. He was a trained covert operative, for goodness' sake. He didn't do crackling sexual attraction, particularly not with civilians.

But then she reached out to *touch* the energy. Her fingertips exactly traced the invisible lines arcing back and forth between them. *Crud.* Could she physically see the attraction between them? Did that mean she was crazy, too, or was it just him losing his mind? Either way, charges zinged through his body, drawing him to her as if they were opposite poles of human-size magnets. The pull was inexorable and irresistible. And hot. Shockingly hot.

Lust for this woman shot through him along those strange ley lines of sexual energy, and it was all he could do to keep his hands off her. Only the sure and certain knowledge that he would be no better than that sicko stalker behind them kept him from seriously contemplating dragging her up against him, kissing her until she begged him to bed her, burying his body in hers and inhaling all that crackling sexual energy flowing from her into him.

"I'm not a superhero, you know. I'm just a guy."

"You're *my* superhero."

Huh. He liked the sound of that. Enough that he ordered his raging libido in no uncertain terms to take a hike. Enough that he volunteered to hold the basket for her as he trudged around a local convenience store behind her.

Grocery shopping was a domestic task he had never done before with a woman. It was surreal. Terribly domesticated. So very normal. He had to admit it held a certain charm. Weird charm but charm nonetheless. Or maybe it was just the company he was keeping that made it seem so damned fantastic.

Gah. This was an anomaly. He would deliver her to Bastien in the morning, she would make her statement, the bad guy would go to jail for a good long time and Max would get back to his regularly scheduled life as an undercover agent. Stalking her.

In a state of minor shock, he carried her plastic grocery bags back to Callista's Curiosities of the Magical and Macabre and dutifully stood at Lissa's side as she fumbled at the door with a big old-fashioned key.

"You should let me install a decent security system and a good lock on that door," he commented.

"Is that what you do? Security systems?"

"Something like that."

The door lock surrendered just then and granted them access to an incredibly cluttered space. Floor-to-ceiling junk crammed the store. It was enough to make a person feel a little claustrophobic. "Hell of a name this place has. Quite a mouthful."

"I call it C2M2 to myself," she replied.

He stopped in the doorway. It felt odd to be entering the place he'd been doing surveillance on for weeks.

"Come in. Please."

Dammit, if he hadn't detected that hint of fearful pleading in her tone, he'd have refused her. But as it was, he had no choice. He'd promised Bastien, after all. And truth be told, he wasn't the kind of guy to leave a woman in the lurch.

She wound across the crowded and cluttered space, heading for a narrow staircase near the back of the store. "I'm sorry in advance for the chaos upstairs. I just inherited this place, and it needs a ton of work."

She said that as if the downstairs wasn't a colossal, messy hoarder's wet dream. He hesitated to see what she considered trashed enough to apologize for. He rounded the corner into her second-floor home and stopped cold. It was a war zone.

The place had been stripped down to the lath and plaster wallboards, and in some places down to bare brick. Corroded copper plumbing was exposed, ancient electrical wires hung in dangerous festoons, bare light-bulbs hanging from the ceiling provided the only light and the floor was scraped boards. The angle of his surveillance cameras on the shop didn't capture any of this.

"What the hell happened in here?" he blurted.

"The previous owner started renovations, and I haven't had time to finish them yet," she threw over her shoulder as she headed over to a corner that contained a 1950s vintage refrigerator with a rusted door, a hot plate on a wooden milk crate and a metal washtub on the floor under two bare faucets.

"Where did the kitchen go?" he asked cautiously.

"In the Dumpster out back. It was disgusting. I tore out what was left."

"So I gather." He picked his way around a pile of debris and across a canvas painter's tarp stretched over the floor. "And your workmen left the construction site like this? Fire them. I know some good contractors—"

"I'm doing the work myself."

He stared at Lissa as she shed her coat and hung it on an elaborate wood-and-iron coatrack in the corner. In a properly restored home, it would be a lovely piece. In this chaos, it was wildly out of place.

Good Lord. She was even tinier than he'd imagined, a mere slip of a woman. And she was capable of the heavy labor involved in a complete home restoration? Color him impressed.

"I'm sorry. I didn't realize you were a contractor."

"I'm not," she answered cheerfully. "But how hard can it be? It's only hammers and nails and saws."

Oh, my dear God. Was that what she thought? "And you know how to weld copper and run wiring and hang drywall and know the New Orleans building codes, then?" he asked lightly. He'd renovated his condo when he bought it, but he'd paid experienced professionals to do it and it had still been a nightmare. He'd pitched in to help the crew and had learned a ton about construction, but he wouldn't know where to begin with this disaster.

"No, but I'll figure it out."

He managed to get his hanging jaw closed before she turned around, a small bowl of tuna fish and mayonnaise in hand. Other hand on her hip, she asked, "Now where has Mr. Jackson gone off to?"

If he were this Jackson guy, he'd have run away from home and not come back until this place was put back together. Belatedly, Max answered, "Can you call him on his cell phone? Find out where he's gone? I know some guys who could pick him up and bring him back here."

Lissa frowned at him as if he'd lost his mind.

Hey. He'd just offered to burn a hard-won favor from his employer for her.

"I'm sure that won't be necessary," she said slowly, as though he were some sort of ignorant child. "Mr. Jackson," she crooned. "I made you your favorite. Tuna salad."

Something landed on his shoulder from above, and he dived for the floor, rolling and coming up ready to kill. *Jeez.* Where had that guy come from? Stunned at the surprise attack, he looked around wildly for his attacker.

Nada. What the hell?

For her part, Lissa laughed and scooped up a…

Son of a bitch.

A cat. Small and black. With one white front paw that looked just like a feline glove. "Mr. Jackson, I presume?" he said drily, lowering his fists to his sides.

"Would you like to pet him? Although I don't know if he likes men or not. You're the first one I've seen him around. I inherited him with the store."

"Along with this disaster zone?"

"I prefer to think of it as a project with unlimited potential."

A cold knot of suspicion started to form in his gut. Had she actually, literally, inherited the place? From whom? And how recently? He'd been under the impression that the store's namesake would be returning at some point. "Exactly how long ago did you inherit this place?"

"Let's see. It's been almost a month."

He closed his eyes in chagrin as acid frustration ate its way through his gut. A month. The past few weeks of grueling round-the-clock surveillance had been for naught. She wasn't the person he was supposed to be following. She wouldn't have any contacts. She was useless to him. Worse, the trail had gone cold, then.

"Who owned this place before you?" he asked in resignation.

"My aunt. Callista Clearmont. She willed it to me right before she died suddenly."

His one and only link to the next level of hierarchy in the mob he was infiltrating was dead? A stream of violent swearing erupted inside his head.

"I'm sorry for your loss," he murmured automatically. *Crap, crap, crap.* How was he going to track down Callista Clearmont's mob connections if the woman was dead? Why hadn't anyone told him?

Unless the niece had inherited the mob contacts, as well…

Lissa turned away. Her shoulders gave a suspicious heave, and she sniffed loudly. *Oh, no. Not more female tears.* He had no defense against them. They scared him to death. Frantic to distract her from launching into full-blown waterworks, he asked quickly, "You said she died suddenly?"

His question did the trick. Lissa turned back to face him, another one of those delicate frowns of hers puckering her creamy brow. "She called me. Told me she was going to die any minute and that she'd willed everything she owned to me."

"Was she sick a long time?"

"Oh, no. She was in perfect health. We all thought she was going to outlive the rest of the family."

His internal antenna wiggled abruptly. Could it be? Had the mob or one of its enemies killed her? "What were the circumstances of her death, if you don't mind my asking?"

"She died in her sleep, supposedly. A customer found her after she didn't come downstairs for an appointment to do a reading."

"A reading?"

"She was a psychic. I think that customer had asked for a crystal ball scrying. She also read palms very well. The last time I talked to her, she claimed she'd had a vision. That a spirit told her she was going to die within a day or two and to put her affairs in order."

A spirit, huh? More like a mob informant, perhaps?

"Who were your aunt's clients? Did she keep a list of them?"

"I suppose so. I haven't found it if she did keep one, though. Her business papers are, well, a little disorganized."

If the shop downstairs was any indication of how the woman had done business, any kind of organized client list was probably a long shot. With a list, though, he could maybe identify Callista's mob contact and find the next level of hierarchy in the secretive Russian gang he'd spent the past two years infiltrating.

"Are you hungry?" Lissa asked, startling him out of his train of thought.

"You don't have to feed me. I'll grab something on the way home."

"It's the least I can do for you after you saved my life."

"I wouldn't go that far in describing what I did. I only interrupted a mugging. Any passerby could have done the same."

"They could have, but that doesn't mean they would have. He was going to kill me."

How did she know that? Was she a psychic, too?

"I was just planning to heat up some leftovers. Let me fix you a plate."

"Can I help, umm, prepare it?" He eyed the hot plate and metal washtub askance.

"Nah. I bought a Monte Cristo sandwich earlier and I'll just pop it in the microwave. It's a lot more than I can eat alone. I'll split it with you."

"Sure. If you'll let me buy the next meal." The words were out of his mouth before he stopped to think about them. There couldn't be a "next meal" for the two of them. She was an innocent, not mixed up in her aunt's mess and of no use to him. He would deliver her to Bastien in the morning, and then he would get the hell out of her life and never look back.

Chapter 2

Lissa's hands still shook a little as she handed a paper plate with the batter-dipped, multilayered, fried ham-and-cheese sandwich to "Max Smith." Which totally wasn't his name. It didn't take special powers to hear the evasion in his voice when he'd given her the name.

She was more rattled by tonight's attack than she wanted to let on, even to herself. Thank God this stranger had been there to swoop in and save the day. She didn't want to think about what would have happened had he not come along.

Speaking of which…"I'll be right back," she blurted. "There's something I have to do."

Max looked up at her in alarm. "You're not leaving, are you?"

"Heavens no." She ducked into what would have been the spare bedroom had her aunt not gutted it and dug around in her big trunk of art supplies for a sketch pad, pastels and her set of drawing pencils. Tucking that under her arm, she scooped up her easel and wrestled it out into the main room.

Max leaped to his feet to rescue the easel from her. "Where do you want this?"

"Over by the lamp. I'll need the light."

"Drawing something, are you?"

Crap. She couldn't admit she wanted to capture the face she'd seen in her attacker's mind as he'd attacked her. "It's, umm, therapy. Helps me calm down when I'm upset."

"You're an artist, then?"

She shrugged. "Not really. I'm just a dabbler."

She pulled a stool over in front of the easel he set up for her. In a few minutes a face started to take shape. She turned out to be a pretty girl, not unlike herself in features and overall coloring. Which was frankly creepy. Was her attacker a serial killer, maybe?

Once she'd captured the girl's initial bone structure, she pulled out the pastels and really brought the face to life, drawing quickly and surely from memory.

"Who's that?" Max eventually murmured from directly behind her.

She jumped, startled. She'd been concentrating so hard on the picture that she'd forgotten he was there.

"I have no idea."

"It's just a random sketch?"

There was no way she could explain it without sounding like a crazy woman, so she didn't even try. Instead she lied. "Yes, it's just a face." And if she were a normal person, that was all it would be. Right, then. She'd determined to be normal; therefore, this was just a face.

Except why did the girl's eyes stare out at her from the paper beseechingly, following her as she shifted right and left, checking the sketch's perspective and making tiny corrections to the features?

It. Was. Just. A. Face.

Max moved in close behind her to study the sketch. "She's pretty. You have a good hand for portraiture. You're sure you've never seen this person before?"

Rather than answer his question, Lissa leaned forward to release the sheet of paper from the easel's clips. "Here. Lay this on the floor in the corner and spray it with the fixative in the can over on the end of my work table while I put my art supplies away."

It physically hurt Lissa to deny the girl's fear and pain coming off that sketch. She had to get away for a minute and catch her breath. *You poor, poor thing.* Lissa jammed her pastels and pencils in a drawer in her dresser and slammed it shut. She wasn't a psychic anymore. She didn't listen to dead people anymore, and she didn't draw the faces of murderer's victims anymore. She was just a regular person living a normal life.

If only her gift didn't seem to be tied to violence. Maybe she would have been able to live with predicting the sex of babies and telling people when to ask for a promotion at work. But her visions were, almost without exception, tied to death. She saw dead bodies. Sensed killers. Heard dead people. Saw death moving in to claim people. With a sigh, she returned to the main room.

Abrupt exhaustion swept over her. It was as if her psyche had held all her reaction to the earlier attack at bay until that sketch was out of her system. Now she felt on the verge of collapse.

"Are you okay?" Max asked quickly. The guy was pretty perceptive himself.

"I'm a little tired all of a sudden."

He nodded knowingly. "Aftermath. The adrenaline drains away, and you feel like death warmed over."

"Yes. That." She sighed.

"Did your aunt leave a working bathtub in this wreck?" he asked.

Normally she would take offense at him calling her place a wreck. Even if it was true. She preferred to think of it as a work in progress. "Aunt Callista left the tub. Probably because it's cast-iron and weighs a ton. I couldn't even move it to scrape the linoleum from under the claw feet."

"Then I suggest you go take a nice, long soak in a hot bath and go to bed."

"Thanks for everything you've done for me. If you don't mind, I'll let you see yourself out. You've been more than kind, particularly since we've never met before tonight…" She trailed off, tilting her head to one side and staring at him as a little voice inside whispered that he knew her better than she could possibly imagine.

What was that all about?

She moved into the master bedroom and closed the door. Callista had not messed with the apartment's original cast-iron claw-foot tub, and Lissa planned to take full advantage of that tonight. A bath was just the thing for quieting the voices rioting in the back of her head, clamoring more loudly than usual for attention.

Max waited until after the light went out under Lissa's bedroom door to get up from the silly Victorian sofa and ease down the stairs. He avoided the step he'd registered as the squeaker on the way up and crept downstairs to the shop. Now to have a look around and see if he could figure out where Callista might have put her complete customer list.

Surely the woman had kept such a thing. Based on the criminal clientele he'd been told she served, she'd have been insane not to keep the names tucked away somewhere for self-protection, if nothing else. Of course, if she'd had a decent dead man's switch in place based on such a list, Callista probably wouldn't be dead now.

He reached the shop floor and looked around in dismay. How did a person even begin searching this maze? He started at the back corner and worked his way around the edges of the surprisingly large space. His mind boggled at the variety of odds and ends. He felt a little like Alice must have when she'd first fallen down the rabbit hole.

He examined an exquisite collection of small enameled boxes. As an art dealer, he would pay double what Lissa had them marked for, and he would mark them up even more for resale. He made a mental note to mention it to her in the morning.

Oh, wait. He couldn't say anything about her merchandise pricing, lest she figure out he'd been snooping.

He refocused his mind on the client list and resolutely ignored a pair of actually quite nice landscape paintings hanging on the far wall from the stairs. They were oil paintings, the technique modern, and the sensibility for light and movement was top-notch. He would love to take a closer look at them in full daylight. If the color held up to bright light, the paintings and the artist could be quite a find.

But he wasn't an art dealer anymore. At least not until he cracked the Russian crime syndicate that had swallowed his entire family whole.

Callista's list, dammit.

He moved to the counter and made a cursory search of the cabinets there. Surely Lissa had already searched this, the most logical place to look for her aunt's business records.

No surprise, he had no better luck than she'd had at locating Callista's books. He looked around the store in the darkness. Where would he hide if he were a ledger, journal or notebook of some kind?

Something shifted in a corner near the ceiling, and he did a double take. For a second there, he thought he'd seen a faint movement. Or maybe a flash of light. Hell, if he didn't know better, he'd say he'd seen a ghost. However, he did know better, and he didn't buy any of that woo-woo stuff. It must have been cast from a passing car or something.

He glanced around behind the counter and spied a short door tucked back under the stairs to Lissa's apartment. *Hmm. A closet perhaps?* He opened the door and was surprised to see another set of stairs, this one leading down. Nobody in New Orleans had basements. The place was built on a swamp, prone to flooding and gradually sinking even farther below sea level than it already was. A waterproof basement would be prohibitively expensive to build, the sort of thing only a bona fide nutball would even attempt.

But as sure as he was standing there, he was looking at stairs leading down. He pulled out the tiny LED flashlight attached to his key chain and pointed it into the dark. A dozen steps led into a low, cramped space that looked for all the world like some kind of vault. The walls looked like steel-reinforced concrete. He felt the nearest one and was startled to register some sort of thick sealant or covering on the surface. Windowless and stuffy, it felt like a prison cell.

Or a secret storeroom. Did the mob move contraband through here? Drugs, maybe? What in the hell was this place?

It was not nearly as cluttered as the shop was. Big wooden crates were stacked along one wall, and several old steamer trunks sat along the opposite wall. He moved to the crates first and was surprised to see everything from wrapped curios to bottles of wine. But not just any wine. This stuff was old, French and had a famous label that would fetch thousands at auction if the dates on the labels were real. The stuff had to be illegal. He was no great connoisseur of wine, but to his knowledge the vineyard itself was the only importer of this brand to the United States. Based on the amount of dust on the bottles, the wine had been there for some time.

He had a look in the nearest steamer trunk. Max opened the heavy lid and was gratified to see the thing filled to the brim with papers. *Bingo.* This was exactly the kind of place Callista might have hidden her client list. He picked up a fistful of papers and began to read.

A magic spell. A recipe for a love potion of some kind. A ritual for luck described in details. *Seriously? C'mon, Callista. Give up your client list already.* A chuckle sounded nearby, making him whip around in the dark, swinging his flashlight wildly back and forth.

And then he realized it was the furnace kicking on. This place really gave him the creeps. That haunting face Lissa had drawn must have gotten under his skin more than he wanted to admit. Those eyes—they watched him pleadingly, begging for help. Thank God he'd gotten to Lissa before that bastard had dragged her off to heaven knew where to do heaven knew what and put a similar expression in her eyes.

He shook his shoulders hard, trying to rid himself of the sensation of something or someone watching him. He was a professional, for goodness' sake. Trained for most of his life in the art of covert operations. He was a man of cool logic and action. He did not do ghosts, and he did not do supernatural. Period.

Lissa's eyes opened drowsily as a hand caressed her forehead. She was too sleepy to bother pushing away the spirits tonight. "Is that you, Aunt Cal?" she mumbled to the room in general. "I'm fine—I promise. That lovely man, Max, or whatever his name is, took care of me. Did you send him to me?"

Another whisper of touch across her cheek. She would take that as a yes. "Thanks." She sighed.

The ghost caressed her cheek again, this time beseechingly. It wanted her to listen. Reluctantly, she woke up more thoroughly, sitting up in bed and speaking directly to the invisible spirit hovering nearby. "Listen, Aunt Callista. About the whole psychic thing. I'm giving it up. I want to know what it's like to be normal. To live like other people. Maybe find a nice guy and settle down. Have a family. I can't keep talking to dead people and have a regular life. I know it's selfish. But I've given my whole life to helping dead people. It's time for me to live a little."

The ghost of her aunt, if that was who'd woken her

this morning, did not deign to answer. There were no more gentle, loving touches on her skin.

Lissa flopped back to her pillow, trying to enjoy the warmth of the morning sun streaming through her window. But that girl's face from her attacker's mind still lingered. She'd dreamed of her last night, too.

It had been awful having to endure the girl's screams and cries for help. Help that had never come. Lissa shoved away the memory of her death, also dreamed about in vivid, high-definition color and surround sound. That was the worst part of dreaming. Lissa had no control over it, and the spirits seemed determined to take advantage of her weakness to torture her.

The nameless, but no longer faceless, girl was dead, and nothing would bring her back. The good news was that her killer was in custody and not likely to go free anytime soon. Lissa could let it go. Justice had been served. So the powers that be could just leave her out of the matter.

She sat up with conviction and threw back the antique quilt that had supposedly been made by a great-great-great-grandmother of hers. She had places to go and things to do. Determined to focus on those, she swung her feet to the cold wooden floor. This room needed a rug. A nice thick Persian one that she could dig her toes into.

What to wear? Max had promised to come back this morning and escort her down to the police station. She wanted to look her best for him, since she hadn't exactly been in top form last night.

Lissa, my dear, she told herself, *you have a crush on Mr. Smith.* A big, fat, juicy one. And normal women acted on their crushes. They put out signals and feelers, and maybe even asked the men they liked out for a cup of coffee or a bite to eat. He did say last night that the next meal was on him. That meant he was open to the idea of seeing her again, right?

If only she'd had a more normal life, maybe she would know how to land a man like Max Smith. As it was, she stood in front of her closet and panicked. Then she moved into the bathroom and stared at the mirror over the sink and despaired. She couldn't do this. He was so out of her league. She was an amateur at romance, and he was obviously a world-class master of the art.

Master of romance didn't quite capture the raw magnetism of Max Smith, or whatever his name was. The Max part felt right, but the Smith part felt slightly off. Although now that she was living a normal life, she probably should ignore the intuition and just accept his name at face value.

Not that all intuition was bad, though. Last night, as he'd walked her to the store, there'd been a moment. The kind of moment she'd fantasized about. That instant of connection as eyes met and instinctive recognition of true love broke over both parties. As angelic hosts sang and heavenly trumpets blared to announce the miracle. *Or something along those lines.*

The moment had left her breathless and thinking the kind of racy thoughts she'd rarely had time for before she'd set aside her unfortunate gift.

Resolutely, she picked up a tube of eyeliner and prayed that it would cooperate with her this morning. The makeup gods were capricious demons from time to time.

As she carefully accented the roundness and width of

her big dark eyes, she allowed herself to remember her other dream from last night. The one about Max. Who knew a girl could make herself blush just by dreaming about a man she'd just met? Except in her dream they'd known each other—or at least had a connection—for a long time.

She stared critically at herself in the mirror and then down at her pitiful selection of lipsticks. She wanted to come off breezy. Demure but sexy—whoa, whoa, whoa. *Back up.* Why was she going to all this trouble for this guy?

She'd always subscribed to the notion that any man worth her love would adore her just the way she was, with no makeup and her curls sticking out all over her head and a smudge of paint on her nose. Apparently that notion had flown right out the window at the first sign of a hot guy. He was *not* out of her league, darn it! She deserved any man she was attracted to.

But an insidious thread of doubt whispered warnings of what he would think if he knew about the circumstances of her conception and birth. She was tainted. Had bad genes. Her stepfather said once that they would come through in the end. The comment, uttered in anger, had stuck with her ever since. Was he right?

The sun shone a little less brightly through her window.

Max was, of course, punctual to the minute. She waited by the shop's main entrance, picking at the black widow's weeds she'd opted to wear. The old-fashioned dress swathed her in gloom and made her look at least a decade older than her twenty-six years.

"Going to a funeral after you make your statement?" he asked drily as he strolled down the sidewalk toward her.

Rendered speechless by his easy elegance in those flannel trousers and crisply starched dress shirt, she could only stare at him. How had she missed these movie-star good looks last night? She'd noticed that he was hot, but not that he was drop-dead gorgeous. She must have been in worse shock than she'd realized.

One of his eyebrows twitched. "Everything okay?"

"Umm, no. Yes."

"Which?"

"I'm a little flummoxed by how handsome you are today."

"Oh." He fingered his jaw. "I shaved this morning. It's nothing."

Right. Because a simple shave had peeled back the troll's face to reveal this prince beneath. She said lightly, "I believe a sincere yowza is in order, sir."

"Well, thank you. And may I say you make a fetching widow."

She grinned up at him. "Nice try."

He shrugged. "Surely you know how beautiful a woman you are. Great bones. Perfect skin. Striking coloring. I have an eye for these things, you know."

"And how's that?" she asked as they strolled down the street.

"I have a good eye for beauty. Ask anyone who knows me. They'll tell you so." He stopped beside a low-slung, sleek sports car and opened the door for her. Startled, she sunk into the plush quilted leather interior. He was wealthy? She hadn't seen that coming. It disappointed her a little. She wouldn't want him to think she found him interesting just because he had money.

"Does your car have a name?" she asked as the vehicle purred away from the curb.

He frowned. "No."

"Every car has one, you know."

"A name?"

"Yes. You're doing this beauty a great disservice by not taking the time to learn hers."

He grinned over at her before accelerating out into a busy thoroughfare. "What would you call my car?"

She leaned forward to lay both palms flat on the dashboard. She listened for a moment and then broke into a big smile. "Of course. Her name is Lola. She's Italian."

"Most Ferraris are."

"You're making fun of me," she accused.

"Are you one of those people who names everything?" he asked, without sounding at all like he was making fun of her.

She shrugged. "Only the things that need names."

"And I suppose you skip people's and animal's given names entirely and make up endearments for them?"

She scowled, sensing that he was subtly poking fun at her. "Yes. And I'd call you Curmy."

"Like Kermit the Frog?"

"No. Short for Curmudgeon."

He laughed aloud. "I could live with that."

"Fine, Curmy. How long till we reach the police station?"

"About…ten…seconds," he answered as he decelerated quickly and swerved into a parking spot in front of a rather nondescript building obviously built in the modern-utilitarian 1970s.

"Lord, that's an ugly building." Of course, it wasn't just the dreadful architecture. An aura of suffering and human evils hung over the place like a shroud. Hastily, she closed her mind's eye, snapping it shut like a cheap door.

"No kidding it's ugly," Max muttered fervently as he helped her out of the car. "You'd think in a town like this that the builder would have given at least a tiny crap about his building not looking like a three-story wart."

His hand came up to touch the small of her back as he escorted her into the police station, and her breath caught a little at the way her entire being focused on that light contact between them.

The actual taking of a statement took about two minutes. But then she came to the tricky part. "Officer Leblanc, have there been other girls in the past few years who went missing?"

"Of course," the handsome Cajun replied.

"I mean any who look like me. You know. Similar height, build and coloring. Close to my age. That sort of thing."

"I don't know. Why?"

"My attacker. He…" She searched for the right words that didn't come right out and say she'd picked a vision out of his brain. "He…indicated that I was not his first victim."

"What do you mean?" As she'd expected, the cop jumped on her comment aggressively.

"I'm not sure exactly," she demurred. "I…" *Crap.* She had no words to get around the truth she was determined not to reveal.

Thankfully, Max dived in and rescued her. Again. "I have to agree with her. I saw the way he was manhandling her. He was no amateur. He knew exactly how to subdue her. Could you just look into other missing persons reports, Bastien, and see if any other petite red-heads have gone missing?"

"Fine. I'll take a look."

They had to wait around for a while as a lineup was prepared for her, and then Detective LeBlanc put her in a nasty little room with no lights and a big window. She knew the drill from watching television. Five surly-looking men filed into the room on the other side of the one-way glass, and she immediately pointed out suspect number four.

She was led out, and Max was brought into the room. He came out in about ten seconds, as well. She didn't even bother to ask him which guy he'd picked. They'd both gotten up-close-and-personal looks at her attacker last night. The lineup was purely a formality.

And then they were done. An odd sense of panic washed over her. There was nothing else to tie Max to her life. He could drop her off at the curiosity shop and drive away, never to see her again. She didn't even have his real name, let alone his phone number. If only she had more experience with men. Maybe she would know a smooth way to ask him for his contact information. Something that would let her keep in touch with him. She had a serious crush on him and craved more of him desperately.

They parked down the street from her shop a little before noon. He did not invite her out to lunch as she'd hoped he would. There was no small talk, nothing to indicate he had any personal interest in her whatsoever. That was what she got for dressing like a mortician. She should have gone with her first impulse to dress up for him.

"Here's my card," he announced without preamble.

"It has my private cell phone and personal email address on it. If you ever get in trouble, ever need help, give me a call."

She took the white rectangle despondently. Not a "Call me if you want to have coffee or go out for a drink." Just a "If you get in trouble…" It was pro forma polite behavior, not a sincere offer to see her again. *Well, hell.*

She climbed out of the car, insisting he not get out and come around to help her. She watched the sleek black car pull away from the curb and dart into the city. And she was alone once more. Except today it hurt even worse than usual.

Max watched the small black figure retreat in his rearview mirror, her shoulders slumped in defeat, her entire spirit shrinking in on itself. He was a horrible human being. She'd obviously hoped he would throw her a social bone and show even the tiniest spark of interest in her.

Thing was, he was interested. And, furthermore, he did give a damn about her. And that was exactly why he had to stay away from her. To cut off even the most casual contact between them. He had to break any link between them before she got seriously hurt. For he and his dangerous, fake life would do just that if he let her into it.

He parked in front of his restored French Quarter condo, pulled out his cell phone and placed a call. In rapid Russian, he said, "Hey, Peter. It's me. There was some trouble last night." Peter Menchekov was his boss nowadays, ever since the mobster who'd controlled Max initially had been killed in a government raid a few months back.

At least he no longer worked for the more violent psychopaths who populated the lower rungs of this crime syndicate. He'd finally moved up the ranks to quiet, thoughtful men who wore expensive suits and weren't prone to fits of temper. But he sensed that he was still far from the top of this sprawling organization. There was someone hiding at the apex of the pyramid. The ultimate predator and mastermind of the whole organization. Until he learned that person's identity, his work was not done.

"What kind of trouble was there, Masha?"

He winced at his childhood nickname. It was the common Slavic shortening of his full name, Maximillian. "The girl, the one whose store you wanted me to watch, is not the person we thought she was. The store's owner died a month ago, and this girl is the new owner. She just came to town. She knows nothing."

"The order I got was to watch the store. Not to watch the store's owner," Peter correctly observed. "Continue the surveillance."

"There's a small problem with that. The store's owner met me last night. It was an accident. A guy mugged her, and I had to stop him from killing her."

A pause while his boss considered that. "All the better. Infiltrate her store. Find out everything she knows about what goes on in the store and whether she plans to continue running it the same way as her aunt did in the past."

An interesting word choice, that. *Infiltration, huh?* That smacked of military training. Or espionage school. Who was Peter, really? Max made a mental note and added it to his growing list of suspicions that this was no simple Russian crime gang.

Why was the crime syndicate so interested in this silly little shop, anyway? What was so special about it?

He'd figured his boss would want him to stay in direct contact with the store owner, now that he'd met her. Which was why he'd put off making this call. The last thing he wanted to do was play Lissa Clearmont. She struck him as a kind and decent soul, innocent and deserving of an honest man. Not a con-man schmuck like him messing with her for his own nefarious ends.

"Understood," he replied shortly. He couldn't bring himself to say any more politely, and he dared not say any more impolitely.

"Good hunting," Peter said briskly, ending the call.

Max jammed the phone in his pocket. Good hunting, indeed. He'd be hunting a babe in the woods. This was going to be a massacre of that poor girl's heart.

Chapter 3

People had a tendency to underestimate her, and Lissa used it to her advantage from time to time. Like the older man in a suit who walked into her store that afternoon, asking after an obscure African fertility statue, almost as though he didn't expect her to have any idea what he was talking about.

She'd seen it in the showcases somewhere, but couldn't remember exactly where off the top of her head. Aunt Cal's ghost was usually around and happy to point out where to find some trinket or another. Not that Lissa particularly wanted any ghost's assistance, no matter how helpful it might be. Sure enough, a light hand nudged her down the second aisle and to the right.

She left the man happily examining the foot-high statue, which she personally considered one of the ugliest items in the entire shop, and returned to the cash register. She was a little disappointed when he didn't buy it but was encouraged when he said he would send his grandson in to look at it the following day to see if it was the one the younger man had been looking for. She could use the sale.

Finishing the renovation that Callista had started upstairs was costing a great deal more than she'd anticipated, and she hadn't even started hiring the various contractors she now knew she would need to finish the job and pass the city building inspection. Yet again, her tendency to leap before she looked had bitten her in the tush.

Business was slow today, likely on account of the football play-offs, and she closed up early. Mr. Jackson shared a TV dinner with her as she settled in to watch an old black-and-white film noir.

Which turned out to be a bad choice. When she had herself properly scared and deliciously tingling, the spirits tended to come to her, whether she wanted them to or not. They were different here in the South, whispering of different pasts and different secrets than the ghosts in her art studio in Vermont had. Not that she wanted to hear any of them.

Desperate to do anything to stave off the insistent murmurs in her mind, she gave in to an urge to read tarot cards. She didn't consider herself particularly skilled with these sorts of readings, but shuffling and laying out the cards gave her restless hands something to do. She cleared the folding table she currently used for eating, painting and balancing business ledgers. The cards all but leaped out of her fingers into a traditional spread. They spoke of four men in her immediate future. A lover. A trickster. A villain. And a hero. But the cards stubbornly refused to tell her which one would win out in the end.

And that was why she didn't like using cards. She couldn't bully them into answering her the way she could stubborn spirits. She tried again, doing individual card turns. She turned over the Prince of Cups from the top of the deck. Then she pulled the Prince of Wands out of the middle of the deck. Then the Prince of Pentacles. She chose a fourth card with great reluctance.

No surprise. The Prince of Swords. *What on earth?* She would end up with all four men? *That* didn't sound like her. She would be thrilled to land one man, let alone four. Although she supposed she could do without a trickster or a villain in her life. She'd already had enough of the influence of those affecting her, compliments of her birth father, whoever he might be.

Her mother never had remembered anything about the night she was drugged at a party and raped, resulting in Lissa's birth. Or maybe her mother hadn't wanted to remember. Not that Lissa blamed her. And not that she actually wanted to know who her birth father was.

Some people argued that Lissa's gift was a result of the great trauma in her genetic past, and others said it was a curse visited on her. No matter its source, she would be glad to be rid of it.

Sometimes, when she'd been little, she'd been able to conjure a shadowy image of a man's face when she thought of her birth father, but she'd never been able to see more than that. The fates had long made it clear that further knowledge of the man was not for her.

As she stared down at the four tarot cards on the table, another man's face swam into view in her mind— this time as sharp and clear as her father's had been indistinct. He had short blond hair, light green-gold eyes that were reluctant to smile and a world of hurts accumulated on his handsome brow. She would love to know what had added such weight to Max Smith's spirit at such a young age. He couldn't be much more than thirty years old. Either that, or the man had the moisturizing regimen of a god.

His face still lingered clear and strong in her mind's eye when she fell asleep. It even followed her into her dreams, promising to protect her and keep her safe.

And maybe that was why she didn't scream when she woke up and heard the noises coming from downstairs.

Max woke groggily as his cell phone exploded into sound. Cripes. What time was it? The face of the phone said it was nearly 3:00 a.m. The caller ID named L. Clearmont as the caller. *What the hell?*

"Lissa? What's up?"

A frantic whisper replied. "There's someone in the shop. And it sounds like he's busting up everything."

Max lurched fully awake. "Go into your bathroom. Lock the door or barricade it with a chair. Crawl into the bathtub, cover yourself with a white towel if there's one in there to make yourself harder to see and be very still and quiet. I'll call nine-one-one. Don't come out until the police identify themselves. I'll be there in ten minutes."

He leaped out of bed and yanked on jeans and a T-shirt, still rattling off instructions to her. "If you have something heavy like a hammer or a wrench at hand, take it with you. Pound the crap out of any bastard who tries to lay a finger on you. Fight like a wildcat if they try to drag you out of there. And scream your head off. Wake up the whole damned neighborhood."

He grabbed his car keys and sprinted for Lola. "I'm getting in my car now. Hang on, Lissa. I'll be there as soon as I can and will kick their asses for you."

He tossed the phone, on speaker, onto the car seat beside him and peeled out, leaving expensive Italian racing rubber on the pavement. It was a fifteen-minute drive normally, but he made it in a shade under eight. The cops were still not there, the bastards.

The Saints had won their play-off game, and the partying on Bourbon Street had to be worse than usual, but still. Lissa lived in this town. She deserved a fast response from the NOPD to a break-in. Especially after the violent attack on her the day before. He'd no sooner had the thought than a pair of squad cars careened around the corner, sirens and lights screaming.

The cops advanced on the store, guns drawn, and he wasted no time moving up behind them.

"I'm a friend of the owner. She's locked in the upstairs bathroom. While you gentlemen clear the main floor and the basement, I'm going for her."

"Sir, we need to clear the entire building before you enter the premises—"

"Just don't shoot me," he tossed over his shoulder, his own pistol drawn from its shoulder holster and at the ready before him in a trained shooter's grip. "I've got the left quadrant and stairs." And with that he spun through the smashed front door.

The cops must have recognized a trained operative, for they let him precede them and ceded the left third of the store to his search.

"Clear!" he called after racing up and down the first

few rows of smashed curio cabinets and overturned display cases. "I'm going upstairs."

"Roger that," one of the cops called back. "Holler if you need backup."

"You'll know if you hear gunshots," he bit out. If whoever had trashed the store had laid a hand on Lissa, there would be no fight. There would be lead flying and dead bastards bleeding out on her floor.

He moved quickly and silently up the stairs and spun into her living room, low and lethal. No movement. He pointed his weapon at each dark corner of the room, searching quickly for man-size shadows or any hint of movement. He'd told her to take Mr. Jackson with her into the bathroom if she could find the cat without having to go looking for him. He'd also suggested that she use the cat as a weapon, to throw it at anyone who tried to break through the bathroom door.

The living room was clear. He spun into the guest room and her bedroom, pausing to check under the bed and behind the armoire before moving to her bathroom door.

"Lissa, it's Max. The police are here, and the intruders have left. It's safe to come—" The door flew open and a soft, slight body flew into his arms, knocking him back a step with the force of her rush.

"I knew you'd come for me. I knew you'd save me. You were there in my head, both of your faces smiling down at me and telling me everything would be fine..."

What the hell was she talking about? Both of his faces?

"We clear up here?" someone called from over by the staircase.

"All clear," Max called back to the cop. "I've got the

owner of the store with me, and she's fine. She'll be down in a second to make a statement."

But for now he was just going to hold her and let their mutual panic subside a little. He was startled to realize his heartbeat was galloping madly and adrenaline screamed through his veins. He hadn't gotten this rattled since he was a kid, before his father starting training him seriously in how to be an undercover field operative. Spies didn't have strong emotions. Or if they did, they certainly didn't let those emotions get the best of them.

Damned if Max's knees didn't feel a little wobbly, though. Was he really that smitten with this woman he barely knew? He lifted his chin off the top of her head to stare down at her, and she leaned back enough to stare up at him. There it was again. That rope of electric attraction hovering right at the edge of his vision, drawing them together.

"Kiss me, Max."

"I don't take advantage of women under duress—"

"Kiss me, dammit, or bend down here so I can kiss you."

"You're bossy for a little thing—"

She looped her hands around the back of his neck and tugged his head down to hers while she stood on tiptoe. And then she kissed him.

He'd had some fine kisses in his day, but this was something else altogether. A movie of their future life together unfolded in his head almost too quickly to process. An entire symphony sound track played in the background, and his soul left his body, joined hers, twined with it. Then both leaped back into his body in the space of time it took to blink once.

Laughter. Love. Loss. Generations before and generations to come all crowded into his brain and then fled again, consumed by the fiery passion that exploded between him and Lissa the moment their lips touched.

She groaned and pressed herself closer to him as his arms tightened around her delicate frame. Although she didn't feel delicate right now. She felt like an untamed tiger in his embrace. And he felt like the one being consumed as she inhaled his soul into herself, stripping him bare and leaving him wide-open to her.

She staggered back from him with a gasp. "I... I'm so sorry... I know better than to cut loose like that."

"What are you apologizing for? Laying the hottest kiss on me I've ever experienced?" He blinked down at her, stunned. "That was incredible."

"You're not scared?" she asked in a small voice.

"Should I be?"

"Well, most people would be a little freaked out by the...intensity...of that."

"Passion is nothing to be afraid of. I mean, I could see some guys being afraid of it. But it takes a lot to scare me..." He trailed off, not entirely certain what they were talking about.

"You have a point." She sounded bemused. A little distracted even, as if she was pondering something else altogether.

"What's going on in that complicated head of yours?" he asked lightly, even though the question was dead serious.

"That's the second time the floodgates have opened around you." She didn't explain her comment.

"Should I know what you're talking about?" he asked.

"No, of course not. I'm just rambling on about nothing."

"What floodgates?" he persisted.

A police officer's voice interjected from by the stairwell. "Ma'am, if you could come downstairs, we need you to make a statement."

Thank God. Saved by the cops.

"Yes, Officer, I know the drill. I was attacked last night on the street."

"Someone got it in for you, ma'am?"

Max froze at the question. He'd been too panicked on his way over there to make the obvious connection between the two attacks. He looked down at her, still nestled in his arms. "Who wants to hurt you? Do you have enemies?"

"Not here. I just got to New Orleans."

Did that mean she had enemies elsewhere? Mad enough to follow her and take their revenge on her in the Big Easy? "We need to talk," he murmured.

She nodded once, reluctantly.

The vandals had been kind enough to leave a calling card in the form of gang symbols spray painted on the walls and windows of the shop. This was retaliation for Julio G.'s capture. Max's jaw went hard as he stared at the damage. Julio G. wasn't the only guy in town who could call in muscle to make a point.

He asked the police tersely, "Do you know where this gang has its headquarters?"

"Hey, now, buddy. We don't want no retaliation from the likes of you. Besides, these punks are a big, powerful gang. Lots of guys. Lots of guns. You stay away from them. Ya heah'?"

"I hear," he replied evenly. He *ignored*, but he heard.

Julio G. and his boys were about to deeply regret messing with one Lissa Clearmont.

Tonight's police interview took considerably longer than last night's. Not only were the police less concerned about her mental well-being, since she hadn't been physically attacked this time, but they were highly suspicious of two attacks by a notorious gang in such quick succession. They probed at length for some connection between her and a gang member, some enemy, some ex-lover or disgruntled customer who could have caused Julio G. and his boys to target her.

Dawn was breaking by the time the last law enforcement professional packed up his tools and left. Max carried down a sheet of plywood from upstairs and sawed it to fit in the frame of the broken shop door. "You're going to need a new door. While you're at it, you should upgrade to something with a wrought iron security grill."

"I'd have no idea how to go about finding something like that."

"Then you're in luck. I know every antique and secondhand dealer in town. We'll find you something. But first, breakfast."

Lissa looked around the interior of one of New Orleans's most famous restaurants in dismay. They were the only customers. "Is this place even open for breakfast?"

"It's open for us. I did the owner a favor a while back."

"What kind of favor?"

Max grinned across the white linen tablecloth at her. "A big one, *chère*."

She subsided, knowing an evasion when she heard one. Max ordered eggs Benedict, bacon, sausage, grits and fresh fruit for two, and then leaned back to study her intently enough that she started to squirm a bit.

"About that kiss last night," he started.

Oh, Lord. She'd been hoping he wouldn't bring that up. She had no idea why such a massive flood of impressions, images and information had come over her when they'd kissed. Her big visions were always tied to violence, not to hot kisses.

Maybe it had been her own fear that triggered the sudden onslaught of psychic emanations in her head. She'd probably just been too scared to put a lid on the vivid emotions that had flooded her. That was all it had been—emotion. Physical attraction and arousal. *Not* anything psychic. She was done with opening herself to those energies.

Max leaned forward curiously. "What happened? Is that what it's always like to kiss you?"

"I wouldn't know. I've never kissed myself."

"*Something* happened when you kissed me, Lissa."

He hadn't picked up on some of the visions that had shot through her when they'd kissed, had he? "You mean the earth moved under your feet?" she joked.

He frowned across the table at her. "I'm serious."

She really wished he would drop the line of questioning, but she sensed there wasn't a chance in hell he would do that. Instead she asked, a shade shortly, "Describe *something*."

"It was like my imagination went crazy. I saw all kinds of images and felt all kinds of feelings. Hell, I even thought I heard music. But it all happened in, like, a millisecond."

She swore under her breath. Did he have a gift of his own, then? Most mundanes were lucky to catch tiny snatches of her vision flow. Nobody saw the whole unedited show inside her skull. She leaned forward. "Has anyone ever told you you're empathic?"

He frowned. "As in the woo-woo kind? An empath?"

She smiled broadly. "That, or merely that you have a talent for picking up on other peoples' emotions."

He leaned back hard in his chair. "I'm a—" He broke off and started again. "I have some experience in watching other people's body language. Reading facial expressions. But that doesn't make me some kind of psychic."

He said the word as if it were filthy. A momentary knife of pain twisted in her gut. *No.* It was all right. She wasn't part of that world anymore. He could despise it and not despise the most important piece of her.

"Are you a cop?" she blurted.

"No," he answered promptly.

He wasn't an FBI agent, was he? That would be disastrous. He'd be an easy phone call away from talking to the feds she'd worked with in the Northeast, finding kidnapping victims and murder victims over the years. Heck, he would probably already know some guys out of the Boston office.

"Are you FBI?" she asked reluctantly.

"Nope."

Thank goodness. But then her confusion returned, bigger than before. "Then how did you know how to drop Julio G., and how did you know all that stuff you told me to do on the phone last night? And now that I think about it, you came into the store at the same time as the police. How did they let you do that?"

"I got to your place first. They just followed me in."

She sensed evasion in his voice. "And the other stuff? About how I should hide and defend myself from an intruder in my house. How did you know about all that?"

He grinned at her. "Easy. I watch a lot of cop shows on TV."

That was *totally* more evasion. She started to challenge him but was interrupted by the arrival of their breakfast. The food was beyond delicious, and she dug in with gusto.

Eventually Max said, "Tell me more about your aunt. I gather she was some sort of psychic? What's up with that? That stuff's not real, is it?"

She'd had this argument so many times over the years that she'd long ago learned just not to go there in conversation. "I am no scientific authority and can't comment on that one way or another. Each person sees and believes whatever they want to regarding psychic phenomena. As for my aunt, most people who knew her believed she was not only psychic but *very* psychic."

"And you? Do you believe that?"

She shrugged noncommittally. "She knew some stuff that was awfully hard to explain any other way."

"There's always an explanation. Scientists can always successfully debunk anyone who claims to be psychic."

She stared at him intently, willing him to understand. "Many people use mundane skills to pass themselves off as psychics. The technique is generally referred to as cold reading. I do think that some people who actually cold read believe themselves to be genuinely psychic. In point of fact, they're picking up on subtle body language signals from their subjects."

"Like your aunt?"

He sounded as if he was trying to make a joke, but she answered seriously. "Most people who saw her in action believed she had a genuine gift. It's not possible to cold read the future, but she could predict it spot-on. She could give uncannily accurate readings to people she'd never met, over the phone, in a different part of the country from her. And she never did it as a parlor trick or for financial gain."

To his credit, Max didn't make any snarky comments. He actually seemed to take her at her word when she claimed her aunt had possessed out-of-the-ordinary skills. At least he didn't disbelieve her outright. That was more than she could have asked from him.

"If you're not psychic," he remarked lightly, "then I guess you're simply a spectacular kisser."

She shot him a damning look. "You don't believe that."

"I dunno. That was a pretty hot kiss you laid on me. Perhaps we ought to try it again and see if the same thing happens."

"We're in a restaurant, sitting in front of the window on a crowded street!"

"All those folks out there have seen kissing before."

"I'm still hungry," she declared, her stomach doing flip-flops at the idea of kissing him again. And this time when she wasn't scared out of her mind.

"Afraid to kiss me?" he teased her.

"You have a sister, don't you?" she accused.

He glanced at her a shade too quickly. "Did your psychic powers tell you that?"

"No. That annoying big-brother tone you just took with me told me," she retorted.

Grinning, he lifted his orange juice to her. "Touché."

An urge filled her to know this man, to understand what made him tick, to know how he'd become the confident, self-contained man seated before her today. "Tell me the three most important things that have ever happened to you," she asked impulsively.

"You first," he returned.

"Fair enough." She thought for a moment. "In no particular order, the circumstances of my conception—"

He interrupted her. "Elaborate on that."

"My mother was drugged and raped at a party when she was nineteen. Her attacker was never caught. I was the result of that event. But it means I never knew my birth father." She added reluctantly, "And it means my mother was plagued by conflicted feelings about me and my existence throughout my entire upbringing."

Which was the understatement of the century. No matter how hard her mother had wanted to love her, some part of her had never been able to break through the trauma of the rape to truly, unconditionally love Lissa. Her mother's head was willing to love, but her heart was not entirely.

Max looked as though his mental wheels were turning a hundred miles an hour, and she continued hastily before he could ask her any more probing questions about that exceedingly unpleasant detail about her past.

"Number two most important life event—inheriting the shop from my aunt. It gave me an excuse to move across the country and start a new life."

"Why didn't you just sell the shop and stay where you were? That building has great bones and is in a neighborhood that's gentrifying fast. You could turn a nice profit if you sold it."

"I needed the new start more than I needed the money."

"Why?"

She was careful not to even think about her real reasons for the abrupt move, lest they show on her face and Captain Perceptive Pants pick up on them. "My life wasn't heading the direction I wanted it to in Vermont."

"And what direction would that be?"

She shrugged. "The normal one. A decent living, some friends, a nice guy. Maybe settling down someday." Suddenly panicked that he would think she was making a pass at him, she added in desperation, "You know. The whole 2.1 kids, dog and a Volvo station wagon routine."

He smiled gently at her attempt at humor. "And the third most important thing to happen to you?"

"I'm still waiting for it." She wasn't about to admit that meeting him was rapidly climbing its way onto the list. And she bloody well wasn't confessing that talking with dead people was the real third thing on her list. "Okay, your turn," she blurted.

His facial expression went stone cold, locked and barred, no entrance. When he spoke, it was with great reluctance. "My parent's divorce changed the course of my life. My father tried to steal my loyalty away from my mother, and the result was that he and I spent a lot of time together when I was a kid. He tried to teach me to be like him."

She sensed darkness in that statement. Were she still a practicing psychic and he a client seeking a reading, she would dive into that darkness and explore it, but she was not and he was not. "Did your father succeed in making you like him?" she asked quietly.

"That's an excellent question."

Good grief. Wave upon wave of darkness shrouded that answer. Clearly Max was deeply conflicted about his father and not at all enamored at the idea of being like him. She noted that he declined to answer her. He continued with his list.

"The car accident that almost killed my mom and little sister was the second big milestone. It left my mother paralyzed from the neck down. I had to move back home from college and care for her around the clock for four years until she died of complications."

"Oh, Max. I'm so sorry."

He shrugged casually, but she didn't have to be psychic to feel the pain in the gesture.

"And the third event?"

He opened his mouth. Started to say something but stopped. A voice in her head filled in his unspoken words. *Meeting you.* Was that for real, or was that just her own desires whispering what she wanted to hear?

"My work, I suppose."

"And what exactly is it that you do?"

"I'm a finder. I locate things for people with a lot of money burning a hole in their pockets. Art, antiques, furniture, information, you name it. I make connections and fulfill wishes."

Interesting. "Tell me more about yourself, Max."

"Nope."

She blinked, startled at the bluntness of his reply. He sounded like he meant it, too. "Gonna make me discover more the hard way, huh? Pass me your hand, palm up."

Smirking, he held his hand out to her. She studied the lines on his hand for a long moment. *Oh, dear.* There was much more than just a split family in his childhood and the tragic loss of his mother. Suffering. Loneliness. Hatred. *Hatred?* That was interesting.

His money line was strong. However, his love line was all but nonexistent. She saw a radical life change in his near future. Love was possible, but at great personal cost. And where his passion mound should be, there was only a hard callus at the base of his thumb. She knew from entirely mundane means, namely, working with the FBI for the past decade, that it meant he shot handguns on a regular basis. The irony of a callus over his heart line was impossible to miss, however.

"See anything interesting?" he finally asked.

"I see lots of interesting things. That doesn't mean I plan to share any of them with you."

"Hey!" he protested.

"I thought we already established that all that psychic mumbo jumbo is pure poppycock," she declared.

She was saved by the arrival of breakfast dessert crepes, which were as scrumptious as they sounded. She and Max dived in to the clotted-cream-and-strawberry-filled confections in companionable silence for the most part. And what conversation there was stayed safely on small talk.

She was stuffed when Max finally held her chair for her to stand up. She was going to have to diet for a week to work off that meal. But it had been worth it to get to know Max a little more.

He drove her back to the shop and dropped her off, and she commenced the tedious process of cleaning up after the damage done by what must have been baseball bats or steel pipes. The vandal or vandals had been thorough. Even the walls had gaping holes in them.

Once the debris was swept into a single pile, she

began the even more tedious process of inventorying everything that remained and then guessing at what had been broken based on the bits she sifted through. If only she knew the inventory better. She was sure to forget something, and without a list of merchandise made by her aunt, she was bound to lose a fortune in any insurance claim she filed.

Where had Max run off to, anyway? Hopefully, their conversation over breakfast hadn't scared him. She'd gotten the impression that he liked kissing her nearly as much as she liked kissing him. But he'd driven away from the shop a couple of hours ago like the devil himself had lit a fire under him. Like things were moving too fast for him. Like she'd spooked him.

Chapter 4

Max jogged up the front steps of a conservative, yet opulent, house off Saint Charles Avenue, uptown. The neighborhood was known for its grand mansions and Old South elegance. This home fit right in.

In stark contrast, however, a pair of thugs, dressed in the requisite leather coats and sporting shaved heads, stood on the Grecian portico, guarding the double entry doors. They were an ugly accoutrement marring an otherwise beautiful work of Southern architecture. But then, he never had gone for the whole Russian mobster look, personally.

"Masha!" Peter Menchekov greeted him warmly. "What brings my special problem solver to see me at my home on a Sunday morning like this?" Although Menchekov's tone was jovial, a warning that this interruption of his personal life had better be important underlay the words.

Briefly, Max told him about the break-in at Lissa's shop and the calling card left behind by Julio G.'s boys. He finished with, "Here's the thing, Peter. If we want this shop to stay alive as a dead drop for our people, we need to back off Julio G. and his gang and make it clear they are not to mess with this place."

"An excellent point. Above my pay grade to make the call on whether or not we keep it as a drop location, though. I'll have to pass the question up the chain of command."

He would take that as confirmation that his conjecture had been correct. The curiosity shop was important to the mob because of its value as a place where messages could be passed securely.

"Thanks, sir." It was frustrating not knowing whether or not the higher-ups would choose to protect Lissa. The police were right. He couldn't take on an entire gang by himself. Not that it would stop him from trying, of course.

Peter was speaking again. "Callista Clearmont was a longtime friend of the family. I expect the bosses will take care of her niece. Particularly after the way Callista died."

Max went on mental full alert. He asked carefully, "Was there something unusual about the way she died?"

Peter shrugged. "Word on the street was that she was murdered."

"The way I hear it, the police didn't think so. They didn't even order an autopsy."

Peter shrugged again. "I'm just saying. I personally find the circumstances of her death suspicious. I saw her one week before she died, and she looked to be in perfect health to me."

Lissa had hinted that her aunt's death had come as a surprise. "Would you like me to look into her death further, sir?"

Peter's eyebrows lifted. "I was not aware you had those kinds of resources. But by all means, yes. If you can find out exactly how she died, I would be interested to know the cause. And I know the big boss would love to know what really happened."

It was right on the tip of his tongue to ask who the big boss was and why the man would love to know how Lissa's aunt had died. But Max bit it back. He dared not raise any suspicions in Peter's mind.

He pondered how to pull Peter back to the main topic, which was identifying why Lissa and her shop had been targeted. Had it been a random chance kind of attack, or had someone else pointed and shot that psycho at her?

He probably ought to take the attacks at face value and let it go, but his instincts suggested that perhaps there was more than met the eye here. He didn't want to traumatize Lissa any further by spouting conspiracy theories about the mugging and break-in without any proof.

"It is possible that Julio and his boys are attempting to test the boundaries of our territory and are probing a perceived weak spot in the wake of Callista's untimely death?" he asked Peter.

Max watched Peter's face closely. The man gave away no hint of having been behind the woman's death. But then Max hadn't expected that he would give anything away.

"Another interesting question. I will have some people put out feelers into the other syndicates operating in New Orleans. We took a big hit when that arms deal last year turned out to be a federal bust. It is possible that Julio might perceive us to be weak. We must, of course, counter this notion. Strongly."

Thank God he'd risen above the level of hit men and street soldiers in this gang. He hesitated to think about the orders that might have already gone out to that cadre to reassert the position in New Orleans of the Bratya— the Brothers, as this particular crime organization referred to itself.

"…having a party next week here at the house," Peter was saying. "You should bring the niece with you. What's her name? Lissa? Yes, bring her along. We'd like to meet her."

We, who? Would one or more of the upper-level executives of Russian Crime, Inc., finally show themselves, perhaps?

Max smiled pleasantly. "Of course. She'd love to meet you, I'm sure." But inside he cringed. No way did he want to embroil Lissa in whatever might have gotten her aunt murdered. But it wasn't as if he had any choice now. Peter had given an order, ever so politely but an order nevertheless. He showed himself out of the house and left Peter to his brunch.

Max had two more errands to run today, and the first took him to Bastien LeBlanc's auto shop. It was a big metal building with living quarters built into one corner of the spacious shop. The guy loved restoring cars better than life, supposedly.

"Hey, Bass!" he called as he stepped into the shop.

Bastien, tank-shirted and bleary-eyed, poked his blond head out the living area door. "What do you want on a Sunday morning, bro? I ain't feedin' y'all. I'm too damned hungover to cook." The Cajun was also re-nowned among his peers as a hell of a fine Creole chef.

Max grinned. "I was hoping I could talk you into looking at the death of a woman named Callista Clearmont. She died about a month ago. Was there an autopsy?"

"The aunt of that girl you rescued? Why you pokin' aroun' in her business?"

"Humor me, will you?"

"I'm not your personal research service, bro. Call Jennie and Perriman if you want that. They'll hook you up after you helped them out like you did last year."

He sighed. He had considered calling the navy special ops support team. Their computer wizard, a young woman named Jennie Finch, was the best researcher he'd ever run across. She could tease information out of a computer like nobody's business. And the unit's leader, Navy Commander Cole Perriman, was as sharp a special operator as he'd ever met.

But it was a favor he was loath to burn just yet. As he neared the top of the Bratya organization, he wanted to know he had a SEAL team in his back pocket if the need should arise. After all, his own covert employer had declined to support this op he was running on his own.

"Or you could call your own government agency," Bastien suggested.

"I'm deep undercover. Can't break cover to talk to them," he replied. In truth, it was more complicated than that. He'd tried to sell his employers on his theory that a Russian crime syndicate might actually be funding a much more sinister ring of Russian spies, but the CIA had completely discounted his theory as ridiculous. His handler thought he was running the op for reasons of personal revenge and had wanted no part of it.

Truth be told, that had probably been an accurate observation by his CIA handler. Hence, this op was completely off the books. The CIA didn't know about it, and he intended to keep it that way.

"What are you messin' around in, anyway, bro? Dis' swamp you swimmin' in dangerous?"

He'd discovered that Bastien's Cajun drawl grew noticeably thicker when the guy was at his sharpest mentally. "Nah. No gators in my swamp." He added drily, "But thanks for asking."

"Look. I know you're deep inside the Russian mob. I know you had Commander Perriman and his boys arrest you and throw you in jail along wit' them other mobsters to protect your cover. But that was almost a year ago. How long you plannin' to stay undercover? A man can only take so much before it starts to mess wit' his head."

And therein lay the crux of his dilemma. He still had more to learn about the mob his father had been so closely tied to. A mob that his father had trained him to run one day. A mob that he believed had killed his mother and might even have killed his father.

Max declared, "I'm all right, man. I've got you to keep me sane, right?"

Bastien snorted. "Callista Clearmont, huh? Was it classed a homicide?"

"I don't think so."

"Great. So there's not even an autopsy to look at." Bastien shrugged. "I'll see what I can dig up. Don't get your hopes up, though."

Max thanked the cop and left quickly, taking the

back alley out of Bastien's place. No sense making it easy for anyone to tie him to one of NOPD's finest.

Now to find Lissa a decent door. One that would keep out thugs intent on scaring the snot out of her and ruining her life. He planned to order the installation of cameras and a loud-ass alarm system for her, too.

And while he was out, he needed a sniper tripod that would fit in the window of the place across the street from the curiosity shop. He'd rented the place a few weeks back and had set up a one-man surveillance operation on Lissa Clearmont. He was going to turn it into a one-man protection operation, now. If anyone tried to mess with her a third time, they were in for a nasty surprise.

Next time any of Julio G.'s boys came around to mess with Lissa, they'd have him and a custom Barrett sniper rig to contend with.

Lissa looked up as Max called out a greeting from the front of the shop. "I'm back here," she told him. She climbed to her feet, her back creaking from a long day spent picking up broken bits off the floor. A thrill raced through her at the sound of his voice, erasing the day's aches and pains from her mind.

"I brought you a present."

"Please God let it be painkillers and a bottle of bourbon," she joked. She rounded the big armoire at the end of a row, and there he stood, with a giant door propped beside him.

"It'll need trimming down to fit, but I've got a circular saw in the truck and all the hardware we'll need to hang it."

"You have a truck?"

"I use it in my work. Most pieces of furniture and art won't fit in Lola."

She stared at the beautiful oiled oak door panel. A large oval glass inset was covered with an intricately patterned wrought iron grill that she could hardly fit her pinkie finger through. Nobody was breaking through it anytime soon. It was both beautiful and functional. "Where on earth did you find that, and on such short notice?" she asked.

He shrugged modestly. "I told you I find stuff professionally. I know people who can get me pretty much anything if it's to be had in New Orleans."

They spent the next hour measuring, cutting, drilling and screwing. At the end of it, she had a very fancy new door for the curiosity shop. It added an air of elegance to the whole place that she thought the resident ghosts would rather like. Even Mr. Jackson gave it an approving sniff and rubbed up against it briefly.

"What do I owe you for the door?" she asked Max after they'd stood back to admire their work.

"Nothing. Consider it a housewarming gift."

She frowned. "I'm not broke, you know. And my insurance will cover most of the damage in here."

"I believe you. But truly, it makes my life easier if you have a secure front door."

She glanced at him, perplexed by his comment. But then he added, "I suppose you could kiss me by way of a thank-you."

"Ha! There it is. The hidden motive. My mother always told me to be wary of men who come bearing gifts." She wagged an accusing finger up at him.

He grabbed the offending finger and kissed the tip of it before turning away quickly to survey the damage in the rest of the store. Her heart skipped a beat at the brief flirtation.

"Was anything stolen, or was it straight-up vandalism?" he tossed over his shoulder as he looked around at the wreckage formerly known as her shop.

"As far as I can tell, stuff was just busted up. Although I think I'm missing an ugly African fertility statue. It was stone and I doubt it would have been broken by a baseball bat. An arm might have come off, but the bulk of it should have stayed intact."

Max turned to face her. "Anyone show any interest in it recently?"

"Funny you should ask. A man came in yesterday to look at it. He said he would have his grandson come in and look at it today."

"And has the grandson shown up?" Max asked quickly.

"Not that I'm aware of. But then, I've had a closed sign in the window all day while I cleaned up. He could have come by, seen the sign and left without me ever knowing it."

A heavy frown knit Max's brow. Heavy enough that she refrained from asking about it and just let him think out whatever quandary had so arrested his attention all of a sudden.

"Was the statue hollow?" he bit out.

She frowned. "Yes. The head screwed off so shamans could put talismans inside it specific to whomever the statue was supposed to help be fertile. Is that important?"

Max smiled, but it didn't reach his eyes. "It's nothing. I just saw a fertility statue once that came apart."

"Where did you see a fertility statue?"

"I happen to have a professional interest in art, in case you forgot."

She might have scoffed, except he sounded serious. So many secrets this man kept. It was enough to make her a little crazy. "I guessed I pictured you as a European old masters kind of guy and not an African fertility statue kind of guy."

He opened his mouth to respond, but his cell phone rang just then, silencing him. He pulled it out to see who was calling. After glancing at the caller ID, he said, "I'm sorry—I have to take this call. I'll stop by later to check on you."

She watched his broad shoulders and athletic frame retreat from her store, which suddenly felt empty without his magnetic presence. With a sigh, she got back to work sorting through the rubble.

"Yo, Bastien. What have you got for me?" Max strode down the street and around the corner. He ducked down a side street and toward the back entrance to his hidey-hole.

"Two things. First, that woman you asked about—Callista Clearmont—donated her body to science upon her death. It was taken to Tulane University so her brain could be studied. Apparently, she was some famous fortune-teller. Anyway, they've still got her corpse. You want me to order an autopsy on whatever's left after they sliced and diced it?"

Color him shocked. "Yes. That would be great."

He slipped into an alley one block over from the curiosity shop and jogged up the long stairs to his surveillance blind. He unlocked the door and let himself inside as Bastien continued, "And about that suggestion your girlfriend made—"

"She's *not* my girlfriend."

"So then you won't mind if I make a move on her? She's hot. Sweet little tushy, and those big do-me eyes. And that head of hair of hers—I bet she's a wildcat in bed—"

"You stay the hell away from her, LeBlanc. She doesn't need some idiot loving her and leaving her just now. Her life's in enough turmoil without you—"

Bastien broke into laughter in his ear, and Max cursed him out soundly.

Eventually, the cop quit chuckling long enough to say, "Yeah, well, your non-girlfriend's suggestion to look for young women who've disappeared recently having matching descriptions to her turned out to be a good one. We've had two more petite, dark-eyed red-heads disappear in that part of town. One about two years ago, and one almost exactly a year back."

Max frowned, seeing where this was going. "So Julio G. was after her for her appearance and nothing else?"

"No, man. He had plenty else in mind besides her appearance. We put a police informant in a holding cell with him, and he got to bragging to our guy. Bastard claimed to have done some seriously twisted stuff to a couple of girls. He didn't confess to killing any of them, but NOPD's psychiatrist thinks we've got ourselves a serial killer."

In a weird way, that was good news. He would actually rather have Lissa victimized by a serial killer—now in custody—than have her be the target of some power play by a rival gang to the Bratya.

Bastien was speaking again. "We got our best interrogators making a hard run at Julio. I'll let you know if he cracks."

"If the cops don't break him, are you going to give it a try?" He knew full well that Bastien's SEAL training included what the military liked to refer to as EIT— enhanced interrogation techniques—and then some.

"One step at a time, bro. In the civilian world, we have to keep an eye on how we get confessions out of perps. I'd hate to have this jackass get off on a pesky technicality."

One corner of Max's mouth turned up. He'd had the same interrogation training that Bastien had. Max sighed. "Keep me informed, will you?"

"You got it, bro."

He hung up and moved over to the window. From this third-story vantage point, he had a clear view into the curiosity shop, which, up until now, had been his main focus. Now he adjusted two of the cameras to look into Lissa's trashed apartment. He pointed one at her living room and another at her bedroom. It wasn't that he wanted to be a voyeur and spy on her private life. But he was determined to keep her safe, and that meant having eyes on her at all times.

He turned on the video cameras and set them to record anyone coming or going from the store. Then, he moved to the table in the corner and settled into the Zen patience of a surveillance operative.

Except the usual waiting calm would not come today. It felt wrong to be sitting there spying on Lissa Clearmont. He knew what she smelled like. What she felt like in his arms. Hell, he wanted to know a lot more than that about her. This was wrong.

But not wrong enough that he stopped. He was closing

in on the bastards who had killed his mother, and they would pay. Nobody, not even Lissa, was stopping him from catching them. If he had to be a disgusting Peeping Tom and invade her privacy in the most unspeakable ways, he would do it. He'd devoted most of the past decade to uncovering the identity of his mother's killer, and he wasn't about to stop now.

Lissa looked up from the pile of debris, arrested by an image in her mind's eye.

A dark night. Raining. Skid marks barely visible on the wet pavement. A broken guardrail. Way down a ravine, the undercarriage of an overturned car visible. Faint moaning filled her ears, even though she was too far away to hear it coming from that car. And the whimpering of a frightened child. She couldn't tell if it was coming from the crashed car or somewhere else in her vision.

A blonde woman terribly injured, more dead than alive, frantic about her own survival, but even more panicked about her daughter's safety. Someone had run them off the road, the blonde woman was certain of it. And she couldn't seem to move any of her limbs. She would not be able to protect her daughter if the would-be killer came down to finish them off.

Horror at the thought of watching them murder her daughter in front of her was worse than the thought of dying herself. A thousand times worse. And her son. So much responsibility already had fallen upon his young shoulders as he struggled to become a man...

Hot, silent tears ran down the woman's cheeks as life faded from her broken body.

Panic rushed through Lissa. She couldn't tell if it was

her own reaction to the horrifying scene or someone else's panic being projected to her. Were she with the FBI, she would merely relay to them the word *panic*.

A replica voodoo doll slipped out of her fingers and thudded to the floor. The sound startled Lissa out of the disturbing vision and back into the curiosity shop.

She'd never noticed until today the series of small shelves mounted around the shop about seven feet up, mostly tucked behind the tops of cabinets and stuff hanging from hooks in the ceiling. They hadn't been disturbed in the break-in, and she found herself staring at one of the shelves now. A large chunk of some clear rough-cut stone sat on the shelf. Quartz maybe.

Her gaze slid along the wall to the next small shelf, where she spotted the two halves of an amethyst geode resting side by side. The next shelf on the adjacent wall held a magnificent piece of fluorite with shards of blue and purple and green flecked throughout it. The next shelf held a bloodstone, more rust colored than red and deeply veined with black.

The entire store was set up as a ritual circle, ringed with magic-enhancing crystals. *Huh.* And then there were those lines she'd found. Today's cleanup had forced her to slide many of the big display units and antique cabinets aside, revealing a network of faded lines painted on the floor. They looked as if they'd been there for decades. Now that she thought about it, they formed a circle edged with some sort of intricate knot-work pattern.

Even the lamps in the store were carefully placed at the eight compass points of a ritual circle. *Son of a gun.* No wonder her psychic talent went crazy whenever she stood in the exact center of the store like she was doing now. The whole space was a focused ritual circle pointing at that one spot.

The more she learned about her deceased aunt, the more secrets she uncovered. And that worried her. What other secrets had Callista been keeping all these years?

Other questions had crowded forward today, too, disturbing ones that Lissa had spent most of her life trying to ignore. Like why had her mother left New Orleans as a teen and never, not once, come back to her hometown? Even after being attacked as a newly arrived girl in New York, why hadn't her mother ever come back here? What had driven her completely away from her own family? For that matter, why had the rest of the family moved away from New Orleans, leaving only Callista behind?

Max intently watched the image on his monitor of Lissa, turning around slowly in the middle of her shop. What was she doing? It was as if she'd suddenly realized she was lost and was trying to get her bearings. As he stared at the computer screen, the image fuzzed out, replaced by a memory of his father abandoning him in the middle of a bayou with nothing but a knife and his wits, and telling him to find his way home or die.

He'd been blindfolded in the car, and they'd driven for hours, whether in circles or hundreds of miles from home, he'd had no idea. It had been dark and scary as hell. There'd been bugs and snakes, which he ate; alligators, which he ran from; bogs, quicksand and swarms of mosquitoes that he'd been convinced before the end of the ordeal would make him lose his mind.

God, he'd hated his father for that trip into hell and back. The man had driven him relentlessly, never cut him any slack. Always he'd been training Max, cramming information down his throat. And all the while, he'd spewed hateful things about the United States, criticized democracy, forecast its failure, propagandized and bullied and harassed Max into saying that he despised America and that the government needed to be taken down.

He actually hadn't figured out that his old man was a spy for Mother Russia until he was about fourteen. The same age his sister had been when she and their mother had been in the car accident that paralyzed her mother and eventually claimed her life.

He blinked at the monitor, and Lissa came into view once more, her sweet face rescuing him from the memory.

A boy. Naked. On his hands and knees. Taking a beating being given to him for no reason other than it taught him how to withstand pain. To show him how much pain he could take without passing out.

Lissa reached out for the boy to shield him and comfort him in her mind, but he looked up at her, his tearstained face defiant.

"No!" he shouted silently at her. "Leave me alone. I can do this. I must do this. If I want to be strong, I have to do this."

Lissa shuddered at the madness of it. Her store swirled into focus once more. Was that a vision from the past, something happening now or a glimpse into the future? She couldn't tell from that brief snippet. And who was that boy? She hadn't gotten a good look at his face, and mostly she'd just noticed the tear-streaked cheeks and grim clenching of his jaw against crying out.

* * *

Max stared down at Lissa in her apartment. It was dark outside, and her living room was an island of light against the night. She looked exhausted. The poor girl had been working from dawn till dark cleaning up the shop for two days straight. She was making progress, but the sheer amount of inventory that had been stuffed into every nook and cranny of the shop was mind-boggling.

Her shoulders started to shake. She was crying. He swore aloud at being forced to sit and watch her suffer and do nothing to help her. His father might have made him torture animals and kill them by all kinds of horrible means, but he'd never stopped being secretly sickened by what his father made him do. Sickened at his father for demanding it of him, and sickened at himself for doing it.

It felt like that now, letting Lissa cry without reaching out to help her. He ought to call her. Distract her and make her laugh. Offer her a little understanding and human compassion. But instead, he sat, paralyzed by his own self-hatred.

He was a monster. Maybe not of his own creation, but a monster nonetheless. He'd let his father turn him into this. He'd been a willing participant in being trained as an undercover operative of the worst kind. He was honest enough with himself to admit that he'd wanted to be like this once upon a time. He'd thought it would be cool. That he would end up like James Bond. But it hadn't turned out to be sexy and exciting and sophisticated. It had turned out to be brutal and soul sucking and humanity robbing.

Lissa was better off without him. As miserable as

she might be down there right now, sobbing alone and hugging herself like a lost child, she was still better off.

After all, what kind of person spied on another one and reported on her to an employer who would kill her without a second thought if she accidentally got in his way?

Kill me, please. I'm begging you.

The blonde woman from the car accident lay in a hospital-style bed that looked out of place in a regular bedroom. The woman's limbs were oddly shrunken, the muscles atrophied away to nothing, and the woman lay unnaturally still. Only her head and face seemed to move. *Paralyzed.* The word burst into Lissa's mind. The woman was paralyzed from the neck down. She looked up at Lissa pleadingly, begging silently for release from her private hell. Or maybe the woman was not looking at Lissa, but at whoever's mind this vision had come from.

"I can't take this anymore," the woman wailed. *"I can't take what it's doing to you, how I'm ruining the lives of everyone around me. Put me out of my misery and end my suffering. Please. I can't do it myself. I'm too weak and too afraid. But you're not. You're strong. I know you know how to kill. Use your knowledge for good. Kill. Me."*

The woman's agony was so intense that if felt as if Lissa's insides were being torn out and tossed on the floor. Or maybe that was the agony of the person whose memory this was—a caregiver to the crippled woman. Either way, it was unbearable.

Lissa gripped her middle desperately, holding in the suffering as tears streaked down her face. Her tears or the woman's tears or the watcher's tears, she had no idea. They were all one and the same she supposed.

Where on earth were all these terrible images flooding in from? Whose were they? Not once had she seen a face she recognized. The visions came without a time context, without a call to action. The spirit sending her these images didn't seem to want anything from her at all, which was a first.

Normally dead spirits wanted their bodies found, wanted their killers brought to justice, wanted revenge. Others wanted to find closure. To let go of something preventing them from leaving behind their mortal existence and resting in peace.

But the source of the flood of images from the past several days remained elusive, not revealing himself or herself, not asking for anything. It just poured out, vision after unwelcome vision.

Maybe it was leftover visions stored in the magic circle of the shop. Perhaps as she cleaned out the stock, she was cleaning out old ghosts. Except they didn't feel old. If she were still into that stuff, she could do a séance to actually contact the spirits hovering so close. She could ask them directly where they came from and what they wanted from her.

In the past, she would have led an FBI team to a hidden grave and helped the spirit find peace enough to move on to wherever spirits went. No more, though. She'd given up that life. The work itself had been too stressful, and the impact on her personal life had been catastrophic. Everyone in seemingly the whole of New England had known her as the crazy girl who found dead people.

She no longer spoke to ghosts. She'd embraced the

normal. But apparently it had yet to embrace her. Maybe if she just ignored the visions and spirits, they would eventually give up and move on. After all, she couldn't possibly be the only person in this mystically charged town who could see and hear them.

She was glad Max had been leaving her alone. She was so rattled by the images that had been flooding her the past two days that she probably wouldn't have made the slightest sense if she'd tried to talk with him. She would have babbled like a madwoman, and he would have run screaming from her apparent psychotic break.

She'd had some genuinely rough patches in her life when in the thick of an FBI investigation, or the time she'd gotten the bright idea to contact her birth father's spirit and find out just how psychic he was. All she'd learned from that one was just how criminally insane the man had been. It had taken her two weeks to speak again after swimming around in his diseased brain.

Maybe this batch of violent, disturbing images was a result of her encounter with the mugger. Maybe these came from his head. Or maybe they were imaginary, conjured by her own brain to cope with the stew of terror and rage she was experiencing after nearly becoming the man's next victim.

That was the problem with a gift like hers. There was an inevitable gap between *believing* in it and *knowing* it was real. She was too logical a soul, too much the product of her skeptical family to entirely set aside her doubts about it. No matter how many bodies she found, or how many future events she correctly predicted, a little voice in the back of her head always was there, murmuring that maybe she'd just made a lucky guess. That maybe she was a fake.

She didn't understand why she kept having the visions, when she didn't entirely believe in them. Over the years, she'd hoped they would go away of their own volition, fading to nothing in the face of her refusal to believe them. Sometimes she thought that skepticism was the only thing keeping her tied to reality. If she let go of it, she would lose herself entirely in the meanderings of her own disordered mind.

At least a dozen customers came in each day and asked for her to do a reading of some kind. Apparently, Madame Callista had steady business as a fortune-teller in the New Orleans woo-woo community. The customers were all about her taking over where Callista had left off. She could no doubt make a good living telling fortunes to the steady stream of customers who asked. But she really, really didn't want to go there. Yes, she could technically do it, but (a) it wasn't her forte, and (b) being normal in no way included becoming a well-known fortune-teller.

Despite her efforts to contain it, though, her power kept growing stronger, the visions becoming more vivid and frequent over time. Moving to New Orleans had done nothing to curb it, and, if anything, the shop seemed to enhance her abilities.

Hence, the radical decision to make a conscious break with that part of herself and refuse to read for anybody. She could only hope that if she ignored the spiritual voices in her head for long enough that they would fade away. This move to New Orleans had to work. It *had* to.

The middle of the week came and went. Max watched Lissa reopen her shop, and a stream of customers trooped through her doors. The place did a fairly brisk business, in fact. Maybe she would even make enough money to finish renovating her apartment sometime this century. He had to give her credit. She was brave to pick herself up after the attack, and then the break-in, and press on like she had.

She'd rearranged the layout of the shop, leaving an open space exactly in the middle of it. She'd set up a small table and covered it with a painted tablecloth covered in stars and moons, unicorns, fairies and an array of mystical symbols. He'd watched her paint it the past few evenings upstairs. People came in daily to gaze into the crystal ball sitting on the table or to fool with tarot cards. And they seemed to be taking whatever they saw seriously.

Max continued to be amazed that so many seemingly sane-looking people frequented the shop. All that mystical stuff was smoke and mirrors. Everything he'd ever seen that had been attributed to the occult could be explained away by overly vivid imaginations, clever charlatans or random chance.

On Friday afternoon his cell phone rang, an unwelcome intrusion into his private purgatory. Hell would be not being able to see Lissa at all. But watching her like this, *spying* on her, was not far behind.

The caller was Peter Menchekov. "Hello, sir. What can I do for you?" he asked in reluctant Russian.

"I just wanted to remind you to bring your girlfriend with you to the house tomorrow night. Some of the higher-ups want to meet Miss Clearmont. Her aunt was rather famous, and people are curious to see if the niece inherited the same talent for fortune-telling as Callista had."

Great. Not only was he supposed to expose her to danger, but she got to perform like a trained monkey while he was at it. "I don't know if she can make it. Her schedule is quite full with clients—"

"These clients are more important. See to it she's here tomorrow evening," his boss ordered brusquely.

"Of course," he answered smoothly.

Now to talk Lissa into it—and find a way to warn her subtly what she was walking into—without scaring her half to death. She was never going to forgive him for this.

Chapter 5

Lissa looked up from the unidentified gadget on her counter as the bell over the shop door rang. A tall silhouette was highlighted in the entry, golden hair shining in the sunlight coming from behind him. *Max*. Her heart jumped, and her hands developed a sudden tendency to flutter up toward her hair.

"Can I help you?" she asked breathlessly.

He grinned. "Indeed you can."

She planted her elbows on the counter and leaned forward, blatantly flirting with him. "Do you need me to read your fortune?"

His grin widened. "I'll pass, thanks."

"You know, just because you don't ask me to do it for you doesn't mean I haven't or won't read your future to satisfy my own curiosity."

"Wouldn't that be unethical?"

"It would be unethical of me to tell anyone what I see or for me to take advantage of precognition in some way."

"Yeah? So what do you see in my future?"

A dark vision of him standing over a man he'd just shot passed through her mind's eye for a moment and then cleared as she shook her head. She smiled playfully at him. "I see dinner at a *very* expensive restaurant with an exotic and slightly Goth redhead in the very near future. And you're paying."

He grinned down at her. "Wow. You *are* good at that psychic stuff."

"I know. Right?"

He glanced down at her fingers, which at the moment were toying with some electronic doodad she'd found in the debris. She had yet to identify which piece of the inventory it could have come out of. It looked like a speaker of some kind. Maybe a recorder from inside one of the dolls? She hadn't been aware of any of the antique dolls in the store being able to talk.

"What's that you've got there?" he asked.

"No idea. I thought maybe one of the smashed dolls might have had some sort of voice-activated speaker in it. Maybe you can figure it out?" She held it out to him, and he lifted the gadget from her fingers lightly.

He turned it this way and that and then asked, "Do you have a magnifying glass?"

"Sure. Just a sec." She fetched one for him. He examined the thumbnail-size bit of black plastic carefully. He even pulled out his cell phone and typed a string of letters and numbers into it.

"Well?" she demanded. Curiosity always had gotten the best of her.

"Where did you say you found this?"

"In the mess I swept up on Sunday. I didn't find it digging through the pile of bits and pieces until Tuesday, though. Why?" Her curiosity was quickly being replaced by apprehension.

"I'm going to be honest with you. It's a bug of some kind. I've copied down the serial number and will research what it's used for and who might have bought it."

"A bug?" she echoed blankly. "Like spies use?"

"Or police or criminals or rival business owners just trying to get a leg up on the competition."

"That's crazy." But as she said the words, a flood of images raced through her brain. Men and women coming into the curiosity shop over and over through the years, leaving notes and messages, even envelopes of money, stashed around the shop. More images of other people retrieving the dead drops flashed across her mental movie screen. The clothing changed through the decades, but the shop remained mostly the same.

She gripped the edge of the counter until it dug into her palms, the pain anchoring her once more in the present. For a person who'd given up doing the whole psychic thing, her powers were bloody well not giving it a rest. Worse, the powers that be seemed to delight in amplifying her sensitivity every time Max was nearby, watching her with that intent gaze of his that missed nothing.

Speaking of which, he was staring at her quizzically now. She gave him a lame smile and prayed he wouldn't question her any further. No such luck.

"I know you haven't been in New Orleans long, Lissa. But have you run into anyone hostile since you came? Someone who was unpleasant with you or threatened you? Or was there someone back in Vermont who might have followed you down here to get revenge for something? Maybe an ex-boyfriend or someone you crossed in some way?"

"Nobody," she answered firmly. Please God, let him believe her. For goodness knew, it was a bald-faced lie. Urgency to distract him from this line of questioning coursed through her. "Is that bug thing still working?" she asked nervously.

He dropped it on the floor and stepped on it hard with the heel of his shoe. "Nope. Not anymore."

"That's so creepy. Why is all this stuff happening to me all of a sudden?"

"Why, indeed?" he echoed cryptically. He sounded almost as if he had some idea of who could be doing all this awful stuff to her.

"And you're sure you're not a cop or an FBI agent?" she asked, glancing down at the remains of the crushed bug.

"Positive."

His unspoken thought popped into her head. *Right government, wrong alphabet letters.* That was weird. She'd never been able to read peoples' minds before.

"Ex-military, then?" she asked.

"Definitely not." She didn't have to be very psychic to sense him projecting with all his might his unwillingness to talk any further about himself.

"Then where did you learn about bugs?" she demanded.

He sighed. "My father was into such things. He taught me about radios and stuff, whether I was interested or not."

She studied him for a moment, weighing his words.

They were not a lie. They just weren't the whole truth. She took pity and let him off the hook, changing subjects. "You said there was something I could do for you, Max. Name it. I owe you big-time for all the help you've given me."

If she wasn't mistaken, he cringed a little at her gratitude. Now, why would he react like that? Most men would kill to have a reasonably decent-looking single woman beholden to them. Was he up to something more than met the eye? What? He'd been nothing but protective and helpful to her.

He spoke up with obvious reluctance. "There's this party I have to go to tomorrow night. A client is throwing it and has insisted that I come. Furthermore, he's demanding that I bring a date."

Her breath caught. Was he asking her out on a date?

"Some of the people there were friends of your aunt. I thought you might like to meet them."

Her interest perked up even more. A date with the hot guy *and* she got to learn more about her cryptic aunt? Sounded like a win-win situation.

"It's formal," he continued. "You'd need to wear a long gown. But the food will be great, and there will be some interesting people there. And we'd get to spend some time getting to know each other better."

Her heart leaped. He wanted to know her better? *Awe. Some.*

"Would you by any chance be willing and able to rescue this knight in shining armor, fair damsel?"

"Well…" she drawled. "I do have a fair bit of damsel stuff to do this weekend, but I think I can manage to squeeze in a knight rescue. And goodness knows, you've rescued me enough times already. I owe you one back."

His eyes lit with enough heat to curl her toes into little ecstatic knots of pleasure. A surprising amount of relief flooded his face, as well. She'd have thought he would be more suave and confident about asking a woman out. As handsome and experienced a man as him...

"I'll pick you up at eight, then."

"Great."

The shop door had not finished closing behind him before she panicked. What on earth was she going to wear? She couldn't afford to spend a bunch of money on a fancy gown she'd wear once this century. Not with the repair bill for the shop yet to pay off and the upstairs apartment waiting to be renovated.

She remembered Callista's trunks in the basement. One of them held some old clothes. Maybe there was something in there that she could make work. She rushed downstairs and threw open the first trunk on the right.

And frowned. It was full of papers. But they were neatly organized and stacked. Which was weird. She distinctly recalled all this paperwork being strewn in here willy-nilly in a chaotic mess.

Okay. Ghosts might be able to whisper to her, but since when did they sort and organize business papers for her? She lifted out the first pile to check it out. Sure enough, all the random sheets of paper, notebooks and file folders from before appeared to have been sorted and categorized. All of these were potion recipes, for example. She lifted out part of another stack. All magic spells. *What on earth?*

She spoke to the ceiling. "Look. I'm willing to concede that ghosts exist. But I've never seen a ghost do anything like this before. What's up?"

Silence.

The darned voices in her head wouldn't shut up all week, and now that she finally asked them a direct question, they clammed up as if they didn't exist. *Jerks.*

She opened the next trunk. This one was similarly organized and sorted, too. Although its contents now appeared to be composed solely of business records. *What. The. Heck?*

Perplexed and more than a little weirded out, she opened the third trunk. At least it was still a mess, full of dresses, coats, old shoes and who knew what all. She reached in and pulled out the first dress, a floral cocktail number that looked vintage 1955 or so. It screamed of Doris Day or June Cleaver. Not sexy enough, and it wasn't long enough.

She had a great time looking through the collection of old clothing, some of it dating back to the 1920s, but nothing came even close to being right for a fancy date with Max. And then she lifted out something black and satin from near the bottom of the trunk. This garment was carefully folded, and she shook it out with a gasp of wonder.

It was a strapless ball gown, slim and simple and classic. Whalebone stays gave the bodice structure, and the neckline was modest. Timeless. It looked like something Grace Kelly would have worn. Please, please let it not be too small. She could always take it in, but she probably wouldn't be able to let it out.

She shimmied out of her T-shirt and jeans and into the gown. She had to contort herself to zip the thing, but it hugged her body as though it had been custom-made for her. It dragged the floor, but that would be easy enough to fix. Overjoyed, she took her find upstairs and plunked down on the floor of her apartment to hem her treasure. Oh, this date was going to be fun.

Max tugged at his tuxedo jacket impatiently and opened the curiosity shop door. This was going to suck. Not the part about spending the evening with Lissa, but everything else about it.

Normally, he didn't worry about maintaining his mob member persona, but tonight? With a woman he genuinely liked on his arm? How was he supposed to balance his tendency to be his real self around her with his tough-guy act?

Lissa emerged from the stairwell, and all thought of acting flew out of his head. "Wow. You look fantastic."

She smiled shyly, which only made her look more spectacular. Her black dress was narrow and simple, skimming down her slender curves as if it were painted on her body. It was strapless, which left lots of perfect porcelain skin bare. She'd swept her striking curls up into some sort of loose twist that managed to be both soft and formal at the same time. As she turned her head, he couldn't tell where dark brown stopped and that deep red color started in her hair. He'd never seen anything like it before in art or in life. Her eyes looked huge and mysterious. The only splash of color against her pale skin was her red lipstick.

She looked dramatic, a creature not entirely of this world, every inch the seer she was. Nobody was going to be able to take their eyes off her. Which was both good and bad. It would make her a star among his new mob bosses, which might serve to protect her from their violent whims. But it also would draw a ton of attention to her. Which might, in turn, draw the attention of some of the more unhinged criminals in the organization.

"You're going to make it damned hard for me to keep you to myself, looking like that," he commented as he waited for her to lock the front door and activate the new alarm system he'd hired workmen to install after the break-in. He held out his forearm to her, and she laid a light hand on his designer wool sleeve.

"I won't even know there's anyone else in the room," she replied stoutly.

They strolled slowly down the sidewalk in consideration of her high heels. "Here's the thing. This is a bunch among whom you'd do well to keep your eyes open. Wide-open. They may look polished and classy, but most of them are not. Do not be fooled by the clothes and jewels."

He helped her into his Ferrari and went around to climb in beside her.

"But what if, when I look at a person, I don't see their exterior. What if I see their soul?"

"Then prepare to look at a whole lot of darkness tonight."

"Who are these people?" she asked in alarm.

"Just be polite and be careful what you say."

She fell silent beside him, for which he was both grateful and worried. In his experience, a brooding woman was never a good thing.

"Did you mean that thing about looking into a person's soul?" he asked, curious.

She momentarily looked alarmed. "Nah. It's just that people expect me to say stuff like that when I'm work-

ing in the shop. I slipped and fell into the eccentric
mystical shop owner thing for a second. I apologize."

"No apologies necessary."

Was that relief in her voice? Not that he wasn't experiencing the exact same emotion. There were things
about his soul that he seriously didn't need her to see.

Sure, most people kept secrets. And he did his best
not to pry into them in real life or otherwise. After all,
he had some whoppers of his own that he would prefer
to keep buried.

No one must ever know that he was a fraud. That he
was living a lie. The CIA must never find out he was
running his own undercover op off the books during
what they thought was an extended leave of absence.
And Peter Menchekov and his cronies must never suspect that he was burrowing into their crime ring with
the intent to find and take out their leader. He was a
dead man if they even suspected he was not exactly
who he said he was.

And Lissa… His motives for her not finding out that
he'd been lying to her from the very beginning were
purely selfish. She was the most fascinating woman he
could ever recall meeting, not to mention sexy as hell.
He still shuddered a little remembering what she felt
like plastered up against him. And that kiss—he fell
asleep thinking about it every night.

He steered the Ferrari to a stop in front of Menchekov's
opulent mansion. Tonight it was lit up like a freaking opera
house, which was funny since the man couldn't tell a tenor
from a trombone.

A valet took his keys and left Max to escort Lissa up
the steps. He ushered her into the foyer, and she looked
around at the gaudy, mismatched antiques and florid

decor. He had to suppress a shiver of distaste every time he set foot in this place. He missed his own spare and intensely elegant home.

Lissa leaned close to him, her breast brushing against his arm and sending his every sense onto high alert. She murmured, "This is wonderfully dreadful."

He chuckled under his breath. "That's one way to describe it. I might go straight to hideous."

She smiled up at him and from behind unmoving lips murmured, "Behave."

He mentally snorted. She was the one he was worried about behaving tonight. The people here would assume she had the same kind of psychic ability her aunt had apparently had. Whether real or imagined, it had the potential to cause serious trouble in this crowd.

Belief in the occult was a time-honored tradition in many Slavic cultures. And some of the people here tonight could emphatically not afford for her to pick around in their noggins and uncover secrets best left totally covered.

Lissa gasped beside him. He leaned down instantly, murmuring in her ear, "What's wrong?"

"I...wow... Umm, that's bizarre."

"Talk to me, Lissa," he said in burgeoning alarm.

"To put it in lay terms, I just felt a great disturbance in the life energies around me."

At least she had the good grace to sound reluctant to say something like that. "What kind of disturbance?"

She turned into him, and his arms came up around her to hug her lightly. She spoke quickly, under her breath. "Someone here just reacted in violent shock to the sight of me. I have no idea why."

"Is this person a threat?"

She frowned against his tuxedo jacket for a moment. "Not directly, but potentially he could become one. It's definitely male energy. Look, I know this sounds crazy, but you have to believe me. I'm never wrong about this stuff."

All undercover operatives developed finely tuned senses of intuition. They felt danger coming before it showed itself. They had uncanny knacks for finding and following people they could not see. They just knew when something wasn't right about a place or a situation. Hence, he was not about to discount her declaration that someone in the room had just taken an extraordinary and not entirely innocent interest in her.

"I've got your back, Lissa. I won't let anyone hurt you. And nobody would do anything here with all these women and outsiders present, anyway. You're safe. I swear."

"Stay close to me?" she asked in a small voice.

"Of course."

She took a deep breath and straightened beside him, and they moved deeper into the crowded house.

Who had reacted so violently to her that it had triggered her internal alarm system like that? Someone who'd known her aunt maybe? Someone who'd been into the curiosity shop since she had taken over and recognized her? But if it was someone who fell into either of those categories, why the violent reaction to her? How was Lissa connected to the Russian mob, knowingly or unknowingly?

As he'd expected, many of the men present paused to take note of the unusual beauty on his arm. Lissa was not the least bit conventional with her pale skin and stark coloring. A certain dark vibe clung to her, a sense of mystery. The possibility of her being able to see into peoples' hearts and minds, their pasts and futures, was exotic and unsettling. She was ethereal and strange, and she was arguably the most captivating woman he'd ever met.

Maybe that was what the nameless shocked person had reacted to. Unfortunately, his own gut told him there was more to it than the simple flesh impact of a beautiful woman walking into the room.

Peter, predictably, rolled in on them the moment he spotted them. "So. This is the new owner of Callista's Curiosities. A pleasure to meet you, mademoiselle."

Lissa's hand tightened on Max's forearm for a moment. Was this the man who'd zeroed in on her presence and unsettled her so badly?

He glanced down at her. She smiled politely enough and extended her hand to his boss. "Thank you for inviting me to your party, Mr. Menchekov. Your home is beautiful."

Max's lips twitched. He caught the faintest hesitation before she uttered the word *beautiful*. She really meant to say garish. Horrid. Trashy. He put a supportive hand lightly on the middle of her back.

"Miss Clearmont, may I call you Lissa?" Peter boomed in an excess of joviality. "I feel like I already know you. I knew your aunt. Remarkable woman. You've got the look of her about you."

Lissa's spine stiffened against Max's hand. "Oh? Were you a client?"

A cheery laugh from Peter. "You might say that."

"You haven't been into the shop since I took over. You should stop by," Lissa replied politely.

"You share your aunt's particular talents, then?"

"No two psychics' powers are exactly the same, of course. And even among psychics, she was considered to be unique," Lissa replied.

Nice evasion. She didn't come right out and say whether or not she was psychic. He relaxed fractionally at how well she was handling herself with arguably one of the most dangerous men in the room. For Peter was nothing if not highly intelligent.

"Maybe you will give us a sample reading, Miss Clearmont?" He raised his voice to the crowd in general. "Who here would like to have their fortune read by a genuine psychic?"

Good Lord. She dared not give the whole room readings. Even if she was totally making up everything she predicted, slipping up and saying the wrong thing could be deadly. This crowd might be entirely funded by criminal money, but they obsessively played a game of pretending that all their wealth was legitimate. Privately he considered them the worst sort of nouveau riche pretenders. Which was probably a shade snobbish of him, given that his own parents had been cut from the exact same cloth as these people.

But, like a school of starving piranhas, this bunch would devour anyone who dared to expose the fiction of their place in society.

A general cry of approval went up at Peter's suggestion that Lissa read fortunes. *Crap, crap, crap.* "No, Lissa—" he started.

"I've got this," she muttered out of the side of her mouth.

"You have no idea—"

"Actually, I do," she retorted, cutting him off.

Peter ordered one of the waiters to set up a table in

the middle of the living room. A chair was brought for Lissa, and she settled into it while Max hovered anxiously behind her. She must not accidentally say anything to make these people think she saw their true professions. And yet he was helpless to stop her at this point.

For her part, Lissa opened her purse, pulled out a well-worn deck of tarot cards and began shuffling. The cards leaped in her fingers, flashing pictures not quite seen in a dancing fountain of color.

"Who's first?" she said confidently.

A blonde woman stepped forward, giggling. Peter's latest trophy wife. Max gave her two years before she was dumped for a new model. Menchekov liked them young, and she was starting to show a few years around the edges.

Lissa had the woman cut the cards and then expertly dealt a tarot layout. He caught the infinitesimal tightening of Lissa's shoulders as she studied the cards, but then she smoothly launched into basically meaningless patter about examining life choices and lessons waiting to be learned.

Another woman sat down at the table, and Lissa predicted a grandchild within a year, which made the woman ecstatic and sing Lissa's praises as a fortune-teller. After that, a line of people formed, waiting their turns eagerly to hear what Lissa saw in their futures.

She started to droop after an hour or so, and Max left her side briefly to fetch her food and something to drink. When he got back, Peter was seated at the table, and there was no sign of the tarot cards. Lissa was looking down at the man's palm. A tiny frown of concentration knit her brow. She was speaking very quietly to Menchekov.

So quietly Max couldn't hear her as he set down the plate and bottle of water beside her. Both she and Peter leaned back abruptly, as if some important agreement had been reached. The Russian nodded and rose to his feet, staring down at her as she turned her attention to the hors d'oeuvres Max had brought.

Peter glanced up at Max and jerked his head to indicate that his employee should come with him. He really didn't want to leave Lissa.

She pulled a card from the deck, glanced down at it and then up at him. "I'll be all right while you're gone," she said confidently.

Seriously? Because of a card she pulled randomly from a deck. He needed to have a talk with her about trusting her safety to random chance. "I'll be back in a few minutes," he murmured. "We have a little business to discuss. Don't get in trouble while I'm gone."

"I could say the same for you," she replied a bit tartly.

What was that about? He followed Peter to the man's office and was alarmed when the Russian closed the door behind him.

"Drink?" his boss offered.

"Sure. Whatever you're having."

Peter poured two neat whiskeys into crystal glasses and passed him one. He sipped at his while his boss tossed back the entire contents of his. Max picked up the decanter and refilled Menchekov's glass. Peter downed that one, as well. *Wow.* Something had him rattled. What in the hell had Lissa said to him during that palm reading? Max poured him another double shot.

"She's the real deal," Peter announced.

"You mean Lissa?" he asked cautiously. Peter sounded none too happy about his declaration. And how did the guy know something like that, anyway? He'd just met her. "That's good, right?"

"No. That's bad. She will see things."

"Well, yes. It is part of her job description. She does run a magical curiosity shop, after all."

"Most psychic readers are rubbish. But that girl… she's worrisome. She's every bit as gifted as the old lady."

"You mean the deceased aunt?"

"Yes." He paced his office for a moment and then stopped to stare accusingly at Max. "What if the niece picks something out of my brain that's confidential?"

"No problem. Don't let her do any more readings on you."

"You don't understand. She's the kind of seer who visions will come to whether a person is standing in front of her or not. That girl's freaking powerful—I'm telling you."

Peter didn't seriously believe in all that psychic powers tripe, did he? Max was severely tempted to ask the man why he was so sure about all of this mumbo jumbo and Lissa. The guy wasn't sharing everything he knew about the girl. Had Peter talked to one of the mysterious higher-ups about Lissa? Maybe one who'd known Callista well?

Max asked cautiously, "Do you want me to have a talk with her? Suggest she stay away from poking into your business…you know…psychically?" He tripped over the last word a little. It was hard to believe he'd just said that aloud.

"Would you?" Peter tossed back the last of his latest

shot. "Be subtle about it, though. If you make a big deal over it, then she'll be bound to poke around and try to find out what I'm trying to hide."

Which begged the question, what *was* the guy trying to hide so hard?

"I'll take care of it, sir," Max declared, since Peter seemed to expect some kind of response.

The Russian jumped up off the leather sofa and paced the office restlessly. "If I'd had any idea how good a psychic she is, I never would have let her near me." He swore luridly and waved his whiskey glass around in agitation. "What if she picks out faces from my brain?"

The memory of Lissa sketching that girl's face the night of her mugging flashed into his mind. Was that *not* a random drawing as she'd claimed? Was it possible Lissa had plucked that image from her attacker's mind? No sooner had the questions occurred to him than he discounted them impatiently. There was no such thing as psychic power. The drawing had been exactly what Lissa said it was—just a random face. A way to blow of stress after a scary event.

"Do you have any idea how much trouble I would be in if your girlfriend starts seeing the faces in my head?"

He opened his mouth automatically to deny Lissa being his girlfriend, but Peter talked over him heedlessly, caught up in his own thoughts.

"The big boss would kill me in a second." Peter shuddered. "I don't even want to think about how he'd do it."

This was the second time Peter had mentioned a big boss, and Max's gut leaped. Was Peter finally letting down his guard and trusting Max enough to let him penetrate the organization even more deeply? Was this the break he'd been waiting for? He spoke soothingly to the Russian. "The big boss would never take some crazy psychic chick's word over yours. You're a smart and loyal employee."

"I dunno. I've been on thin ice with him since that mess last year with the Who Do Voodoo club getting robbed and then raided."

"That mess happened way below your pay grade," Max responded disdainfully. Of course, he refrained from mentioning that his own sister and her fiancé were behind the investigation and raid that had closed the club and relieved its management of nearly a half-million dollars in cash.

"The big boss says we need this girl's shop to stay safe and not get busted up. We lost an information drop there in last weekend's break-in, and the boss doesn't want it to happen again."

Max was startled. This was the first he'd heard of a dead drop being stolen. Was *that* why Lissa's store had been trashed? To cover up a theft? It seemed like a rather extreme tactic, when shoplifting something or just intercepting the dead-dropped item would have been so much easier and drawn so much less attention.

"What was stolen, if you don't mind my asking? I'm happy to keep an eye on future dead drops if I know where they're stashed in the shop."

"A voice recorder was lost. It had a recording in it of sensitive information pertaining to an ongoing business deal."

Had the bug that Lissa had found actually been placed in the shop for someone else to pick up? Or... *holy crap*...had the recording actually been made in the shop of a conversation that happened within the range of the recorder? As soon as the thought occurred to him, he knew it to be the truth. Someone had been set up to be recorded inside the shop. The store was much more deeply entangled with the mob's operations than he'd begun to imagine. Which meant Lissa was in a great deal more danger than she knew.

"Speaking of the break-in, do your police contacts have any idea who vandalized your girlfriend's place?" Peter asked.

He let the second girlfriend reference slip by uncorrected. Now that he thought about it, the closer Peter thought Lissa was to Max, the less likely he would be to kill her out of hand. At least that was what Max hoped.

He answered his boss's question. "Beyond the obvious? Julio's gang marks were spray painted on the walls, after all. But as for the individuals who actually broke in and trashed the place? No. The police have no identities. They're convinced it was retaliation for Julio's arrest by members of his gang. It could have been any of dozens of thugs.

"The police are convinced it was three young men. But that's about all they've got. Traffic cameras in the area showed their faces to be covered with bandannas. They came and left on foot." He omitted the part where the cameras were his and the footage the police had provided by him.

"That sounds like Julio's boys. Bunch of…" Peter devolved into foul Russian epithets.

When the tirade wound down, Max commented grimly, "Whoever it was had better hope the cops catch them first. Because if I get my hands on them, I'm gonna mess them up real bad."

He expected the Russian mobsters above his pay grade shared the sentiment. It was one of the few perks of working for an organized crime syndicate. They did protect their own. Peter flopped onto the leather sofa and sprawled on it, squinting up at Max.

"The big boss wants you to keep watching her shop. Sit on top of it if you have to. Don't let anybody mess with it or with the girl again. Got it?"

"Sure. No problem." Not that doing surveillance on Lissa was going to mess with his head any less because his employer had ordered it.

He threw out a trial balloon. "If someone would tell me when a drop's coming in, I can watch it until it's safely picked up. For that matter, if I know who's supposed to make the pickup, I can make sure the delivery is not intercepted." He added hastily, "It's just a thought. I don't want to overstep my bounds."

"No, that's a good idea. I'll let you know when we've got a drop coming in."

Peter said it importantly, as if he was an intimate insider to the big boss's private affairs. But Max strongly suspected that was the whiskey talking and not at all based in truth. Still. If he could get his hands on one of the drops, maybe he could get a better idea of what this secret "big boss" was up to and who the guy might be.

"As for the girl," Peter announced, his words starting to slur as the alcohol hit his brain and tongue. "You keep a close eye on her. Stick to her like glue. If she says anything about seeing into my private affairs or she starts talking about people and places she's never seen before, I need you to take her out."

"Excuse me?"

"You heard me. If she starts seeing strangers in her head…" Peter drew a finger across his throat.

Chapter 6

*W*hat. *The. Actual. Hell.* His boss had just ordered him to *kill* Lissa—a woman Peter believed to be Max's girlfriend—if she stepped out of line? Shock slammed into him.

As if he'd ever lay a finger on her. The mere idea of harming her offended him deeply. Who did Peter think he was to give an order like that? It was monstrous. Callous. Horrendous. An urge to jump Peter and silently strangle him here and now nearly overcame Max.

Dammit. His boss was staring at him quizzically, as if noticing his violent reaction.

"But I thought the big boss wants me to keep her safe," Max said carefully.

Peter frowned. "Nothing is more important to the big guy than protecting himself. No matter how much he wants this girl to be protected, if she poses a threat to him, she's toast. Got that?"

Max blinked, taken aback by Peter's vehemence. "Yeah, sure. No problem." He swore aloud, faking his own whiskey slur. "But I gotta say, I hope she doesn't do any weird psychic stuff like you're talking about, because she's hot."

"I'll bet she's a firecracker in the sack," Peter declared.

So did he, but he wasn't crude enough to talk about her that way, not even behind her back and not even for the sake of maintaining his cover.

Peter waved his glass around some more, announcing importantly, "Nobody sees the big boss's face. It's his number one rule. Anyone who sees him without his express permission is killed on the spot."

Cripes. No wonder he'd been having such a hard time figuring out the identity of the shadowy figure at the apex of the entire crime syndicate. "Is he that ugly?" Max joked.

"Nah, man. He's just that freaked out over no one finding out who he is. He's got this paranoid obsession with protecting his identity."

"Well, yeah. I would, too, if I were him. He'll go to jail for the rest of his life and then some if the cops catch up with him."

Peter's voice dropped into a conspiratorial tone. "It's the feds he's terrified of. The stuff we do at our level of the organization—that's just a moneymaker for the real stuff he does. It's not even his actual business."

Max nodded slowly as if the news were a revelation to him. "I've always said that knowledge is a hell of a lot more valuable than cash. It's all in who you know and what you know."

"You got that right." Peter stood up abruptly. "I gotta take a leak."

Max took the opportunity to leave the office behind his boss and rejoin Lissa. Apparently she'd read the fortunes of just about everyone at the party, for she was now having the guests around her try to guess which tarot card was dealt facedown before she turned it over to reveal it.

She handed the deck to a man Max knew to be a high-level enforcer for the Bratya and had him deal a card facedown for her.

"Nine of Pentacles," she announced.

The thug flipped the card over, and everyone gasped as the Nine of Pentacles did, indeed, stare up at them.

"Again," Lissa ordered the guy.

He dealt another card facedown, this time out of the middle of the deck.

She studied it for a moment and then grinned. "What else could it be? It's the Magician."

The Russian flipped over the major arcana card of a man wearing a wizard's robe and wielding a magic wand. A deeper gasp went up from the gathered crowd of onlookers.

If they all believed, as Peter did, that she was the real deal, there would be more than one person in this bunch who would react the same way Peter had and see her as a threat to their deepest, darkest secrets. The kind of secrets they would readily kill to protect.

"Show's over, folks," he announced. "The lady hasn't had a break all evening, and she needs to spend some time with her handsome, charming escort."

The crowd dispersed, and Max gathered Lissa up against his side, publicly staking his claim on her for anyone in the house who mistakenly thought she might be a free agent or without protection. He led her over to the catered buffet that was laid out in the gaudy dining room, with its gold leaf moldings and naked cherub frescoes on the ceiling.

"Michelangelo it isn't," Lissa said under her breath.

"I like to think of it as high bordello couture," he muttered back.

She giggled, and the sound shot through him like a bolt of lightning. It was joyous and carefree, a glimpse of an entirely different woman from the one he'd met last week in the arms of a killer. He wanted to hear that sound again.

"Let me give you a tour of the place. It's really quite a remarkable home, and chock-full of history."

They strolled around the ground floor of the mansion while he regaled her with the antebellum home's early history. And in its defense, the bones of the house really were magnificent. It was just that the current owners had done up the grand old lady with a face full of garish clown makeup. Max had faith that the house would outlast the current residents and someday be restored to her original glory.

For her part, Lissa's eyes sparkled with interest as he told her stories about famous parties and guests, showed her where the duel had been fought over the daughter of the house who ultimately refused the suits of both duelists, and relayed the history of New Orleans, and the South itself, written in the home's walls.

"I'd love to come here sometime when no one is home and just sit and listen to this house," Lissa murmured.

He frowned, bemused. What did a house sound like,

anyway? Did she really fancy that she heard ghosts, after all? She'd been throwing him mixed signals about her belief in her own psychic powers or lack thereof ever since they'd met.

He led her down a brick path into the moonlit garden, which was shockingly well designed, in contrast to the home's interior.

"Tell me something, Lissa. How did you know what cards were facedown on the table?"

She laughed under her breath. "Easy. The deck is marked."

"Really? How?" He'd stared at the card backs carefully and had seen no sign of the usual telltale nicks and ink ticks of a marked deck. As an art dealer, he had a pretty good eye for such details.

She leaned close to him, her exotic perfume wafting to his nose and straight to other parts of his body. Who knew that a whiff of scent could turn him on like that? Or maybe it was the sleek feel of her body brushing against his side that made hot blood surge through him.

"Promise not to tell my secret?" she breathed.

Lord. Her breath caressed his neck almost as if she'd kissed him right there where his pulse throbbed in his throat. And it was throbbing noticeably faster than a few seconds ago.

"I promise," he managed to choke out, his voice unaccountably rough.

"I've handled those cards for so many years that the edges are all frayed and bent. Each card in the deck is banged up a little differently. The gilding has worn off the edges unevenly, and the corners are tattered differently. Since I know the deck so well, I can tell which card is which from the tiny variations and blemishes."

He released a slow breath, seeking calm that did not come. "And what about the tarot readings you did for everyone earlier? Were those fake, too?"

"Tarot cards all have specific meanings. When you lay them out in a spread, they tell a story all by themselves. I don't have to make up anything. I merely have to read the cards and relate the connections they've already lined up."

The sound of burbling water became audible, and he and Lissa turned down a path in search of the source. A fountain with water leaping from one bowl to the next came into sight. A live oak spread its branches over the tiny courtyard and the fountain like a protective mother embracing the secret spot.

"Oh, Max. It's so beautiful here," she breathed.

"You're the most beautiful part of this place."

She paused and turned to look up at him. "I don't know. You wear a tuxedo very well, sir."

He stared down at her, the smile fading from his cheeks as he took in the wonder of her. An urge to kiss her came over him, so strong it was as if a hand pressed between his shoulder blades, compelling him to go to her.

"Would you mind if we kissed again?" he asked quietly.

"I thought you'd never get around to it."

He ran his palms up her slender, cool arms and slowly drew her forward to meet him. The night, the moonlight and the mystery of the woman in his arms all wrapped around him in a net of magic.

Their lips touched, and Lissa exhaled in soft surprise that mirrored his own. He thought he'd known what to expect this time, but this kiss was nothing like the last one. Tonight, it was as if a million tiny fairy lights exploded around them, showering them with sparks. Everywhere they touched his skin, they licked at him like tiny flames, making him tingle from head to toe.

He deepened the kiss slowly, coaxing her into the magic with him, losing himself in the champagne and berry taste of her. He wasn't sure what he'd done to deserve a woman like her, but he wasn't about to question whatever force in the universe had sent her to him.

Her arms came around his neck, and he encircled her slender waist, raising her up to fit their bodies together more closely. His palm slid over the satin of her dress effortlessly. She was air and light in his arms, insubstantial and fleeting. Even though she molded herself to him from the hem of her gown to its arcing neckline covering her small, firm breasts, it felt as though she would slip away at any second.

His arms tightened around her, and he kissed her more deeply still, attempting to anchor her to him with a desperation that was shocking. Was he really that lonely, or was she really that incredible? He prayed it was not the former and wished hard that it was the latter.

The tip of her tongue touched his, startling him. Soft fingers twined in his hair, tugging his head down to hers, and she murmured against his mouth, "Quit over-thinking this and just kiss me."

How does she know?

Who was he to question her wisdom?

A barrier of some sort fell away from his heart, and he plunged into the kiss with enthusiasm then all but drawing her into him body and soul. His hands ranged over the curves of her body, enjoying the fullness of her hips, the plumpness of her buttocks, the inward dip of her spine. His fingers swept up her ribs and brushed the swell of her breast, and Lissa gasped.

"Are we okay?" he asked, his hand freezing.

"Yes. Oh, yes. Don't stop."

And then she was kissing him with as much fervor as he felt, nipping at his lower lip, her hands roaming restlessly across his back.

"Would you mind if we got out of here?" she asked breathlessly. "Maybe go back to my place or yours?"

"Definitely my place," he replied between kisses. "Yours is a war zone."

She smiled against his mouth, her lips curving up deliciously. He kissed the corner of her mouth and then couldn't resist kissing his way along her jaw to her velvety-soft earlobe. "Ahh, Lissa. What are you doing to me?"

"I'm using my supersecret magical powers to ensorcell you. How am I doing?"

"Fantastic. Let's get out of here."

He tucked her under his arm and strode back the way they'd come, suddenly in an all-fired rush to get her alone and in private. And, God willing, naked. He realized belatedly that she was struggling to keep up with him, what with his long legs and her tight dress hampering her stride.

"I'm sorry," he muttered. "I'd pick you up and carry you out of here if I didn't think the people inside would say something totally inappropriate to you about it."

"That's so romantic."

Startled, he glanced down at her without breaking his now slower stride. "How's that?"

"Literally swept off my feet by a big, handsome stranger in the night and carried to his secret lair—" She broke off. "You do have a secret lair, don't you?"

"Most assuredly."

She resumed. "Swept away to his secret lair like a fairy-tale princess for a long night of—" She broke off again. "Oh, dear. I have let my imagination run away with me, haven't I?"

"I like where it's running. Don't stop. A long night of what?"

"Passionate lovemaking?" she asked in a very small voice.

"Your wish is my command. After all, you're the princess."

He opened the French doors into the house and a wall of sound slammed into them. It was crass and harsh after the enchantment of the garden. Lissa recoiled against his side, apparently as jarred by it as he was.

He leaned down to murmur in her ear, "Stay with me, Princess. I'll have you out of here in a jiffy."

They stepped back into the dining room, and Lissa staggered slightly against him. "There it is again," she muttered.

Without making a big deal of it, he let his gaze sweep the room. Nobody appeared to be paying particular attention to Lissa. "The shocked reaction you felt before?" he muttered without moving his lips.

"The very same."

"Who is it?" An itch to shield her from harm burned through him. *Sheesh.* This woman provoked his protective instincts like no one he'd ever met before.

"Get me out of here," she breathed.

"You've got it."

"Ooh, ooh, look at me. I'm psychic!" a drunk-sounding brunette squealed from nearby. "He just told you he wants to take you back to his place and screw your brains out!"

Max smiled at the woman, but the expression felt brittle on his face. He threw a protective arm around Lissa's shoulders and hustled her through the house and out the front door with slightly more haste than decorum allowed for.

He waited impatiently while a valet brought around the Ferrari. Lissa was silent beside him, and he could only hope the spell from the moonlit garden wasn't entirely broken. It wasn't that he was desperate to get laid. He was just desperate to be back in that magical moment with her again. It had been pure and clean and untouched by the filth of the world he lived in.

Lola purred to a stop, and he passed the valet a folded twenty-dollar bill. The valet beat him to opening the passenger door, but Max personally helped her down into the low-slung vehicle. He was antsy to get her away from there.

"Do you have any idea who was so interested in you?" he asked her as soon as they were well away from the mansion.

"Just that it is a man. He was stunned to see me and intensely interested in my presence…not necessarily in a good way."

He made a mental list of the party's attendees. Unfortunately, he only knew about half the guests. And he couldn't exactly ask Peter who the other half were.

The drive into the French Quarter took a while on account of Saturday night traffic and the approach of Mardi Gras, but at long last they pulled into his garage— an expensive modification to the building he owned but well worth every penny.

The automatic door closed behind Lola, and darkness shrouded them. "Stay there," he murmured, getting out and moving around to the passenger door in the dark. "Let me go first up the stairs. I'll need to disable the security system." Particularly some of its more aggressive features, which would stop an intruder in no uncertain terms.

"Okay, you can come up now," he called down the staircase. Lissa joined him, rising out of the darkness like Venus from the sea.

He stepped into the foyer and announced, "Lights on." The computerized switches illuminated the entry softly with spotlights aimed at the art hanging on the long white hallway's walls.

"Wow," Lissa breathed behind him. "And here I thought you were just some nice guy. I had no idea…"

He frowned over his shoulder at her. "I am just a nice guy." Although he knew the words were a lie when they came out of his mouth. He knew how to kill—had killed. He knew how to lie and steal and deceive, and his life at the moment consisted of all three. Sometimes he wondered if finding his mother's killer was worth it. But as quickly as the doubt entered his mind, he shoved it aside. Men like him had no time for doubt.

"If I pay you a dollar, can I get the special tour?" Lissa murmured playfully from beside him.

He glanced down at her. "For you, the special tour is free of charge. But you have to take those ridiculous heels off. It feels strange having you be so tall. You reach practically to my nose in those things. Besides, there's no need to be formal with me."

With a sigh of relief, she kicked off the stilettos and wiggled her toes. It turned out her toenails were painted a sassy shade of scarlet. He didn't usually consider himself a foot man, but hers made him reconsider. They were small and shapely and perfect, just like her.

He strolled through his home with her, pointing out his favorite pieces of art and standing quietly beside her while she studied a number of them intently, as if listening to them speak to her.

"Your collection is extraordinary, Max."

"Thanks. I'm fond of it."

"Where's the pièce de résistance?"

He frowned at her. "I beg your pardon?"

"Surely you saved your favorite piece of art for your bedroom. It is a person's private sanctum, after all."

His eyebrows lifted. "Are you trying to get me into bed, Miss Clearmont?"

Her dark eyes sparkled. "What if I am?"

"Then come with me." He threw open the double doors to his bedroom, which was a study in darkness compared with the rest of his apartment. In here, the walls and carpet were charcoal gray, the furniture was dark and the decorations were monochromatic. The only splash of color in the room was a large painting, hung at the foot of his bed and bathed in bright light.

It was a picture of a mother hugging a chubby little boy in her lap, painted in the late impressionist style.

"That looks like something Mary Cassatt would have painted," Lissa commented.

He smiled. "She did paint it."

"Oh, my God. That's an original?"

"It is."

With a gasp, Lissa moved to stand in front of the piece. As was appropriate with great impressionistic art, she examined it up close and then stepped back to look at it from a distance. The back of her thighs bumped into the foot of his bed.

"You have to be lying in bed to look at it properly," he said drily.

She looked up at him, awe written in her expression, and all thoughts of Cassatt and impressionist painters exploded out of his mind. This woman was here. With him now. And looking at him as if he was some kind of conquering hero.

He stepped close to her and tucked a stray curl behind her ear. He ran his fingertip lightly around her earlobe and savored the shiver that passed through her whole body. "Are you cold?" he murmured, taking note of the goose bumps rising on her arms.

She laughed a little. "Not in the least. In fact, I was wondering how long it's going to take you to unzip this uncomfortably warm dress."

He took another step forward until her chest touched his and reached behind her for the offending zipper. "It is a hot dress, by the way. It's going to look fantastic in a pool on my floor."

Staring deeply into her infinitely dark gaze, he slowly pulled down the zipper. It was the only sound in the room besides her light, rapid breathing.

"You're sure about this?" he asked.

Her lips turned up in a wise, mysterious smile. "Oh, yes. Very sure."

He let out the breath he hadn't realized he was holding. "You have no idea how glad I am to hear that."

"Would you really have let me go and taken me home if I said no?"

"Absolutely." He stood straighter, a little offended that she would even question him.

Her arms went around his neck. "Come here, you, and kiss me. I didn't mean to offend you and your unshakable honor."

She might as well have stuck a knife in his gut. If he was truly honorable, he would tell her to leave his condo right this second. But instead, he leaned his head down and kissed her hungrily.

If he was a good man, he'd walk her to the door and call her a cab. But he invaded her open mouth with his tongue, sipping at the sweet taste of her and loving the way she groaned in the back of her throat.

If he had integrity, he'd tell her to stay far, far away from him for her own safety. But instead, he slipped his hands inside the gapping bodice of her gown and skimmed it down over her hips, letting it slither to the floor at her feet.

Oh, hell. She wasn't wearing a bra. And that sexy little black thong hardly qualified as underwear.

If he was a decent man, he'd warn her that being with him was a one-way ticket to disappointment and heartache. But instead, he let her untie his bow tie and pull it from around his neck. He let her pop the studs out of his shirtfront and cuffs and strip the starched shirt off his shoulders.

She stood back in admiration to stare at him, and he took advantage of the moment to do the same. She didn't seem the slightest bit self-conscious, which was rare in his experience with women. Who needed beautiful paintings to look at when she stood before him, nearly naked, and every inch a sexy, confident, beautiful woman, inside and out?

Then she stepped close to him again and pressed her

lips against the center of his chest, murmuring, "I just want to eat you up."

He laughed a little painfully. "I know the feeling."

Her clever fingers undid his belt buckle and pulled the leather from around his waist. His own zipper went down, and then her warm hands were plunging inside his trousers and boldly cupping his privates.

"Oh, my," she declared.

"Lights dim," he declared. The spotlight on the Cassatt painting diminished to a bare hint of light, casting the room in deep shadows and Lissa's face into sepia silhouette. He took both of her cheeks in his palms and stared down at her for a long time, drinking in the magnificent lines of her brow and nose and lips. And then he kissed them all, while she shoved his pants down over his hips.

Impatience overtook him, and he swept her off her feet and up into his arms, carrying her to his high king-size bed. He didn't bother pulling back the comforter, merely deposited her on its cool raw silk surface and followed her down, covering her body with his.

"We're good?" he murmured in her ear as he nibbled at it, enjoying the little sounds she was making in the back of her throat.

"You don't have to keep asking me," she replied.

"Yes, I do. It's called rolling consent, and it's important. I don't ever want there to be any doubt that you're enjoying yourself and want me to keep doing what I'm doing."

"Thank you, Max. Please keep doing that."

"Which part? This?" He nibbled on her earlobe lightly. "Or this?" He cupped her breast in his left hand

and let his thumb drift lightly across the eager tip that rose to meet it.

"Both!"

"Or maybe you'd prefer this…" He kissed his way down her neck, across her collarbone and down to the gentle valley between her breasts. At the same time he let his free hand drift lower, skimming down her hip and thigh to the back of her knee, which he raised. His fingers traced back up the inside of her thigh.

"Umm, yes. That's better. Oh, my. Much better…"

He smiled against her velvet skin as she gasped and arched up into him.

He was surprised, however, when she returned the favor and reached for his stomach with her hands. Her fingers explored him every bit as boldly as he was exploring her until he was the one gasping in surprise and delight.

When he could take no more, he grasped her wrists and pulled them up by her ears, pinning her hands in place by twining his fingers with hers. He pinned the rest of her in place with his body, but he was careful not to crush her.

"Are we—"

She cut him off. "We are *not* going to be good if you don't get busy soon. I've been thinking about this nonstop ever since the night I met you, and my patience is wearing very thin! I'm on birth control, I don't have any sexually transmitted diseases and there's no one else in my life. Now can we get on with this?"

He grinned down at her, enthralled by her frank desire for him. She rose up off the pillows to kiss him, and he rolled onto his back, taking her with him, wrapping her in his arms and reveling in how her breasts pressed against his chest.

Despite the difference in their physical statures, they fit each other perfectly. She crawled all over him and covered his body with hers as they explored each other with growing intensity. He met her boldness with his own, claiming her body with gentle force and claiming her sighs, and then cries, of delight with his mouth.

They reversed positions, and she arched up against him eagerly, meeting his thrusts with her own, helping him drive deeper and deeper into her body and soul. And, oh, how she welcomed him in, surrounding him with love and acceptance and joy…all the things he'd been denied his entire life. She wrapped him in her arms and showered him with it all, and he was powerless to do anything but let down his guard and humbly accept it.

At some point, they pulled back the covers and ended up between his black Egyptian cotton sheets. She straddled him and drove him into oblivion at another point, and he returned the favor at yet another.

They made love for hours, resting and making out in between more athletic bouts, but the end result was complete and total satiation of body, mind and soul. As Lissa sprawled across his chest, exhausted, he stroked her hair and murmured, "Sleep."

"Mmm. Hmm."

So. Was this what happiness felt like?

And that was the last thing he remembered thinking before blessed darkness claimed him.

Lissa woke gradually, perplexed by the various aches and pains of having exercised excessively until she regained enough consciousness to recall the exact form said exercise had taken last night. And then she popped to full awareness all at once, simultaneously registering smooth, warm flesh beneath her cheek, the smell of aftershave and the caress of cotton against her skin. All of her skin. *Oh, right.* She was naked in bed with Max Smith in his magnificent condo full of art after an even more magnificent night with him.

Well, then. This normal life thing was going smashingly well, if she did say so herself.

And to that end, she eased carefully off his outstretched arm and out from under the covers. He deserved breakfast in bed after the spectacular night he'd gifted her with.

She picked his discarded tuxedo shirt off the floor and slipped it on. Buttoning it absently, she padded down the hallway in search of a kitchen. Woo baby, did the man ever have a kitchen! She looked around in delight at the high-tech gadgets tucked neatly into alcoves all along the quartz counters.

One of the gadgets was a coffeemaker, and she fiddled with it until it flashed to life and commenced what appeared to be the preliminary steps of making coffee. As best she could tell, it already had coffee beans and water in it. That was Max. Always thinking one step ahead.

For the first time since Max had swept her off her feet in the garden, she had a mental moment to herself to ruminate on last night's revelations. Almost all the people at that party had known her aunt. Some of them well. Which was a shade alarming given that she'd picked up a strong impression that most of the partygoers worked for the same illegal criminal organization.

Oh, they thought they were being tricky and secretive about how they couched their questions to her about their psychic readings. But they didn't seem to grasp that she could see a great deal more than their words revealed. Interesting business associates Max had. Was he one of them? And if so, why hadn't being around him flooded her with the same violent images and nefarious intent? Did having the hots for someone blind her to his true nature? Alarm exploded in her gut at the notion of being blind like that.

Whoa. Wait. She wanted blind. *Right?* Blind meant normal. How did regular people live like this, not knowing for sure who they were dealing with? Panic rippled through her.

Desperate to distract and calm herself, she turned her thoughts to the last set of psychic images to come to her, clinging to them like the lifeline they were. No matter that they were the pile of violent images that had flooded her last night.

One in particular had struck her. It was an image of a young girl, a teenager with a mop of bright red curls, who looked a lot like Lissa, crying.

If she didn't know that Julio G. was safely in police custody across town, she would have wondered if maybe she'd picked up on another one of that guy's victims. Although the impression of the crying girl didn't feel recent.

As Max had told her the stories of the mansion last night, she'd assumed the crying girl must have lived in the home at some point. But now that she thought about it without Max's distracting presence nearby, she revised her conclusion. That image of the crying girl had come out of someone's mind at the party, not out of the walls of the house. Of course, that didn't explain why the image had struck—and stuck with—her so strongly.

She opened Max's refrigerator door and was pleased to find eggs and bacon within. She popped a whole pound of bacon into the oven to bake, because there was no such thing in life as too much bacon, and wandered out into the condo while it got a head start on the eggs she would fry up.

There was a small painting in Max's office she wanted to look at again. For all the world, it looked like a Picasso sketch. She was no great expert on art, but she wasn't a complete ignoramus about it, either. She'd taken as many art classes in college as she could fit in around the entirely boring degree in business that her parents had forced her to get.

Max's office was as sleek and neat as the rest of his house. It looked as if the man didn't actually live there. It was decorated too well to be labeled sterile, but the white walls, pale bamboo floors and modern furniture were only a step or two short of it.

She glanced at a perfectly stacked pile of papers on his desk and picked up the top one out of curiosity. It was written in what looked like the Cyrillic alphabet. Of course he spoke Russian, too. She started to put the paper back, but the next letter in the pile caught her eye.

Dear Mr. Kuznetsov, Thank you for putting us in contact with the auction house...

Kuznetsov? Who the hell was that? He'd told her his name was Smith. Max Smith. It was one thing to suspect his name wasn't Smith. But it was another to know for sure that he'd lied to her.

This "being normal" crap was for the birds. In the future, she would rip into the mind of every man who got close to her whether they liked it or not. Normal human judgment was horribly, fatally flawed, and, furthermore, she clearly sucked at it.

Particularly after last night. How could he sleep with her, when he hadn't even told her his real name? What else was he lying about? And what about the things he'd said while they were making love? Things about never having known a woman like her. Had any of that been real, or had the whole thing been nothing more than a casual hookup to him?

Chapter 7

Fury and fear and humiliation mingled in her gut, and an urge to flee overtook her. But her clothes were in his room. Scowling, she found a laundry room just past the garage entrance and a basket of laundry. She didn't care if it was clean or dirty. She just grabbed a pair of sweatpants and a sweatshirt and yanked them on, her hands shaking she was so mad.

Granted, she'd suspected Smith wasn't his real name, or at least not all of it. Why hadn't she listened to her instinct? It had been trying to tell her. But no. She had to go and be all regular and gullible and trusting.

She needed a ride home. Her place was miles away from here. The keys to Lola were on a credenza in the front hall where he'd tossed them last night. She scooped them up and raced down to the garage, frantic to get out of there before Max or whatever his name was woke up.

She hit the garage door opener and started the car, then backed it out carefully into the street. A moment's awareness that she was engaging in grand theft auto passed through her mind, but she angrily dismissed the misgivings that came along with the revelation. He deserved it.

She touched the accelerator, and the Ferrari jumped forward, scaring her into yanking her foot off the pedal. She tried touching the pedal more lightly, and the sports car accelerated more cooperatively. Gingerly, she guided the car across town. Intuition tickled her spine, and she angrily and eagerly tuned into it. A vision of Max royally pissed off that she'd taken his car flashed through her head. *Good.* The least she could do was repay his lie with a big scare. *Jerk.* And she would return the darned car to him, anyway. But not now. Right now, she was so mad she could spit.

Max woke up to the smell of fresh coffee—and was that bacon?—and smiled up at the ceiling lazily. That had unquestionably been the best night he could ever remember. He'd searched his entire life for a woman who could love him for himself, just the way he was, and he'd finally found her.

He jumped in the shower. When he emerged, he wrapped a towel around his hips. *Hmm.* The bacon smelled a little burned. But his euphoria was such that Lissa could serve him charcoal this morning and he wouldn't care. He padded toward the kitchen, where the burning smell became more pronounced.

"Lissa?" he called.

No answer. Maybe she was in the guest bathroom washing up. He opened the oven door, and smoke poured out. He swore, grabbed a hot pad and pulled a cookie sheet covered in strips of blackened bacon out. The smoke alarm let out a piercing scream, and he dived for the kitchen window, opening it wide. He turned on the ceiling fan and went into the dining room to open that window, as well.

His eyeballs actually hurt from the piercing noise by the time the smoke alarm finally went silent. That crisis solved, he headed for the guest bedroom and bath. Odd that Lissa hadn't come out to see what all the fuss was about—

He frowned at the open bedroom door and darkened attached bath. *Huh.* Where was she? He backtracked into the main hall, and that was when he noticed Lola's keys were missing. His frown deepened. Last night she'd expressed nervousness at the idea of driving a vehicle like the Ferrari. Surely she hadn't just gone out to make a quick grocery run. Besides, there was a place on the corner she could have walked to.

He headed for his bedroom and his cell phone and dialed her number. It went straight to voice mail. "Hey, Lissa. Where are you? Did you have someplace to be this morning that I didn't know about? I miss you. Last night was really special, and I'm looking forward to spending more time with you. Call me."

He waited ten minutes, and when she didn't call back, he called her again. Still no answer. Cold fear took root in his gut then. Something was wrong.

He finished dressing and jogged to his next-door neighbor's garage. He rented the space to park his pickup truck. He used the vehicle in his antique business to haul large pieces of furniture and art. Fury beginning to tickle his gut, he steered the truck toward Lissa's place.

He breathed a sigh of relief to see his Ferrari parked in front of the curiosity shop and still in one piece. But hard on the heels of that came more unfolding anger. Why had she ditched him like that?

The shop door was locked, but he still had a spare key from when they'd installed the locks. He let himself into the shop.

"Lissa!" he shouted up the stairs.

She appeared at the top of the staircase swimming in a pair of his sweats and looking about twelve years old. "What are you doing here?" she demanded truculently.

He reached for reason and managed to reply relatively calmly. "Getting my car back for one thing. And worrying about your safety for another. Why did you take off like that without saying anything to me?"

She glared down at him and planted both fists on her hips. "How come you didn't tell me your real name?"

Her question froze his burgeoning anger like a blast of liquid nitrogen. "I beg your pardon?" he finally managed to choke out.

"You heard me. What's your name?"

"Max. Max Smith—"

She made a buzzer noise. "Wrong answer. I was wandering around your place looking at the paintings again, and I saw a letter on your desk."

He closed his eyes. An acidic wash of chagrin passed through him. "It's complicated, Lissa—" he started.

Again she cut him off. "No, it's not. Every human being has one first and one last name. Their real one. What's yours?"

"I can't tell you."

That stopped her head of steam a little. "Why not?" she asked.

"It's complicated."

"Try me."

"Can we not do this shouting up and down a flight of stairs?" He pinched the bridge of his nose, feeling the beginnings of a headache coming on.

"No. I like having the high ground. And you deserve to be shouted at. You lied to me. I can't believe I made love with a man whose name I don't even know!"

It sounded as though she'd found her mad mojo again. She reached out of sight with one hand and when it came back into sight, she threw something down the stairs at him.

Surprised, he snagged something fuzzy and fist-size. He stared down at the wad of fake fur in his hand. "Earmuffs?" he asked incredulously.

"I'm from Vermont, you idiot! It was December when I left there to come down here."

Something else sailed down the stairs at him. This time a small folding umbrella. He started up the stairs toward her. Lissa's arm was cocked back to throw some other piece of weather gear at him when she froze. Based on long years of threat training, he froze, as well. He listened hard but heard nothing in the sudden and deafening silence.

When she didn't say anything and remained motionless, he finally asked, low and urgent, "What?"

She snapped out of her reverie and shocked him by whispering, "If I told you we have to leave the building right this minute, would you just take me at my word and go with me?"

He frowned, glancing around the interior of the

shop, looking for any threats. He saw none. But then she was rushing down the stairs toward him so quickly she nearly knocked him off his feet.

"I'm serious," she bit out as she brushed past him like a gust front. "C'mon."

Perplexed and alarmed, he followed her down the steps to the main floor. She surprised him by veering away from the front door. "Hurry!" she whispered frantically.

Okay, what the hell was going on? She sounded as if armed killers were about to burst in on them. He glanced out into the quiet street in front of her store and saw no movement. What had happened to her tantrum about him lying about his name?

She raced into the hallway housing the customer restroom and a small storeroom, and he followed swiftly. No way was she getting away from him this easily. She burst out of the building's back door into a narrow alley with him close on her heels.

"We have to get out of here!" she gasped.

"Why?"

"No time for explanations. They're almost here!"

His alert level went from alarmed to full combat mode. He grabbed her arm and pulled her into the shade next to a brick wall. First order of business was to get out of this alley. They were fish in a barrel there. He asked her urgently, "Do you know what direction this threat is approaching from?"

She pointed off to their right.

He took off running to their left, never releasing her arm. She kept up with him reasonably well, considering she was wearing only fuzzy socks on her feet. They reached a side street, and he pressed her back behind him as he peered around the wall to clear the thorough-fare. Nothing moved, no cars or pedestrians.

If, in fact, some terrible threat was coming to the shop, the two of them needed to get out of sight and fast. Ideally, they'd get in a car and drive away, but Lola was parked directly in front of her shop, and his truck was parked right behind it.

A squeal of tires nearby caught his attention. It came from around the corner...*holy crap*...in the direction of the curiosity shop.

"Stay here," he ordered.

He crept out into the side street and raced silently on the balls of his feet to the corner. Very carefully, he peered around the brick wall into the street housing the curiosity shop.

A windowless white delivery van was double-parked next to Lola, and four masked men were pouring out of the back of it. The first guy used a lock gun to pick the lock on the front door. The man then disappeared into the store.

Max listened in satisfaction as the newly installed security alarm screamed like a banshee. Two of the men carried small black nylon duffel bags, and the last man carried another semiautomatic weapon.

He'd love to move in closer and figure out who these guys were, but first he had to secure Lissa's safety. He glanced back over his shoulder to gesture for her to join him and jumped to find her not three feet behind him. So much for her following instructions and stay-ing back.

He waited until the last masked man disappeared into the store, then eyed the driver of the van warily. *Ha.* The driver climbed out of his seat and headed for the back of the van—probably closing the rear doors in preparation for a quick getaway.

"C'mon." He grabbed Lissa's hand and they darted across the street, keeping the side street and staying out of sight of the van. He took off running with her.

"Where are we going?" Lissa panted.

"I've got to get you someplace safe. Off the street where you could be spotted." The place he had in mind to take her was going to make her anger at not knowing his name pale by comparison to her anger when she saw it, but he really had no choice. He had to get her under cover and away from the armed intruders in her home. Her safety was much more important than his being in hot water with her.

The shop's security alarm went silent and he winced. Sixty seconds tops to disable the state-of-the-art system he'd just had installed? *Yikes.* These guys were top-of-the-line professionals. So much for this being another hit from Julio G.'s boys. Not unless street gangs in New Orleans had upgraded into world-class paramilitary professionals.

He rounded the next corner and raced to the alley behind his secret apartment. He hustled Lissa up the stairs and unlocked the door as quietly as he could. Thankfully, her socks made no noise, and he knew how to be silent while running no matter what the surface might be. He dialed in the combination on the padlock protecting his hidey-hole and popped it free. He opened the door and gestured with his free arm.

"Inside," he ordered quietly.

She slipped past him, and he eased the door shut, throwing its dead bolts quickly.

He looked up, and Lissa stood in the middle of the

bare living room, staring at the cameras and computer monitors. "What is this place?"

"A surveillance blind," he answered shortly, moving to one side of the window. He swung a camera lens in front of the lower left-hand corner of the window and clicked on the recording button.

She headed for the other window. "We should close the blinds so they won't see—"

"No!" he said sharply. "Stay back. Any movement at all in a window, be it you or the blinds going down, will catch the attention of the driver, who's also acting as a lookout. You're safer over here by me," he told her as he moved over to the table tucked back in a corner by the kitchenette. He clicked on the twin computer monitors, and the front of the curiosity shop jumped into view.

"What is this equipment for?" she asked ominously. A look of dawning comprehension had come over her face.

Crap. She'd figured out that this whole setup was aimed at her shop. The woman was too damned quick on the uptake for her own good.

"Does your Spidey sense say that we're safe here?" he asked her in clipped tones, hoping to distract her and hold off the explosion until after this crisis had passed.

She frowned and paused, as if to listen to a voice only she could hear. "We're safe here as long as we stay out of sight from the men out there. They don't know about this place."

"Does the voice in your head know who those guys are?" Max gestured at the computer monitor in front of him.

She paused again, no doubt to give the powers that

be a second to share anything they cared to with her. She shrugged, announcing, "I've got nothing."

"Lemme see if I can pull a license plate off that van." Using a joystick, he maneuvered the second camera in the far window—the one that normally pointed into Lissa's living room—to capture the back bumper of the van.

"Got it," he muttered, jotting the plate number down on a pad of paper. He readjusted the camera and captured an image of two gunmen moving quickly around Lissa's apartment.

"What the hell are they doing in my home?" Lissa demanded indignantly from over his shoulder.

He caught occasional glimpses of a figure moving past an upstairs window. "They appear to be searching your place. Any idea what they're looking for?"

"None. I don't have anything particularly valuable. Well, some items in the shop are pretty valuable, but there's nothing upstairs worthy of armed robbers. It's not like my house is a bank or a jewelry store."

She stood so close behind him he could feel the heat of her body against the back of his neck. He'd give anything to be able to put his arm around her and draw her against his side for comfort, but he expected she was still too mad about the false name thing to accept comfort from him, let alone the whole spying on her home thing that was just dawning on her.

They watched in grim silence as the gunmen left the shop and piled in the side of the van. Max glanced at his watch. "Three minutes on the nose that they were inside. Professional discipline."

"Which means what?"

"I can say with certainty that those aren't Julio G.'s

cronies. Nor are they random amateur thugs looking to rob your place. They're a highly trained crew of some kind."

"Trained to do what?"

The van pulled away from the curb, and he stared down at Lola, still sitting exactly where she'd been parked before, with not a scratch on her. If those guys had been in the shop to vandalize it, surely they would have put a rifle butt through the Ferrari's windshield. Why leave a four-hundred-thousand-dollar car completely untouched unless they were following specific orders that did not include random vandalism?

Lissa started to ask questions, but he held up a finger and made a fast call to Bastien. "Hey, buddy. Lissa's place just had some visitors..We barely made it out the back before they barged in through the front... I pulled a license plate number off a creepy, unmarked van with no windows... They didn't look like Julio G.'s friends. These guys were pros... Nah, no need to send over a patrol. They didn't appear to take anything or bust her place up... I've got the whole thing on film on my surveillance setup of the shop. I'll let you know if I find anything that will help ID the intruders."

Speaking of which, he couldn't wait to watch a slow-motion playback of exactly what the men did inside the shop and apartment.

He ended the call and looked up into the face of wrath incarnate. "You were *watching* me?" Lissa asked, her voice low and intense.

"Not exactly. I was watching your shop."

"Why? And before you answer this, consider carefully. This explanation had better be good, or else I'm calling the police and reporting you."

He sighed. So much for a perfect emotional connection with the woman of his dreams. "I was just on the phone with a cop and mentioned my surveillance equipment. What makes you think they'd do anything? As a matter of fact, nothing I'm doing here is illegal."

"Quit dodging my question. Why were—are—you watching me?"

"I have reason to believe your shop is being used as a dead drop site."

"As in spies leaving messages for each other?"

"Spies aren't the only people who leave dead drop messages for each other. Criminals also use the technique."

"Why not just text each other, or send an email?"

"The internet isn't as secure as most people seem to think it is. Given the right technology, most electronic communications can be intercepted. Dead drops are still one of the most secure forms of secret communication."

"Who, exactly, is using my shop as a dead drop site?"

"That's what I'm trying to find out."

"And?"

He realized he'd clenched his jaw and had to consciously unclench it. "And I'd rather not get into specifics with you. Suffice it to say they're bad people, and I'm trying to figure out who they are so I can stop them."

She stared at him a long time, weighing his words. "Is this why my aunt was killed?"

His eyebrows shot up. "What makes you so certain she met with foul play?"

"She called me two days before she died and told me she was about to die. I got the distinct impression she expected foul play. Not to mention the woman was completely healthy."

His jaw dropped. He knew that Lissa didn't believe her aunt had died of natural causes. But the woman had known it was coming? That meant Callista had likely known her killer. Which considerably narrowed the list of suspects. "She told you that? Why didn't you call the police?"

Lissa huffed. "Because everyone in my family thought she was crazy. They thought her psychic powers were bogus and credited drug use in her youth for her visions and intuitions."

"And you? Did you think she was crazy?"

"No. She was the real deal."

He tilted his head to one side. "So you think psychic phenomena are real?"

"I'd really rather not debate that at the moment."

This from the woman who'd listened to a voice in her head that had warned her about a van full of armed men on their way to attack her? He had to admit, though, that the accuracy of her prediction did give him pause.

He asked her abruptly, "How did you know those men were coming to raid your home?"

She shoved the curls off her face in exasperation. "I just did, okay?"

They stared at each other in a frustrated standoff. Apparently, neither of them was willing to give up their secrets to the other one. Which left them exactly nowhere. Loss and the old loneliness stabbed his gut. The darkness that descended around him now was much worse for his having glimpsed a tiny burst of light with her last night.

He grimly pushed all his feelings into a mental

drawer and slammed it shut. Men like him did not get hampered by pesky things like feelings.

"Are these things turned on all the time?" Lissa asked, gesturing toward the cameras.

"Yes," he answered shortly.

"And you're recording everything they film?"

"Yes."

"Remember that man I told you about? The one who asked about an African fertility statue. Took a long, hard look at it but didn't buy."

He leaned back in the folding chair and stared up at her, waiting to see where she was going with this line of reasoning.

"That statue was hollow and too ugly for any normal human being to purchase. It was a good bet the thing would sit in the store forever. If I were going to make a dead drop in the curiosity shop, that's where I would have put a message."

"What time of day did he come into the shop?" Max asked, pulling up the digital record of that day.

"Late afternoon."

It took him a few minutes of fast-forwarding, but eventually a man in a business suit, which was atypical of her usual clientele, speed walked into the shop. He stopped the tape and backed it up at a more moderate pace. "Have a look at this. Is that the man who made the possible drop?"

Lissa leaned down to take a close look at the computer monitor, a hand unconsciously on his shoulder to steady herself. Against his wishes, his pulse spiked as she glanced sidelong at him and murmured, "That's the guy."

Maybe that hand on his shoulder hadn't been so unconscious after all. A tiny flicker of hope illuminated the darkness in his soul.

Max clicked through screenshots from the video of the man in question until he found a reasonably clear picture of the target coming out of the shop. He copied and pasted it into an email and fired it off to Jennie Finch to see if she could work her computer magic and get him an ID. It was the sort of challenge Jennie would enjoy.

While he worked, Lissa moved away, exploring the corners of the barren apartment. It was two rooms, a living room/kitchen and a bedroom with a tiny, disgusting bathroom. No closets. No furniture except for a clean mattress he'd brought in and put new bedsheets on. There was nothing to relieve the stained walls and even more stained brown carpet that had once been shag and was now just a sad matted mess. It wouldn't occupy her for long.

He worked quickly, rolling back the footage of the most recent incursion into her property. He watched the men burst into the shop. The two with the bags opened the duffels immediately and commenced moving around the ground floor. If he didn't know better, he'd say they were installing surveillance cameras. But they took no time doing wiring... Did they have the wireless, self-contained models that had hit the market recently? Those were not cheap gadgets.

While the guys with the guns stayed downstairs, clearly standing guard, the other two raced upstairs and moved around Lissa's apartment, more obviously planting a half-dozen cameras up there.

He leaned back hard in his chair, staring at the monitors. They *were* installing photo surveillance equipment! *What the hell?* Why would anyone want to watch Lissa Clearmont like that? Granted, he was sitting in front of a camera bank, but he wasn't watching her. He wasn't watching her like some creeper-stalker type; he was watching her shop.

But those guys had placed something like a dozen cameras all over her home and place of work. Lissa was definitely the target of the operation, not her store. Otherwise, they wouldn't have bothered with all those cameras upstairs.

He looked at her. At the moment, she had her palm pressed to the filthy wall of his living room and seemed to be listening to the damned thing speak to her. She glanced up, caught him studying her and jerked her hand away from the wall guiltily.

"You're disturbed by something," she announced.

"Did you read my mind to figure that out?"

"No. I looked at your face. You're scowling like someone stole your favorite toy. And your shoulders are hunched up around your ears."

"We need to talk, Lissa."

Chapter 8

Oh, no. He was going to demand to know exactly what was going on with her mental powers. If only she hadn't gotten that urgent warning to get out of her home…

On second thought, she couldn't be sorry for having gotten a message that could very well have saved their lives.

Thing was, she'd never been able to do anything even remotely like that before. Her powers had never included awareness of current events unfolding around her, and, furthermore, her powers had never extended to her own safety.

Dammit, her powers were supposed to be going away, not multiplying exponentially. But ever since Max had come into her life, the cursed things had been growing like crazy. She just had to persist. If she ignored her powers for long enough, they would fade. They *had* to.

She glanced up, alarmed to see Max studying her in that intent way he did that peeled back every layer of deception and laid her soul bare. She asked cautiously, "What do you want to talk about?"

"This whole psychic thing. Is it really a thing?"

Although this was a conversation she was intimately familiar with, having had it a hundred times, never had so much ridden on her handling it correctly. She shrugged with feigned unconcern. "Depends on who you ask. Most of my family would tell you it's all crap. But you just got a fairly forceful demonstration of it when I got that warning to run."

"And you had no idea whatsoever that those guys were coming for you and your place?"

"None whatsoever."

"Nobody at the party last night said anything to you to indicate that your place might get rolled today?"

"At the party?" she exclaimed. "Do you think someone from there sent those men?"

"It's possible. But we can talk about that later. I want to stay focused on this psychic stuff for the moment."

Rats. Not going to be diverted, was he?

He spoke slowly. "Hypothetically, let's say I have an open mind. Convince me what I just saw is real."

She pulled over the only other folding chair at the table and sat down across from him. She looked him dead in the eye and said, "Here's the thing. It's not my job to convince you one way or the other whether or not my talents are real or fake. You'll see what you see, and you'll come up with whatever explanation makes sense to you. Some people think they see miracles from God. Others see angels. Others see pure coincidence."

"And you? What do you see?"

She winced. In spite of her angry decision earlier to bag the whole normal thing, she hadn't really meant it. She'd just been mad at Max for lying to her. At the end of the day, she really wanted to find a way to have a normal life. Which left her trying to tiptoe between the land mines the man across the table was throwing at her feet. The hot man she'd had amazing sex with last night and whom she'd dearly love to not only bed again but build a real relationship with.

"Okay," she said cautiously. "Let's say that psychic powers do exist. Hypothetically, of course."

"Of course," he agreed quickly. A little too quickly. Or maybe she was just being oversensitive to criticism from him.

"It would follow, then, that these powers could manifest in any number of ways. A person might be able to see past events they were not present to witness at the time."

"Would this power extend to speaking with dead people?"

"Possibly," she answered carefully. She really didn't need him making fun of her. For some reason, she actually gave a darn what he thought of her. Or maybe the reason wasn't that obscure. Making love with him had been as close to life changing as anything she'd ever experienced in her life. Which was saying something, given the course of her life to date.

"How else might these powers manifest…hypothetically?" he asked.

"Well, a person might be able to see the future, as well. And they might be able to pick up thoughts other people are having."

"What else?" he asked. His voice was starting to take on a tone of resignation.

She took a deep breath and went for it. "They might be able to speak with ghosts. Or find lost things. You know, the usual."

"The usual," he repeated slowly. "And you're telling me you can do all these things?"

"I'm telling you that I'm doing my level best to live a normal life in spite of the possible existence of all these things," she replied with more desperation than she cared to hear in her voice.

"Are your hypothetical talents in the field of things psychic well known?" he asked cautiously.

"I was hoping that no one in this part of the country would have heard anything to that effect." God, it was weird talking in circles with him like this. "And, yes, to anticipate your next question entirely without using any hypothetical powers, it was the reason I moved all the way down here from Vermont to make a new start. To escape certain…rumors…about me."

"Like a witch hunt?"

"Nothing that dramatic. Just sidelong looks from strangers and neighbors who avoided me. Enough to make it difficult to meet any guys who weren't already nervous about me. I'm weird enough without the people I date having to worry that at any second my head will start spinning around while I vomit green pea soup."

"What's the craziest thing you've…been rumored to do?"

She had to think about that one. "I suppose it would be finding dead bodies for the FBI. That seems to creep people out pretty badly. Talking to ghosts seems to mess people up, too. I find that most people have skeletons in their closets they'd like to keep hidden."

He nodded, but the man looked a little shell-shocked. "So what are the, um, ghosts, telling you about everything that has been happening to you for the past few days?"

"I wouldn't know."

He stared at her. "I thought you just told me you could speak with ghosts."

"I told you it might be hypothetically possible and that there were rumors to that effect. Besides, just because a person might be able to hear them doesn't mean the ghosts would choose to say anything."

"Why not?"

Dammit, did he have to keep asking such ridiculously perceptive questions? She exhaled hard. "Sometimes an individual's abilities are tied to a specific trigger. For example, children and things pertaining to children might be all a psychic can hear. Or a psychic might only be able to speak to dead spirits. Or only to see the future."

"If you—hypothetically—had these sorts of powers, how do you think yours would be triggered?"

She took a deep breath and admitted the thing to him that she rarely even admitted to herself. The thing that had ultimately made her run away from her abilities and come to New Orleans to hide. "By violence."

Max stared at her for a long time in silence. Finally, he said slowly, "Well, that would suck. Particularly if you found yourself in the company of someone surrounded by frequent violence."

"It would, wouldn't it?"

She couldn't take much more of this conversation. It was time to change the subject. "So, Max. Is that really your first name? What should I call you?"

"Maximillian is my real name. I've always gone by Max, though. If you want to irritate the hell out of me, you can use the Russian nickname for Maximillian and call me Masha."

That made her grin for a moment. He was so totally not a Masha. "And your last name?"

He just shook his head, a stubborn set to his jaw. Kuznetsov was the name she'd seen on that letter. Of course, it could just as easily be a fake name, too.

"Can you at least tell me why you're using an alias?"

"To protect my life and those of the people I love."

"From whom?"

"Nope."

She tried another tack. "Tell me about the people you love." It was a direct request to let her in, past his undercover persona and into his real identity.

Silence stretched out between them as he considered her request. Obviously he hadn't missed the implications of what she'd asked. At long last, he spoke slowly. "My parents are both dead. I have a sister, though. She's younger than me, and a pain in the ass when she gets stubborn. Reminds me a little of you."

Lissa pursed her lips. She could live with being called stubborn. When Max didn't continue, she prompted, "Do you have friends?"

"Yeah, sure."

"Are you from New Orleans originally?"

He hesitated, but then answered, "I am."

"Your accent isn't very thick."

"My family wasn't from here. No Southern drawl in the home meant I didn't pick up as thick an accent as most natives."

"Where was your family from originally?"

"Europe."

That wasn't very descriptive. With Masha as a nickname, she would guess his people hailed from Eastern Europe or Russia.

"Brothers?"

"Just the one sister."

"I could see you being a good big brother."

He merely shrugged, clearly unhappy with this discussion about his origins. Now why was that? She tilted her head and studied him intently. "Where did you learn how to do…this?" She gestured at the surveillance equipment on the table between them.

"Anyone willing to do a little research and spend some bucks on gear can do this."

"That's actually kind of scary to hear you say."

He made a commiserating face. "Most people are blissfully ignorant of the possibilities for invasion of privacy."

She knew quite a bit about regular people being blissfully ignorant of the energies and events swirling around them, invisible and unseen.

Max asked, "So, at the party last night when you were doing all those tarot card readings, was there any…additional element…to the readings beyond you telling people what was on the cards?"

"You mean did I use any psychic skills to enhance the readings?"

"Well, yes."

She shrugged. "Not intentionally."

"Did you happen to see anything beyond the cards?" he asked carefully.

"That's an interesting question in light of my mentioning that my hypothetical skills would be tied to violence."

"And yet, entirely fitting for that bunch," he grumbled under his breath.

In a flash of candidness, she commented, "I saw plenty. Interesting crowd. They had some unusual stuff in both their pasts and futures."

"Like what?"

"Beyond the usual divorces, money problems and family hassles, I saw criminal activity. Violence. Legal troubles. Death."

"Death?" he exclaimed. "Who?"

"Sorry. Client confidentiality. I don't see and tell."

"You didn't tell whoever it was that they're going to die, did you?"

"If you'll recall, you told me to be cautious. I took you at your word. Not to mention that the guests themselves exuded deep reluctance to have me reveal their secrets. Forecasting death and violence didn't seem to be exactly the stuff of light party entertainment. I omitted most of the dark stuff I saw from what I told them. I kept what I said light. Superficial. I forecasted a few weddings and babies. That sort of stuff."

"Thank God," he breathed.

"Why did you take me to that party if you think so badly of the attendees?" she asked, curious.

"I was ordered to."

That sent her eyebrows up. "By whom?"

"My boss."

"That Peter guy who got drunk and started having such violent thoughts?"

Max lurched. "What kind of violent thoughts?"

She shrugged. "He was contemplating killing somebody. Maybe whomever you two left the room to talk about. Or maybe whoever he's so afraid of."

Max's jaw went hard at that comment. He was silent for a time and then said tightly, "As you may have noticed, the people at that party—my current business associates—are not exactly on the up-and-up with the law."

"I gathered that. I did look into plenty of their heads, remember?"

"About that. Did you happen to catch an image of a man from any of them?"

"What kind of image?"

"I wish I knew. My boss, Peter Menchekov, knows what a particular man farther up the food chain of his business looks like. I'm trying to find out the identity of that man."

Pieces of the puzzle were starting to fall into place for her too quickly for comfort. Many of the people at that party had Russian names and Russian accents. Some sort of Russian organization steeped in violence, and for which Max worked under an assumed name.

"Are you *sure* you're not an FBI agent?" she asked sharply.

"I *swear* I don't work for the FBI," he answered emphatically. She watched carefully for tells of lying, but Max seemed to be telling the truth, and her sixth sense for lies didn't send up any alarms.

"Who do you actually work for, then?"

"I'm self-employed in my real life."

He was being deceptive with that statement. But before she could call him on it, he continued. "This investigation is off the books. I have a personal interest in finding the man whom I seek within this organization."

"What kind of interest?"

"It's a long story."

She stared at him, and he stared back stubbornly. The man did not have any intention of sharing his secrets with her. Little did he know that nobody could keep secrets around her for long. Her eyes narrowed. Perhaps a small demonstration of that fact was in order.

She opened her mind, and the images she'd been seeing for the past week flooded in. Those painful scenes had come from Max's life? Her heart physically hurt in her chest at the realization.

She spoke gently. "How about I take a guess? A car crash on a dark road. Two women hurt, one terribly. Hours before help came. Maybe one of them your mother? A little boy in terrible pain. Alone in a swamp. Beaten to prove how much pain he could stand. A cruel father. Blond and handsome, but cold."

"Stop."

She winced at the grief and denial in his voice. *Note to self: Max's childhood is strictly off-limits for the moment.*

He took a deep breath. Exhaled very slowly. He stared at her for a long time, a stew of disbelief, horror and curiosity swirling in his eyes. She swore under her breath, shoving back from the table and surging to her feet.

What the hell was she doing? She knew better than to show off like that. The last thing she wanted to do was scare off Max for good. Yes, he'd lied about his name. And, yes, he had secrets about his life and his work. But if she believed the evidence of her own eyes, he was at heart a decent and honorable guy trying to do the right thing. He'd saved her from Julio G. at personal risk to his own life. He'd come when Julio's thugs had busted up her store and she'd cried out for help. And he kissed like a god.

She turned to face him and winced at the expression on his face. She knew that particular cocktail of emotions. And it inevitably spelled the end of any chance at a real relationship with him.

Oh, God. No.

The knowledge that she'd lost Max made her want to clutch her middle and fold in half in agony. She'd been so close to finding a man she could have a real relationship with. But then she had to go and blow it and be honest with him. Would she *never* learn? This was all her fault, but that didn't make it hurt any less.

She fell back into the flimsy chair, too devastated to stand and look at him any longer.

No sooner had she sat back down than Max jumped to his feet and paced a lap around the tiny apartment, which took about ten seconds total. He stopped, looming over her. "I don't know how you knew so much about my past that I never talk about to *anyone*. Maybe you did your homework insanely well on me."

A frown flitted across his features, and she could tell that he was trying to figure out who'd known about him being abandoned in the bayou naked, or who might have known about the beatings.

She ached to tell him her gift was real. That no one else knew about his private anguish and humiliation. That his secrets were safe with her. But she'd learned over the years that the harder she tried to convince someone that her talent was genuine, the less they believed her. She simply had to wait in an agony of impatience for him to decide for himself if he could accept that she knew things about him that no normal human being could reasonably know.

He took several more laps around the apartment and at length stopped in front of her again. "I'm willing to accept that you know stuff about me. Whether you have a real psychic talent or you're a gifted charlatan, I don't know. And I'm not sure I care which it is. But right now I could use your help. Did you see or hear—or divine—any information about a man, a shadowy figure, who is in charge of a lot of the people at that party?"

"I didn't see any faces that anyone was trying to conceal from me. But now that I know what to look for, if you could put me in close enough proximity to your boss to touch him, I might be able to pick the face you're looking for out of his mind."

"In the first place, is that how it works? You come into physical contact with someone and you get stuff on them? Is that how you got the face of that girl? From Julio G.'s noggin? And is it how you picked up that stuff about me? No. Don't answer that."

Max was babbling, a glaring indication that he was rattled. She started to speak, to promise that she would never reveal his secrets to anyone else, but he cut her off.

"In the second place, I'm not letting you go anywhere near Peter Menchekov again. He's too dangerous."

She reeled as she caught a mental glimpse of an order to kill her. An order given to...*ohmigosh*...Max. "Would you really do it?" she whispered, stunned.

"Do what?"

She shook her head. "Nothing. Just my imagination getting the better of me. It's a hazard of the profession."

"So here's the thing. Peter believes that you're as

psychic as your aunt reportedly was. He's terrified that you're going to have a vision of the apex predator at the top of his organization. Peter has asked me to keep a very close eye on you and make sure you don't 'see' anything you shouldn't." He made air quotes with his fingers as he said the word *see*.

Ahh. That was where the order to kill her must have come in. If she "saw" Peter's boss, Max was to kill her. Was that what had happened to Callista? Had she identified a man who was willing to kill to keep his identity secret? Would the same men ultimately kill her, too?

"Do you suppose she saw him, too?" she asked.

"You've lost me."

Oops. She often had that problem. She would have silent conversations with the voices in her head and forget that other people couldn't hear them. "What if my aunt had a vision of a face that's not supposed to be seen? Would your boss wire my place to make sure I don't do the same thing?"

Max glanced down at the monitors and back up at her. "I doubt Peter has the power to order a crew that professional, and hence expensive, to put high-tech surveillance gear in your place…" His voice trailed off.

"But you know who does have that kind of clout, don't you?"

"Yes. And no. The man I'm trying to identify would have that kind of money and resources. If word got passed up the chain of command to him from Peter that a new psychic is in town, he may be trying to find out just how good you are and how much of a threat you pose to him."

She glanced down at the monitors of her now empty shop and apartment. She knew full well from her previous work with the FBI that a person powerful enough to send armed men to her house to wire it for surveillance surely had the resources to have the same armed men kill her.

In a small voice, she asked, "What are we going to do?"

He stared at her grimly. She didn't need to be psychic to know she wasn't going to like what he had to say next. "I think we need to go back to your apartment and act like nothing's wrong."

"Excuse me?" she blurted.

"Let them watch you. Let them see that you're perfectly normal and you don't talk to the ghosts in the corner. That you don't have visions or see faces. Show them you're a fake and no threat at all to them."

She frowned. It was what she'd planned to do when she'd moved here. But now that she wasn't being given a choice in the matter, she liked the idea of hiding her abilities a lot less than before.

Max was speaking again. "Another problem. Peter ordered me to keep a close watch on you. He may have told his boss he gave me that order."

"Why is this a problem?"

"Whoever is on the other end of those cameras may expect to see me hanging out with you constantly."

Her pulse leaped. Max was going to be spending a lot of time with her, then? She failed to see much of a downside to that. And to think she'd been ready to kill him less than an hour ago. She might be weird, but wild mood swings had never been part of her gig before. At least not until she met a man who completely swept her off her feet.

"So what are we supposed to do when we go back there?" she asked him.

"We play house like any other perfectly normal, boring couple."

She snorted. The two of them were a lot of things, but normal or boring didn't make the list.

"And in the meantime, you keep an eye out for me to start describing or drawing strange men's faces, and you'll tackle me if I start doing anything along those lines."

"That's correct."

"And if I don't go along with this plan?"

"Peter or his boss will have those guys with the guns come back and kill you."

She stared at him, appalled. "And you work for these people?"

"I'm infiltrating these people to take them down. And I need your help."

"How long have you been undercover with them?"

"Approaching two years."

Her jaw dropped. "And you don't have enough to send them all to jail by now? What makes you think you'll ever get enough to put them away if you don't already have it?"

He sighed. "I have plenty to take down all the little guys. In fact, a few of the low-level street thugs have already been taken out. This bunch was using a human-trafficking ring to finance some of their other extracurricular activities. A stop has already been put to that."

That was good news, at least.

"But it's the top man I'm after. And he has yet to show his face. It has taken me a while to work my way up the organizational ladder far enough to get a shot at him and to gain people's trust along the way."

"How have you protected your soul from them for so long?"

He looked at her as if he didn't know how to answer the question. Warning bells went off in her head as he continued to stare blankly at her.

She threw him a lifeline. "So how is this acting like a normal couple thing supposed to work?"

He frowned, thinking hard for several seconds. Then his face lit. "I've got it! I'll help you renovate your place. It'll give me an excuse to spend a lot of time with you."

Her heart jumped before she reminded it that the whole thing would be just an act. "Since I don't seem to have any choice in the matter, I guess I'll have to accept your offer, then."

"Look. I'm sorry to have dragged you into this. I really wanted to keep you out of it. But your aunt worked for these guys for so long that they established her shop as their main dead drop location for all of their most important information exchanges. They don't want to mess up the routine if they don't have to."

"Callista was involved with the Russian mob?"

"Up to her eyeballs, apparently."

"Did *they* murder her?"

"How certain are you that she was murdered?" He clearly was asking if she had special knowledge of a crime. Air quotes around the word *special*.

"I'm not positive, of course, because I didn't witness the crime. But I have a feeling—" She broke off. Then she started again, this time telling the truth. "Fine. Her ghost has been whispering to me. Sending me dreams. I don't normally do the whole whispering ghost thing, but I'm pretty sure it's her. And she wants me to find out how she died."

To his credit, Max only rolled his eyes a little. "If she can tell you all of that, why can't she just tell you how she died?"

She threw him a withering look. "Because I obviously have to have proof of how she died for some reason that counts in this world."

"Well, yeah. If we can show that she was murdered to the police, we can force them to open a murder investigation and possibly expose the guy I'm after."

"There you have it," she declared. "Callista was no dummy in life. She wouldn't be one in death."

Max looked as though a headache was starting up behind his eyes and hammering at his temples. She might be mad as hell at him for watching her, but he was still a human being, and still trying to look out for her.

She moved around behind him to massage his shoulders and neck. It was like kneading rocks. But gradually, some of his terrible tension eased. It wasn't exactly a truce, but it also wasn't open warfare.

He sighed and said, "I've called in a few favors. An autopsy's going to be performed on your aunt's remains. This long after her death, it may not show much, but it's worth a look."

It seemed as if her jaw was destined to be perpetually sagging open today. "Well, okay, then. Um, thanks."

For the first time since they'd come into this surveillance headquarters, he looked her square in the eye. Apology was packed into every corner of his gaze. Her indignation softened even more. Gradually, the apology warmed, shifted. Turned to heat, and then to blazing fires of need.

It was darned near impossible to stay mad at a man who looked at her as though he wanted to crawl into bed with her for a week, not sleep a wink and never crawl out.

He tore his gaze away from hers reluctantly. "If you're going to go back into your apartment with me, there are a few things you need to know."

Rats. They were back to business.

"First, don't ever look for the cameras. You won't find them anyway, and it would tip off whoever's on the other end that we know the cameras are there. If you're tempted to peek, come talk to me instead. I promise I'll distract you. I'm not giving these bastards any excuse to hurt you."

That last bit was delivered with such fierce protectiveness that her heart broke a little. After everything she'd revealed to him, he was still willing to walk through fire for her? Tears pricked at her eyelids, and she sniffed loudly, fighting them off.

"Second," he continued more gently, "you really do have to try to act natural. Just be yourself."

Apparently, her natural self was a weepy mess at the moment. He stopped his lecture and gathered her against his big, comfortable chest wordlessly. He probably didn't even know why she was crying, and he was still willing to stroke her hair and hold her until she felt better.

At length, she gathered the shreds of her composure around her and stepped back from him. "You were saying? Something about acting natural."

"It's a thousand times harder to do than it sounds. You'll essentially become an actor pretending to live your life. It feels weird, so expect that. If you make a mistake, just move on. Don't try to backtrack or explain yourself. People misspeak all the time. Got all that?"

She nodded to indicate that she at least caught the gist of what he was saying. She figured it was going to take just diving into the deep end of this pool to really figure out the whole living-on-hidden-cameras thing.

"If it turns out to be too much for you, we do *not* have to play out this charade," Max added.

Charade? It would all be a charade with him? Such a soft word, but its sharpened edges cut into her flesh, making her bleed inside. Maybe it was for the best. He lived some sort of double life that involved a lot of danger. She didn't need to get mixed up in that.

Except she was apparently already mixed up in it without even knowing it. What had Callista been thinking to drag her down here and throw her into the middle of a giant mess like this?

She stared at Max, and he at her, each lost in their own thoughts. Finally she asked, "And when does this home renovation party commence?"

"Now. I'd suggest we go downstairs and get my truck, make a run to a home improvement store, and return to your place with some tools and supplies that will explain our abrupt departure from your place this morning." He glanced down at her feet. "And we'd better get you some shoes. Nobody goes shopping in fuzzy socks."

He made it sound so simple. Just act normal. Spend time with the attractive guy who was so hot he made her toes curl. Do some renovations. How hard could it be?

Why, then, were warning bells clanging wildly in her head as if the whole city were burning down around them? What wasn't he telling her? What else was going on here?

Chapter 9

Max carried in the last load of PVC pipes and dropped them on the floor of Lissa's living room with a clatter. He'd already spotted two of the surveillance cameras. But he knew what to look for, and with her place gutted like this, spots to hide the tiny gadgets were not plentiful.

In a way, he felt bad for the guys who'd been sent to wire the place for sight and sound in three minutes flat. They had to have sworn up a storm when they saw what they had to work with. They had made the best of it, though, and chosen the same spots he would have. Which told him volumes about just how well-trained those men had been. After all, his own training had been world-class.

"What's first?" Lissa asked cheerfully.

He glanced up quickly. Was she that good an actress, or was she that ignorant of just how dangerous a game

they were playing? One slip. One hint that they knew
they were on *Candid Camera*, and those guys with the
guns would be back so fast that even Lissa's special
powers wouldn't be enough to save them.

"Plumbing and electric repairs. Then we can put your
walls back together."

"I don't know anything about either of those."

"Lucky for you, I do." He was no contractor, but he'd
watched the ones in his condo closely. And for right
now, all he had to do was fake looking competent. He
just had to stay busy. Not think too much about those
damned cameras. But how could he not, with Lissa's
life hanging in the balance?

He enlisted her help in measuring and sawing sec-
tions of pipe. Rather than pull out the old copper pipes,
he was just going to install PVC pipes in the walls beside the old ones. She caught on quickly how to prime,
dry fit and glue plumbing fittings together, and they
actually finished replumbing both the bathroom and
kitchen before it got dark outside and Lissa called a
halt for the day.

They ordered pizza, and when it arrived they sat on
her couch, eating it directly out of the box with cold
beers.

"When are you planning to open the shop again?"
he asked conversationally.

"As soon as I can get iron bars for over the windows.
I'm not having any more thugs break into my shop."

He looked up quickly at her. *Careful, Lissa.* Although
he supposed it was something she could be expected to
complain about. "I can help with that. The same guy
I got that front door from salvages wrought iron from
all over the city. I'll take some measurements in the

morning and see if he's got something that would work for you."

Lissa laid aside the pizza box and scooted forward on the couch until her knees touched his hip. She threw her arms around his shoulders and kissed him soundly on the mouth. "You are the best boyfriend *ever*."

Startled, he kissed her back. "I am, aren't I?"

"Are you too tired to drive home tonight, by any chance?" she asked cajolingly.

"You want me to stay?" He was genuinely surprised by that.

"Yes," she answered firmly. "I feel much safer when you're around."

Ha. For good reason. He was no less lethal than any of the men who'd planted the cameras in her place. "All right, then. A slumber party it is."

"Want me to tell you some ghost stories?" she joked.

"I'm not sure I want to hear the stories you could tell me."

She waved a breezy hand at him. "All that psychic mumbo jumbo is just for show. Callista's longtime customers expect it. Doing the whole woo-woo thing is purely a stunt to keep sales up."

Ironic that his intuition told him her intuition should be taken seriously. But then a whole lot about this situation was pretty damned ironic.

Like allowing himself to be spied on when he was supposed to be the one doing the spying.

Like crawling into bed with a woman he'd love to make love to, and instead letting her fall asleep snuggled up next to his side while he endured the mother of all hard-ons in pained silence.

He eventually managed to sleep. But how long he'd

been out before a cry jerked him abruptly to consciousness, he had no idea. Lissa was thrashing next to him,
clearly in the throes of a nightmare.

"Oh, no," she moaned. "I see them."

Aw, hell. Was she having some sort of vision? He
dared not let her spout out some prediction in her sleep
for the cameras to record. If Peter and his bosses were
on the other end of the surveillance, at all costs she must
not reveal a psychic prediction.

"Lissa, baby. Wake up. You're having a bad dream."

She thrashed against him again. "They're coming.
We're all going to die."

Crap. She wasn't waking up. Quickly, he rolled half
on top of her, gently pinning her in place.

"I see it all. The trees and the water. An ambush—"

Desperate to silence her before she incriminated herself, he plastered his mouth against hers. She jolted
against him and then subsided all of a sudden. Cautiously, he lifted his lips from hers. "Are you with me?"
he breathed.

"I'm here," she whispered back. "Oh, it's awful and
it's com—"

He kissed her again quickly. And this time he didn't
stop. He deepened the contact of their mouths, demanding her attention, calling forth the passion he knew rested
close below the surface with her. In her half-awake state,
it came easily, and she kissed him back, molding herself
to him as her arms snaked around his neck.

Another moan slipped from her throat, this time having nothing to do with nightmares and visions. *Better.*
But then it registered belatedly that her flimsy night-
gown was bunched up around her thighs and that her
sleek legs were suggestively entwined with his. Her lips

were unbelievably soft and tasted like mint toothpaste and Lissa. And her entire body undulated gently against his. She felt like a mermaid in his arms, elusively sexy and apt to slip right through his arms at any second.

She muttered against his mouth, "I have to tell you about my dream."

"Later," he breathed back. Louder he said, "Sweetheart, it makes perfect sense that you had a bad dream after the past week you've had. But I'm here now. I'm not going to let anyone else mess with you. No more muggings—no more break-ins. It stops now."

That last sentence was for the benefit of the bastards on the back end of the cameras as much as her. Although hopefully, they couldn't see much in the darkness and only had audio to go on right now. Ideally, the cameras didn't have some kind of infrared or low-light technology in them.

"I'm not going to be able to sleep again." She pouted against his mouth.

He laughed a little in response. "I think we might be able to do something about that."

"Mmm. I was hoping you'd say that."

She kissed him with enough enthusiasm that he suspected she'd temporarily forgotten about the cameras. Which was excellent. Her life might very well depend on convincing their watchers that she was just a normal woman running a shop she'd inherited. Nothing more.

Except, good grief, she was so much more. Her hands slipped between them, gripping his male flesh in her warm, sweet fists, and then cameras mostly retreated from his awareness, too, replaced by the taste and feel and passion of the woman in his arms.

It was so damned nice, once in his life, to let another

person inside the walls of his world. He couldn't remember the last time he'd let down his guard like this
and allowed himself to enjoy another human being's
company. Not to mention how long it had been since
he'd authentically been *himself* with anyone. It had been
so long, in fact, that he wasn't entirely sure how to be
himself anymore.

But it was as if Lissa sensed his uncertainty and
coaxed him out of overthinking the whole thing with
her sweet mouth and quick, curious hands. And those
little noises she made in the back of her throat—they
drove him out of his mind completely.

Soon the night was filled with warm skin and kisses
and laughter and sweaty passion that drove him beyond
caring about anything except this moment. This woman.
Secrets be damned. If laying himself bare meant his
life could be filled with Lissa and all of this, he would
happily run naked down the street shouting his secrets
to the world.

As if she felt his capitulation, Lissa's arms tightened around him. Her movements became more urgent
against him, her sexy little pants faster. Responding
to her siren's call, he sank into her completely, and all
thought became impossible then. She was dark oblivion,
and he joyfully let her claim him body, mind and soul.

Lissa woke slowly in the morning, something warm
against her back and something heavy across her waist.
An arm. Max's arm. Memories of the passion they'd
shared last night flooded her about one millisecond before she remembered they'd been on camera the whole
time, too. A hot blush suffused her cheeks. She was just

grateful that Max was still asleep and not awake to witness her embarrassment.

Except then his hand crept up to cup her breast lightly, and his lips moved against the back of her head. "G'mornin', sunshine," he murmured.

"It is a good morning, isn't it?"

"Mmm-hmm. What's on your agenda today, Lissa?"

"I have to do some shopping for new stock for the shop. I lost so much inventory last week that there's actual empty shelf space I need to fill."

"That's hard to imagine," he replied drily. "Actually, I know a few places you might want to check out."

She snuggled back against his hard body contentedly.

"I don't know about you, but I'm hungry," Max announced. "Can I interest you in a quick shower, breakfast and then a shopping expedition?"

"I do believe you could. Last one in the shower's a rotten egg!"

She leaped out of bed, taking the bedsheet with her. Max squawked, laughing, and followed her into the bathroom more slowly. He might not care if the cameras caught him naked, but she did.

She turned on the hot water full blast, and under its din muttered to him, "Are there cameras in here?"

"Not that I've found," he mouthed back. "But to be safe, assume there is one."

She shuddered, suddenly feeling horribly exposed. She yanked the shower curtains around the big clawfoot tub and stepped quickly into the protection of the shower. Max joined her and then effectively distracted her by soaping her body down in leisurely and entirely sensual fashion. The quick shower turned into a hot-water-heater-emptying marathon, but she didn't mind.

She was practically purring like Mr. Jackson before they finally emerged, fingers wrinkled and breathless, wrapped in fluffy white towels.

Lissa scrambled eggs for them in a pan on the hot plate while Max insisted on squeezing fresh orange juice by hand. She did have to admit the tangy sweetness of fresh juice was worth the effort.

"First order of business after we get your shelves restocked downstairs is to get you a working kitchen," he announced.

"I couldn't agree more," she declared fervently. She was eager to get out from under the constant pressure of knowing the cameras were staring at her, and she ate and cleaned up after the meal quickly.

She opted to drive his truck back to his place while Max followed in Lola. They parked the sports car in his garage and she slid over in the truck while he slipped into the driver's seat of the heavy-duty vehicle.

"Can we talk now?" she asked as he backed the truck out of the garage.

He started down the street and checked his rearview mirror carefully. "Yes. We can talk."

Thank goodness. She blurted, "I have to tell you about my dream last night. You were in it. Along with some men and women I've never seen before."

He glanced over at her. "What were we all doing?"

"Hiding in tall grass. Carrying guns. Getting ready to be attacked."

"By whom?"

She shrugged. "I have no idea. But everyone was tense. Not scared exactly, but expecting something bad to arrive soon."

"What sort of something?" he asked.

"I couldn't see it, but I get the impression it was people coming. Dangerous ones."

"That would explain the tension and hiding." He grinned at her.

He didn't sound as if he was taking her the least bit seriously. "Look. I'm not making this up," she declared. "I routinely dream about things before they happen, and this was one of those dreams. You and I are going to be in a bad situation sometime soon. We'll be with friends, and we'll all be in grave danger. You have to believe me."

He glanced over at her again, the smile fading quickly from his face. "I hear you, and I do believe you. But you have to understand that I have no intention of borrowing trouble before it arrives. At the moment, I've got an SUV trailing me, and if I'm not mistaken, the driver is the same one from the white van yesterday. I'm much more interested in dealing with that problem right now. I'll worry about your ambush later."

She started to turn in her seat, but he barked at her, "Don't turn around!"

She faced forward, a little offended.

"We can't tip them off that we know they're back there," he explained apologetically.

"Okay, I'm over the whole surveillance thing being an adventure. I want it to stop," she announced.

"If only. Welcome to my life," he grumbled under his breath. "You can at least speak freely in here. It's damned hard to bug a moving vehicle successfully."

"Who *are* these people?"

"What say we draw them out into the open and have a look at them?" he suggested.

That sounded dangerous. "How?"

He grinned over at her. "No sweat. We'll go somewhere where they'll stick out like sore thumbs. And I know just the spot."

He parked a little while later in front of what looked like a huge, ramshackle barn on the verge of falling over in the next strong wind. He came around to open her door for her, and as she slid out of the seat, she asked, "What is this place?"

"Best auction house this side of the Mississippi River. You're gonna love it. Just be careful you don't get carried away. It's easy to spend a fortune in here."

Max led her inside the massive structure, and she gasped with delight as she spied a treasure trove of art, antiques, collectibles and eclectic junk. She temporarily forgot about bad guys following them as they wandered the long tables of items to be auctioned off. She marked at least a dozen lots of quirky knickknacks in her auction catalog that would be perfect inventory for the shop.

Max led her to a collection of bleachers clustered around a small raised stage, and they climbed up high into the seats off to one side of the bidding area. She all but bounced on the bench beside him as the auction got going.

"Never been to one of these before, I gather?" he asked, humor lacing his voice.

"Never. Oh, this is so fun!"

He grinned broadly at her. "You focus on the auction while I watch the crowd."

Oh. Right. Their tails. She glanced around at the clientele, who mostly fell into two distinct camps: well-dressed collectors with money to burn, or the Southern version of beatniks.

She spotted a middle-aged man in jeans and a black

leather jacket. The guy seemed intensely uncomfortable. "There's one of our tails, I bet," she murmured.

"Good eye. See if you can find at least one more like him. These guys are too professional to work alone." Max commenced fiddling with his cell phone and then announced, "There. Got a good picture of the first guy and just sent it to Jennie to identify."

"Jennie?" Her attention snapped to Max.

One corner of his mouth turned up. "Computer researcher I've worked with before. Nice lady. Not my type."

"You have a type?"

"Turns out I do," he replied, his gaze scanning the crowd that was gathering quickly in the bleachers. "And there's number two," he announced. His cell phone pointed in a new direction for several seconds.

"I think I see another guy lurking over by that exit behind the stage," she murmured without moving her lips.

"Yup. Guarding the back door to make sure we don't sneak out and give them the slip."

"So, what's your type?" she asked.

"Petite redheads with quirky ideas about the occult."

"They're not quirky—" she started before she caught him grinning at her. She subsided and merely stuck her tongue out at him instead.

The auctioneer stepped up to a podium and commenced selling items in a rapid-fire staccato that was contagiously exciting. She saw what Max meant by warning her not to get carried away. The first lot she wanted to bid on came up for sale, and she gripped the paddle in her lap tightly. But the opening bid was higher than the maximum price she'd set for herself on the lot and she slumped, disappointed.

A few more lots went by out of her price range, and then the one she really wanted came up on the podium. It was a collection of sundries from the estate of a local man who had passed away recently. The bidding started low and progressed anemically.

"I'm bidding," she whispered to Max.

"Wait," he muttered back. "Let the two serious bidders wear each other down before you jump in."

"But I don't want the price to get too high for me."

He shook his head. "Trust me. I do this for a living. Let them start questioning their commitment to the buy before you enter the fray."

She waited impatiently while two bidders dickered back and forth for several minutes. The auctioneer had to cajole each bid out of the buyers now, and the price was inching up by tiny margins.

"Now," Max murmured. "Barely outbid them."

She raised her paddle hesitantly. All eyes in the place swiveled to take in this new entrant to the bidding. Max reached out casually to put an arm around her shoulder, and an audible sigh of disappointment rose from the crowd.

The auctioneer asked the two other bidders if they wished to continue and both shook their heads, looking disgusted.

"Sold. To the lady on the right."

The gavel dropped, and she let out a low squeal of delight under her breath. "Why did everyone sigh like that when I bid?" she asked Max.

"They all spotted me."

She turned to face him. "And?"

He shrugged. "I'm known to come in here with deep pockets. If I want a piece for a client, no one's beating me out for it. They give up on items pretty quickly when I indicate that I want something."

"Wouldn't they try to bid up the price to get the most money out of you?"

"There's a certain honor among dealers. Artificially inflating the prices of art and antiques benefits none of us in the long run. We all know the fair market value of items. I'm usually willing to pay just a little bit more over that price than the rest of them."

"Well, I don't care if I overpaid. I wanted that chest full of tarot cards, and I doubt I overpaid for it in the least."

"Let's go collect your booty and see what you got."

An employee set the carved wooden box about the size of a bread box on a table and surprised her by saying, "Hey, Max. Haven't seen you around here in a while. Want this charged to your account?"

"Sure. Good to see you, Louis. Anything special sitting in the back room?"

Lissa looked back and forth between the two men, listening to the easy banter between them. Apparently, this man gave Max the occasional heads-up when out-of-the-ordinary pieces came into the auction house for sale.

Max signed a line on a clipboard, and then turned to her. "So. Open up your treasure chest. Let's see what we've got in this box of yours."

"Did you just pay for this?" she demanded truculently.

"I have a credit account here. It's easiest just to throw the charge for this onto it."

"I'll reimburse you—"

"Believe me. This little thing is a drop in the bucket compared to what I usually spend around here. Don't worry about it."

She frowned, prepared to argue the principle of the thing, but she was distracted when Max turned the antique key in the box's lock and lifted the lid. The description in the auction booklet had said the box contained a tarot card collection. But she gasped when she saw the decks of cards neatly stacked to the top of the box.

"There must be a hundred decks in here!" she exclaimed. She lifted out deck after deck, recognizing many of them as rare and vintage decks, some more than a hundred years old. The deeper she dug in the chest, the older and rarer the decks became.

"Oh, my gosh," she breathed as she spied a deck near the bottom. "I do believe this is an original Etteilla deck from France."

Max replied, "I have to plead ignorance of old tarot decks. Is an Etteilla deck a big deal?"

"They were the first mass-produced tarot decks for divination in France. They date to the late eighteenth century."

And then she spied another deck, tucked way in the back corner of the chest. It was old and dirty, and it didn't have a storage box or bag. A simple piece of twine held the cards together. But the power pouring off the deck lit up the chest's interior like a beacon.

"What's that?" Max asked with definite interest.

Does he actually see the power radiating off the deck, too? She picked it up carefully. "It's a Russian deck. Dates to around 1900 if I had to guess."

"Is it a special deck, then?"

"Umm, no. Yes," she mumbled, mesmerized by the magic of the cards.

"Which is it?"

She tore her gaze away from the cards and lifted it to him. "It's not a particularly valuable deck, especially given its worn condition. But the magic in it… I've never felt the like…" She trailed off, lost again in the power emanating from the deck. A folding chair was nearby, and she sank into it, completely immersed in the cards. "I have to do a reading. Right now."

Max glanced around in alarm. "Now's not a good time—"

"Distract them, then. I *have* to do this."

Max swore under his breath.

A wave of violent intent washed over her, followed by the now familiar opening of the floodgates of power. Yet again she choked on the volume of power washing over her, filling her lungs and clogging her throat. Lord, there was so much of it.

She vaguely registered Max muttering, "I'm going to have to draw them off, then. You stay here and do whatever you have to do—fast. I may text you in a few minutes, and if I do, I'll need you to do exactly what I tell you to when I tell you to do it. Will you do that for me?"

"Umm, sure."

"Promise?"

The urgency in his voice made her look up. "Yes, Max. I'll follow your instructions to the letter. I promise."

He nodded tersely and then startled her by taking off quickly toward the very exit one of their tails had been guarding a few minutes earlier. In the presence of her multiplied awareness, the deck of cards in her hand vibrated so sharply that she could barely hold on to them. Her powers extended outward to encompass the entire auction house, and she clearly felt three spirits detaching from the crowd and racing after Max.

Quickly, she shuffled the deck, handling it carefully in deference to its advanced age and generally worn state. *There.* The deck was charged. Whatever it wanted to say to her was ready to emerge. She flipped the cards over and commenced laying them out in an old-fashioned spread that seemed appropriate to the cards.

But then the deck took over, demanding she place cards in no pattern she'd ever seen before. She could no more have stopped the odd spread of the cards than she could have held back a rushing river in full flood. The power of the deck overtook her and swept her away in its massive force.

She hardly had to look at the cards to know what she would see. The four princes of each suit lay stacked neatly, one on top of another in the center of a circle of surrounding cards.

If she read the spread from past to future, she saw her aunt's death clearly. Her own break with an unhappy past. The move to New Orleans. And then that pesky stack of princes bursting into her life. And in the future?

Hesitantly, she read the remaining half of the spread. Danger. Death very close to her. Loss. Her past returned to threaten her. And a very small possibility at the end of it all of a happy outcome.

Well, that sucked.

Impatiently, she asked the deck how to improve her odds of reaching the happy outcome. She flipped over three cards, and the message was as clear as a bell. Her fate was directly tied to the princes. If they succeeded, all would be well.

And who, exactly, were these mysterious princes who held her fate in their hands? She flipped one last card and stared down at the card in shock.

It was the Lovers. A pair of naked people embraced passionately on the card, but that was not what shocked her. The woman had curly, dark red hair, the man was tall and strong with short blond hair. The pair looked *exactly* like her and Max. The faces, the height difference, the body shapes, everything. Identical.

A chill chattered down her spine, and goose bumps raised on her arms. Which was saying something for her. She'd spent her whole life around inexplicable magic, but this freaked even her out.

Somehow, Max was the link to all four of the princes.

Furthermore, their relationship was the key to achieving a happily ever after. *Duh.* It didn't take a tarot deck to tell her that. Although she was surprised at how adamant the deck was that she and Max had a destiny—for better or worse—together. That was reassuring to know, sort of.

Her cell phone buzzed, and she pulled it out of her pocket. Max had texted her, telling her to go outside and meet him in front of the auction house in exactly sixty seconds. She hit the stopwatch function of her phone, scooped all the decks of cards back into their chest and picked up the whole thing awkwardly in both arms.

She had to hustle to make it to the front of the huge auction house in one minute, but she made it with about three seconds to spare. She took a deep breath and stepped outside.

Max's truck screeched up in front of her, all but running over her toes. He leaned over to throw open the passenger door, and she scrambled inside as a dark SUV careened around the corner. Max accelerated away from the auction house before she even had her door properly closed.

Then he surprised her by pulling out into traffic sedately. "They'll totally be able to follow us if you drive like this," she declared, confused.

"Oh, I don't want to lose them. We don't know we're being followed, remember?"

"How will they explain away you sprinting all over the place, then?"

Max grinned. "I know the entire staff at the auction house. I raced out back, grabbed the first female staffer I found and shocked the hell out of her by laying a big kiss on her. I made it look like I'm cheating on you. Then I ran around front and got the truck to meet you out front. Our tails will think I'm a two-timing bastard, but they'll be none the wiser about us knowing they're tailing us."

"What about the woman?" Lissa demanded.

"I've known Margie for years. I told her it was a bet and thanked her for helping me win."

Lissa snorted. She would bet the woman would have let Max kiss her without the existence of a supposed wager. Men didn't come much better looking than him.

"Now what?" she asked him as he drove with purpose toward some destination.

"Now we pick you out new kitchen cabinets, appliances and fixtures. And we see how fast they can be delivered to your apartment."

Her adrenaline still pumping hard, she had trouble concentrating as he led her into a contractor supply store. Finally Max suggested a vintage-look cabinet style in an antiqued wash. A big farmhouse sink, black quartz countertops and a subway tile backsplash completed an updated retro look that was going to make the apartment look better than it had when it was new.

When Max dragged her over to look at flooring, though, her brain refused to function. "Whatever you think best," she mumbled as she stared at a dizzying array of hardwoods, tiles and carpets.

Max quickly pointed out a scraped cypress flooring that managed to look both modern and vintage. She nodded numbly.

"Are you okay, Lissa?" he asked quietly as a salesman rang up their order.

That deck of cards had made a bigger impression on her than she'd realized. It still held her in the throes of its magic, its dire predictions swirling in her mind. A lover. A trickster. A villain. And a hero. Which one was Max?

"I beg your pardon?" Max asked beside her.

She blinked up at him. Had she asked her question out loud? "Umm, the tarot deck spoke of four men coming into my life. I was wondering which one you are."

"What are my choices?" he asked drolly.

She answered seriously. "The prince of each suit turned up last week, and today they revealed themselves again. They represent the lover, the trickster, the villain and the hero."

Max stared at her, his expression troubled. "What if I'm all four of them?"

She stared back at him. Was *that* why the cards had insisted on being stacked, one on top of another? Bemused, she followed him out of the store.

Max took her to a few more wholesale places—antique dealers and local artisans mostly—introduced her to the owners and helped her set up accounts. Along the way, she picked up a selection of magic wands, various crystals and cheap jewelry, and she found a decent homemade candle supplier. All in all, it was a great purchasing trip. But she couldn't get Max's comment out of her mind. What if he was all four of the cards?

She could readily see how he was the lover and the hero. And maybe the trickster referred to his using an assumed name. But how was he the villain? Was he destined to double-cross her in some way?

Chapter 10

Max sat on the sofa at Lissa's insistence to relax and have a drink while she made dinner. The moment of domestic bliss was almost too much for him to stand. He couldn't remember the last time he'd felt this stress free. He'd had no idea how heavy a burden he'd been carrying around until he finally set it down. And he had Lissa to thank for it. The woman was good for his soul on so many levels.

Not only was she attractive as hell but she was smart. Kind. Compassionate. She saw him more clearly than anyone he'd ever known with the possible exception of his father. Hell, she made him see himself more clearly.

God knew, the timing of finding her in the middle of executing his personal vendetta wasn't ideal. But he was just glad she had come into his life. She brought light he hadn't even known he'd needed into the darkness of his heart.

He kicked off his shoes and took pleasure in watching her fuss over the hot plate, seasoning a pot of clam chowder she claimed would make him forget jambalaya altogether. If he were the superstitious type, he'd say she looked like a witch stirring her cauldron.

There was no way around it: her psychic abilities were disturbing. She was so bloody accurate. It would be an easy baby step to cross the boundaries of logic and believe in all her mumbo jumbo.

If only she would try to convince him she was legitimate. Then he would have something to push back against. But she stubbornly insisted on letting him form his own opinions. And his observations kept telling him she was the real deal. Which was, of course, insane.

His phone rang, and he fished it out of his back pocket. It was Bastien. "Hey, buddy. What can I do for you?"

"What do you know about Callista Clearmont?" the cop replied grimly.

"Why do you ask?"

"Her body was stolen from the Tulane anatomy lab. Who the hell was she that someone would steal her corpse?"

He sat bolt upright. "Are you kidding me?"

"I wish, bro. She's gone."

Max's mind raced with possibilities. "Did they do what they said they were planning to, at least?" Aware of the surveillance, he avoided asking outright if the autopsy had been completed before the woman's body had been stolen.

"Nope. They hadn't started the autopsy yet. She was on ice. Literally."

He winced. This was going to upset Lissa something

fierce. Not to mention, it wasn't something he cared to talk about on camera. "Huh. That's bizarre. I don't know anything I haven't already told you."

"Do me a favor, Max. Find out what your girlfriend knows about her dear, departed aunt and what the hell the woman was up to before she died."

"I'll see what I can do. And thanks for the call."

He hung up only to see Lissa standing over her chowder pot and wielding a wooden spoon like a magic wand. "Spill," she demanded.

He reviewed quickly what he'd said aloud and formulated a lie to fit. "That was a client. He thought he'd found a piece he wanted, but it got sold out from under him. He wants me to contact the new owner and see if the guy's willing to sell or not."

"People do that? They buy stuff and then turn around and sell it?"

He grinned. "Anything can be had if the price is right, darlin'."

She rolled her eyes at him. "I'd like to think that at least a few things in this world are not for sale. Like friendship and loyalty and—"

She'd been about to say love before she stopped speaking so abruptly. He knew it. The word was hanging right there in the air between them, practically visible to the naked eye—

He broke off that train of thought sharply, swearing under his breath. Apparently, all Lissa's woo-woo stuff was rubbing off on him now.

Lissa went back to stirring and seasoning, and he let a couple of minutes pass before he obliquely broached the subject Bass had asked him to. "So, tell me more about your shop. How long has this building been around?"

"Well, Callista took it over in the early 1970s, but it had been around for a long time before that, apparently. The building was originally a bank. Sometime shortly after the Great Depression it failed. I think the place has been some sort of store ever since."

Aha. That explained the vaultlike basement. It probably *was* originally a vault. Which meant steel walls. Which meant electronic signals wouldn't be able to get in or out. Which meant he and Lissa could talk down there in safety. *Perfect.*

But first it was time to turn the conversation to innocent topics. "So, *chère*, you got any big plans for Mardi Gras?"

She looked up at him eagerly, her eyes shining. "This will be my first one. I'm so excited to see all the parades and pageants. I understand it's quite a spectacle."

He laughed. "The way people act is the real spectacle. There will, indeed, be topless women running around in the streets and drunk guys throwing plastic necklaces at them. It's some party."

"You sound less than thrilled at the prospect."

He shrugged. "It's not really my speed. When I was sixteen, I enjoyed the education in the variations of the female form."

Lissa laughed gaily. "Is that fancy talk for 'I like boobs'?"

He grinned reluctantly. "Well, yeah."

"Duly noted. Why don't you bring your lecherous self on over to the table and let me show you what real chowder's supposed to taste like."

"You do realize I'm going to have to cook my world-famous jambalaya for you now, right?"

"Done."

He moved over to the card table, which had been made imminently romantic by the addition of a linen tablecloth and drippy candles. He pulled out Lissa's chair and held it for her before moving around to his seat. "It smells delicious."

He sipped a cautious spoonful. "And it tastes even better." He dug in with enthusiasm, and the conversation lagged as he savored the creamy chowder. The crusty sourdough bread she'd paired with the stew was perfect, and the bitter greens in the salad completed a perfect meal.

Lissa looked at the empty plates regretfully a little while later. "All that's missing is a really full-bodied red wine to finish off the meal."

"Ha. I may know just the thing. Stay here." He jumped up and headed down the stairs and into the dark basement. Carefully, he lifted one of the dusty wine bottles out of the crate he'd found the first time he was down there. He blew off the dust and sneezed as he read the label. *Oh, yes. This will do nicely.*

He carried the bottle back upstairs and deposited it in front of Lissa. "Is that the stuff from the basement? I'd forgotten it was there," she said.

"Shall we see if it's any good?" he asked.

"Sure. But I don't have a corkscrew."

"You say that like a proper gentleman wouldn't have one on him at all times," he quipped.

"You open the bottle and I'll get some wineglasses. I think they're still packed in this box over here."

She rummaged through cardboard and wrapping paper while he carefully removed the cork from the bottle. It came out cleanly, and he sniffed it appreciatively. They decanted the wine, let it breathe a bit and then he raised his glass in a toast.

"To luck, love and happy endings."

"Hear, hear," Lissa replied stoutly.

He sipped the wine and sighed in pleasure. Give Callista credit for great taste in wine. "Do you have any idea where your aunt got this stuff from? It's hard to come by in the States."

"No idea. But I imagine she had a fairly eclectic clientele. I remember her saying once when I was a little girl that some of her customers paid her in gifts instead of cash."

"Did you visit here often as a child?"

"Not really. My mother hated New Orleans. I didn't get to come down here at all until I could fly on a plane by myself."

"Why did your mother hate this city?"

"She grew up here. I suppose everyone's childhoods have memories we'd rather forget."

"How old was she when she left?" he asked.

Lissa frowned. "I don't actually know. That's a good question. I'll have to ask her the next time I talk with her."

"Tell me more about Callista. Is she your mother's sister, then?"

"Yes. Callista was the oldest of seven kids and my mother is the youngest."

"So there was quite an age difference."

"Yes. Close to twenty years. Callista was the odd duck in the family. She always claimed to hear voices and see things, but it got worse as she got older. She creeped everyone out around her. Most of the family thought she lost what few marbles she had when she did too many drugs in the sixties."

"And you? What did you think of her abilities?" He sent her a warning glance, reminding her of the cameras listening and watching. This was a perfect moment to debunk the idea of her having special powers.

Lissa laughed. "Well, it's not like any of that stuff is real, now is it?"

Perfect. He smiled approvingly at her.

"Did your aunt ever marry? I gathered she didn't have any kids, since she left her shop to you."

"No. She never married. Although she did mention the great love of her life once. So, I know there was someone at some point."

"Ooh. A mysterious lover. Maybe it was a pirate ghost," he teased.

Lissa grinned widely. "I like how you think, Mr. Smith. Actually, my impression was that there was a lover, maybe a longtime romance. Given that they never got together formally, my guess is she had an affair with a married man."

"Either that, or he wasn't in a position to be seen involved with a psychic."

"Like a politician or public figure with a reputation to protect?" Lissa asked.

Max shrugged.

Lissa's face registered disappointment and hurt that he would suggest being around someone like her wasn't respectable.

He wanted to reach out to her. Take her in his arms and assure her that he thought no such thing, but with those damned cameras recording their every word and move, he couldn't take the chance. He settled on announcing, "You, ma'am, are a hell of a fine cook. I have a friend or two who'd love to try some of that Yankee cuisine of yours."

She perked up a little, but the shadow remained at the back of her eyes. After supper, he suggested they head down into the shop and finish up the last of the painting down there. It had taken several layers of primer and paint to mostly cover up the graffiti left by Julio G.'s buddies.

It took them less than a half hour to roll on one last layer of paint. And then Max commented, "Help me carry these paint cans down into the basement. I'll show you how to seal and store them safely."

Lissa frowned, but she picked up one of the gallon cans of paint. He picked up the other one.

Once they were in the basement, he looked around quickly, checking the corners and crates for any sign of hidden cameras. Sure enough, he found no sign of surveillance gear.

He spoke low. "I'm fairly sure this used to be the bank's vault. It's probably steel lined and impervious to electronic monitoring. We can speak freely, but we'll have to be careful not to spend too much time down here or else we'll arouse the suspicions of our observers."

Lissa nodded and looked around the room nervously.

"What's wrong?" he asked quickly. He was startled to realize just how much he trusted her intuitions.

"Nothing. It's just that someone was down here recently and organized a bunch of the papers in those trunks. It's got me a little spooked."

"That was me," he confessed. "I was looking for your aunt's client list in hopes that it might shed some light on why Julio attacked you."

"You don't think it was random chance that he chose me as his victim, then?"

"I honestly don't know."

"I do know he killed that girl whose picture I drew. And I also know she looked a lot like me. I think I happened to fit the profile of the kind of girl he likes to kidnap, torture and murder from time to time."

The idea of anyone doing any of those things to her made Max's skin crawl. "You're making it hard for me to deny that psychic abilities do exist."

She winced. "If it makes you feel any better, I'd love it if they didn't."

He sighed. "Don't feel like you have to be less than you are on my account."

Lissa turned slowly, staring at him as if he'd grown a second head. "Say that again," she whispered.

"What? That you don't have to be less than you are to try to please me?"

She exhaled slowly and looked as if a ten-ton weight had just been lifted off her.

He frowned. "I don't understand what the big deal is."

"You have no idea how long I've been waiting for someone—anyone—to say those words to me."

"Why? Isn't it kind of obvious?"

"Maybe to a man like you, who always sees more than meets the eye when he looks at people. Which is a pretty extraordinary skill in its own right, by the way," she added.

He frowned. *Extraordinary* was not an adjective he usually applied to himself. He was odd. An outsider. Strangely trained. But not extraordinary. At least not in the way she meant. Looking for a change, any change, of subject, he gestured at several big wooden crates stacked in a corner. "What's in those?"

"Callista's personal effects. Stuff that got packed and moved out of her apartment in anticipation of my moving into it. Her attorney hired a company to come in and crate it up before I arrived."

Interesting. "Maybe that's where her elusive client list is hiding."

Lissa glanced over at the boxes. "Maybe. I haven't had the heart to face her stuff since I came down here."

He moved over to the crates to examine them. "I'll bring a crowbar tomorrow, and we can have a look inside them. She had to have a client list somewhere. It would have been madness not to keep one."

"Madness as a descriptor would not be misapplied to my aunt."

"Tomorrow," he promised.

"We probably ought to head back upstairs if we don't want the creepy peepers to get suspicious."

Grinning at her sobriquet for their watchers, he followed her upstairs to the shop. "It looks better since the break-in. It has a little more room to breathe."

She nodded and looked around. "It feels more like me now. I just hope that doesn't drive off the regular clientele."

"Trust your instincts, Lissa."

She rolled her eyes at him. "Easy for you to say."

They spent the remainder of the evening installing light fixtures and sanding down window sashes. They called it a night early and both collapsed into her big bed, exhausted.

Lissa counted it a win that she slept through the night without any nightmares yanking her from her sleep. It helped greatly having Max sleep with her. She rested easy, knowing he was there to protect her.

Frankly, she was amazed that he hadn't run screaming from her and her oddities already. She could only pray he'd meant what he'd said last night about not wanting her to be less than she was on his account.

Until he'd said it, she'd never realized that was exactly what she'd spent her whole life doing. She'd tried to be a good daughter—not only by suppressing her talents but by suppressing anything about herself that might remind her mother of her conception. She'd tried to be quiet, nonthreatening, to fade into the background as much as possible. No matter that being a dormouse was emphatically not who she really was.

She'd ignored and shoved away all but the most insistent psychic demands, and only when she'd been a teen and able to hide much of it from her parents had she let the visions in. Of course, that had led her straight to the FBI. Ultimately, her gift had been too much to contain, and she'd alienated everyone she loved with it. Until Max. And he was still on the fence about it.

Desperate need to contain her powers, to limit them, to seek and find normal washed over her. She couldn't lose Max to her gift—her curse. She just couldn't.

Max left quickly after breakfast, citing errands to run. She felt bereft without him, and she moved downstairs quickly to open the shop. Thankfully, lots of customers distracted her through the day. He didn't come back until nearly closing time.

He pulled her into his arms and kissed her on the tip of the nose in front of a customer, which made her blush, before he asked, "How was your day?"

"Good. But now it's even better since you're here."

He smiled against her temple. "I missed you, too."

He helped her close up and then led her to the base-

ment door. "Let's unpack that inventory in the basement, shall we?"

It took her a second to realize he meant her aunt's
personal effects. "Right," she agreed belatedly. They
headed down into the cramped, claustrophobic space,
made all the more crowded tonight by copious spirits
hovering close. She huffed at them. Were they out to
ruin her fragile love life completely?

"Which crate first?" he asked.

She stared at the three big crates, and one of them
had a distinct glow about it. She sighed and pointed at
Mr. Glowy Crate. "That one."

Max pried open the lid, and she peered inside. Clothing, knickknacks, books and who knew what else were
a tumbled mess within. Why the glow around this particular collection of stuff? She relaxed her mental guard,
and immediately plunged her hand down into one corner of the box. Whatever she was supposed to find was
buried…right…here…

Her fingers closed on a cloth-covered book. She
pulled it free of the crate and examined a cheap journal that had obviously seen better days. The cloth cover
was a cheesy print straight out of the 1980s.

"What have you got there?" Max asked.

"Looks like a diary."

"Damn, you're good."

She glanced up at Max, wincing at the chagrin in
his words. Did he even know that tone had crept into
his voice?

"Whose is it?" he asked.

She opened it to the first page. "Aunt Cal's. It's dated
one year before I was born." A chill of foreboding raced

across her skin. "If you don't mind, I'd like to take this upstairs and glance through it."

"Of course. It belongs to you, after all. But before we head back up to the shop, is there anything in here you wouldn't mind putting on the showroom floor to sell? We did talk about opening up crates of inventory before we came down here."

She gestured at a dozen porcelain figurines of birds.

"Perfect," he declared. "Help me carry them upstairs."

They deposited the statues on a shelf and headed up to her place. She slid over close to a lamp at the end of the couch and opened her aunt's journal in the bright light. She frowned. "Look at this, Max."

He leaned close, and she was momentarily distracted by the masculine scent of his aftershave. "Dang, you smell good," she breathed.

He glanced over at her from a distance of about a foot, and she was arrested by the golden flecks in his hazel eyes. "Stop that," she muttered.

"Stop what?"

"Distracting me."

A smile curved his beautiful mouth as he turned his attention to the journal. She exhaled carefully. Wow, he was hot.

"Can you read this?" he murmured.

"No. Can you?" It looked like regular cursive writing, but the letters were unlike any she'd ever seen before.

"After a fashion. It's cursive Russian."

"What does it say?"

"How about I take it home with me and have a go at translating it for you?"

"You have to go home?"

He dropped a light, quick kiss on her lips, too fleeting to satisfy the ever-present craving pounding through her. Lord, the effect that man had on her.

He murmured regretfully, "My dictionary is at home. I'm a phone call away. If you get scared or want some company, just call."

She couldn't blame the man for wanting a break from her and her general weirdness. He surprised her, though, by wrapping her in his arms and laying a smoking-hot kiss on her. That was more like it. She felt boneless and pulsing from head to foot before he finally loosened his arms and set her gently away from him. At least he had the good grace to look regretful while he did it.

"Call me before you go to bed, Lissa. I want to hear your voice one more time tonight."

She blinked up at him, thrilled and a little amazed. Was he really developing feelings for her, after all? She mumbled something affirmative as he swept out of her apartment. Moving to the window in a fog of desire, she watched him climb into Lola and disappear into the night like some sort of mysterious superhero. If only he weren't so skeptical of her gift. Maybe they'd have a real chance. But if she was being totally honest with herself, she would admit that they were doomed, whether she liked it or not.

Max settled in at his desk with a mug of coffee and a strong work light. *All right, Callista Clearmont. Time to cough up your secrets.*

He opened the journal and started reading the Russian script. It had been some time since he'd read the language, but it came back to him quickly. Before long, he was skimming through the pages rapidly.

Callista was in love with a mysterious man she only referred to as Y. Max gathered the lover was Russian. Which maybe explained why Callista was writing the journal in Russian—to practice her rusty skills with the language. Indeed, the text was riddled with grammar errors and misspellings, and sometimes she resorted to writing English words in Cyrillic letters.

A sad story unfolded before Max of her realization that her lover was both married and involved in criminal activity. But Callista went on at length about how beautiful his soul was in spite of his visible character flaws and how his spirit sang to hers. This was exactly why he worried about Lissa's reliance on intuition and vague feelings to make important life decisions. The heart could so easily mislead the mind.

He turned more pages and then came to a passage that made his blood go cold. He backed up and read the entry again. Callista was upset because a close friend of her lover had taken advantage of Callista's little sister. The sister wasn't named, but Max had a sneaking suspicion he was reading about the sexual assault of Lissa's mother. The same assault that had resulted in Lissa's birth.

Near the end of the journal, there was a reconciliation between Callista and her lover. Y had apparently promised to make the rapist, who was never named in the journal, stay the hell away from Lissa's mother and from the baby that had unfortunately been conceived in the attack. Callista expressed dismay over the fact that the rapist was not going to be brought to justice, but she had clearly failed to sway her lover into taking legal action. She railed in her journal about stupid codes of mutual protection among thieves. Apparently, Y had referred to the attacker as a prince of thieves and his brother, which had infuriated Callista. Personally, Max had to agree with her.

But then it dawned on him. The Russian reference to a "prince of thieves" might very well refer to the man having been "royalty" within the Russian mafia brotherhood. *Good Lord.* The "prince" would be the heir apparent to the mafia empire, with only the "czar" or "king of thieves" outranking him. Was *that* why nothing was ever done about Lissa's mother's rape? Had the man who attacked her been at or near the very top of the mob organization and, hence, untouchable? Who in the hell *was* he?

For once in his life, Max regretted that his father was dead. He'd known everyone in the Russian mob structure in southern Louisiana. If anyone could have identified both the mysterious Y and Lissa's father— this prince of thieves—it would have been his old man.

Which made him frown. Was it possible that his father had kept a written record of his mob contacts somewhere in his personal papers? Max knew the code that his father had used to make most of his personal notes. It was worth a try. He would have to ditch anyone who was following him before he drove to the storage unit where he'd stashed his father's personal effects after his death. The materials that proved his father had been a spy for Russia were too incriminating for him to store inside his own home. He had no desire to go to jail for his father's crimes. After all, he had his own crimes to answer for. Being a spy was a dirty business in the best of circumstances. But being a spy off the reservation and two years undercover with a mob outfit was an even dirtier business.

The very last entry in the journal reported that Callista's lover had started using her store to pass messages to his cronies and that he wasn't aware she knew about it. Callista seemed to think it was humorous that her lover thought he could keep any secrets from her. Max reread the final paragraph in the journal again, his blood running cold as he translated it in his mind.

The more deeply Y tries to hide his secrets from me, the more clearly I see them. My gift cuts through every layer of deception and deceit, whether I want it to or not. If I love a person, I see everything about them. Everything.

Could Lissa do the same to him? He didn't dare let her love him and strip him bare. At all costs, he must prevent that.

Chapter 11

Lissa was busy in the shop the next morning, when a delivery truck arrived with her new kitchen cabinets, appliances and quartz countertops. How on earth had he pulled that off? She'd expected to wait weeks for her new kitchen furnishings. Knowing him, he'd called in some rich contact to get instant service. She instructed the crew to carry everything upstairs, and she didn't pay much more attention to them because she had her hands full with customers.

But when she finally closed the shop and stumbled upstairs that evening, exhausted, she rounded the corner into her digs and stopped in shock. The kitchen was fully installed. And it was gorgeous. Max had impeccable taste as it turned out. Stunned, she went over to the sink and turned on the faucet. Actual water ran out of the tap and disappeared down the drain. Delighted, she turned on the stove, opened the dishwasher and stuck her head in the brand-new *cold* stainless steel refrigerator.

She pulled out her cell phone and dialed Max's number. "Hi, Max. It's me. Do you by any chance know anything about my kitchen being completely functional? I was under the impression the stuff was just supposed to be delivered, not fully installed."

"Merry Christmas a little early," he replied. "I was tired of worrying that you were going to burn down your place every time you used that hot plate."

"I'd like to pick a fight with you over this, but I expect I'd lose."

"Did your Spidey sense tell you that?"

"No. Plain old common sense."

"Smart girl. It's done and paid for. Discussion closed."

She huffed. "Thank you, you wonderful, exasperating man."

That made him laugh.

"So, are you going to come over here and help me christen this gourmet delight?" she demanded.

"I'll bring the steaks if you'll cook them."

"Deal."

He added, "There's someplace I want to take you after dinner, though."

She had time for a quick shower before he arrived, and she stepped out of her bedroom feeling refreshed to the sound and smell of steak sizzling on the grill-top feature of her new gas range.

Max pressed a glass of wine into her hand and recruited her to help tear fresh herbs into a salad. She'd just finished tossing the lot when Max plated up two magnificent steaks at the brand-new kitchen island with its matching bar stools.

"Wow," she remarked. "This is so civilized, I'm not sure I can handle it."

"Stick with me, kid. I'll have you brushing your teeth in a real bathroom and sleeping in a bedroom with actual walls in no time."

She stuck her tongue out at him before diving into the delicious meal. Max didn't seem to be in a talkative mood, which was just as well with her. She was starving after skipping lunch.

But after the meal was over and the plates were rinsed and deposited in the dishwasher—with the appropriate amount of fanfare—Max headed for the stairs. "C'mon."

She followed him downstairs and outside, where she was surprised to see his truck and not Lola. They hopped in and headed into evening traffic, which was still heavy after rush hour. She became aware of Max paying close attention to his rearview mirror. "Are we being followed?" she finally asked.

"Doubtful. But I'll take evasive measures anyway."

Unlike television, it didn't involve much dodging in and out of traffic or red light running. He did wind all over downtown New Orleans. But eventually he got onto a highway and accelerated.

She had to confess to being disappointed when they pulled up at the gate of a storage facility. It was a multistory indoor place with a security guard and a bunch of protocols Max had to go through before they were finally let into long hallways lined with gray metal doors.

Max unlocked the door of a dark room. She stepped into the long, narrow space while he closed and locked the door behind them. She commented, "If you're planning to kill me, may I compliment you on your precautions not to get caught."

Shelves lined the space, crammed floor to ceiling with books and plastic bins full of gadgets, notebooks and papers. Four tall filing cabinets took up the corner, and it was to these that Max moved.

"What is this place?" she asked. "And what's all this stuff?"

"Welcome to my father's personal and private effects," Max replied.

"And we're here why?"

"I'm looking for some information that might be pertinent to you. And I thought you might like to get out of the surveillance spotlight for a few hours."

"What on earth could your father have had that would apply to me?"

"The identity of your birth father."

She stared at Max in shock. "I beg your pardon?"

"Didn't see that one coming?" he asked drily. "I thought for sure your psychic mojo would have warned you."

Nope. The powers-that-be had apparently thought it would be hilarious to spring that bombshell on her.

He opened a file drawer and rummaged through it, emerging with an old ledger. He moved over to the tall workbench in the opposite corner and turned on the work light over it.

"What are you hoping to find in there?" she asked.

"Lists of names. My father took notes on everything and everyone he saw and met."

And somehow Max was going to know which of those names was her birth father's? More agitated than she wanted to admit, she moved beside him. He threw open the book, and she stared down at meaningless scribbles. They didn't even look like letters. How in the hell was that jumble supposed to reveal the identity of her father?

"What's that?" she blurted.

"A code," Max answered shortly. "And, yes. I know how to read it. My father taught it to me." He scanned the pages, turning them quickly until he found what he wanted. Drawing one finger across the lines of scribble, he seemed to be deciphering whatever was on the page.

Did she even want to know who her father was? The statute of limitations had long ago expired for prosecuting the man. And her mother certainly wouldn't want anything to do with the bastard at this late date. Probably not even to punch him in the face. Lissa's stepfather might get some satisfaction from shooting him, but that would be the extent of her family's interest in the guy.

"This isn't necessary, you know," she declared. "I don't really need or want to know who he is."

"I need to know."

Okay, color her surprised. "Why?"

"I think he may be the man I've been trying to identify for the past two years."

"You mean the head of the big crime ring you've infiltrated?"

Max looked up from the ledger. "I don't think it's just a crime ring. I think whoever's running the outfit is a spy. The obvious conclusion is that the ringleader is doing it for Mother Russia."

"You think my biological father is a Russian spy?" she exclaimed.

Max grimaced and then muttered, "Welcome to my life."

"I beg your pardon?"

He looked up, a chagrined look on his face, as if he'd just revealed a lot more than he'd wanted to.

"Your father was a spy? For Russia?"

He stared at her for a long moment. Long enough that he didn't have to answer her question aloud. The truth was all too clear on his face and in his thoughts. Which, of course, her Max-amplified powers were having no trouble picking up at the moment.

"Yes," he answered heavily. "My father was a spy for Russia. My mother, too."

She was so shocked at the revelation she blurted the first thing that came to mind. "Are you kidding me?"

"You have no idea how much I wish that were a joke."

The pain in his reply was almost too much for her to bear. She actually had to take a physical step back from it.

Max's expression darkened, and abrupt violence blossomed in his thoughts. "And now their legacy is going to cost me you, too, isn't it?" he asked bitterly.

Oh, dear. He'd interpreted that step back as her rejecting him. "Max, it's not like that—"

"Don't," he bit out sharply. "Don't give me lame excuses and try to explain away your horror with some logical argument. I get it. Traitor's blood runs in my veins. Like father, like son, and all that rot."

She had no immediate retort for that, and he turned his back on her, hunching over his father's notebooks, shutting her out both physically and emotionally. She stared at his back thoughtfully. That certainly explained a lot. Like how he knew so much about surveillance and taking down thugs and losing a tail. But it also opened a whole new can of worms in understanding who he really was.

She asked cautiously, "And you? What about you? What country are you loyal to?"

He turned slowly on the stool and stared at her, rage and resignation swirling in his gaze. She wasn't sure he would answer her.

But eventually, he spoke grimly. "God knows, I had plenty of opportunity to follow in my parents' footsteps. But they made one serious miscalculation in raising me. I was born in America and grew up here. My dad took me back to Moscow when I was about twelve, and that was all it took for me to know where my heart and loyalty would always lie."

She needed to hear him say it. This was too important for her to rely solely on her psychic impressions of what dwelled in his heart. "And where does it lie?"

He looked at her candidly. "It doesn't take a rocket scientist to know how much better life is in this country than in Russia. I fundamentally believe in this way of life and not the ones my parents grew up in. I'm American all the way to my bones."

He returned to perusing the coded text.

"Well? What are you reading?"

"I'm reading about my father's financial dealings with the Russian mob twenty-seven years ago. He laundered money for them by buying art at auction for large sums of cash. This is a record of transactions. But he's made a number of notations about his various clients. I'm interested in those."

"Did something in my aunt Callista's journal make you think my father is Russian and/or a mobster?"

Max winced as he looked up at her. "Your aunt wrote about her long-standing affair with a man she only called by the English letter *Y*. She made it clear that she believed him to be a member of a Russian crime syndicate. She thought it was very swashbuckling and romantic."

Lissa rolled her eyes. "She always did have a special fondness for pirates."

Max snorted. "She made it clear that her lover knew your father. He claimed that your father was untouchable after the attack on your mother because of his high rank within the mob."

An uncomfortable feeling crawled up her spine. The more she focused on the idea, the more certain she was that Max was exactly right. Her birth father had been a high-ranking member of the New Orleans mob run by Russians. She'd known all along, deep down in her gut, that he was a dangerous man, and the revelations from her aunt's journal only confirmed that long-held feeling. But then something else dawned on her.

"Are you telling me Callista knew who my birth father was?"

"I got that impression, yes."

"And she never told my mother?" Lissa demanded in outrage.

"Did your mother actually want to know who it was? DNA testing was available to determine paternity," Max replied gently. "Every guy at that party could have been tested pretty easily."

Lissa had to set aside her knee-jerk anger to think about Max's question. Her mother never talked about the rape, never questioned who did it, never expressed any desire whatsoever to know who Lissa's father was.

Max continued. "It might have been incredibly dangerous to your mother—and you—to know who her attacker was. If he's who I think he is, the man is a cold-blooded killer. It's entirely possible your mother suspected that."

Was it possible her mother had known her attacker was someone powerful and violent? Was that why she hadn't pursued discovering his identity? Did she fear for her own, or her child's, safety? She couldn't fault her mother for the sentiment. If Lissa thought that pursuing her attacker's identity would endanger her own child, she would back off pretty quickly, too.

In the rare instances when the topic of her rapist's identity had come up over the years, her mother's only response was to insist—adamantly—that Lissa's stepfather was her real father.

Which was true for the most part.

Except for the little bit of both her parents that could never forget how Lissa had come into being. Oh, they'd never blamed her for being the daughter of a rapist. But it had always been there between all of them, the unspoken gorilla in the corner that kept her from feeling entirely loved and accepted.

"Why so quiet?" Max queried cautiously, startling her out of her depressing thoughts.

"How much does it bother you that my father is a rapist?"

He frowned. "Not enough to blame you for something you had nothing to do with." He paused. "My father was a spy and a murderer. How much does that bother you?"

"Not enough to walk away from you. You're nothing like your father."

She glimpsed a dark shadow filling Max's troubled gaze as he turned away to study the ledger some more. *What on earth?* She could fully believe that Max was a spy of some kind. But a murderer? The protective, funny, considerate man she knew? Every instinct she had shouted that it could not be.

Or was that just desperately wishful thinking?

She'd seen the way he'd taken down Julio G. when the guy had mugged her. Max had been efficient and violent, and he had shown no stress whatsoever at having nearly killed a man.

While Max continued to read, she moved around the space, absorbing images and feelings emanating from the collection of gadgets and gear. Max's father had clearly been a hard man. Angry. Which made Max's innate decency even more remarkable. No matter what violent skills his father had taught him, she could feel Max's heart, and it felt nothing like the vibe in this room.

Assuming her psychic abilities weren't either lying to her or deserting her and leaving her with nothing more than blind faith in superstitions.

Max had made his opinion of that choice abundantly clear. Was he right? Was she losing herself in meaningless and wildly unreliable impressions, feelings and guesses?

When she'd been young and naive, she'd never stopped to question her gift. She'd bombed around confidently, telling law enforcement officials where to find dead bodies as if it were the easiest thing in the world to do. But now she knew how strange and unscientific an art it was. Now, with the wisdom of adulthood, she doubted it.

Eventually, Max tore a piece of paper out of an old notebook of his father's and jotted down several words in Cyrillic lettering that looked like names.

"Is one of those my father?" she asked hesitantly.

"Maybe."

He might be trying to fake casual unconcern, but his entire being was vibrating like a tightly stretched wire. He'd found something.

"Are you ready to get out of here, then?" The closeness of the space and the accumulated hatefulness of Max's father that filled it were starting to feel oppressive.

He spoke reluctantly. "There's one more thing we need to talk about without an audience eavesdropping on us."

She turned to face him, alarm chattering down her spine. "Do tell."

"I asked my buddy on the New Orleans police force to look into your aunt's death for me. See if he could find any evidence that she might have died from something other than natural causes."

"I remember you mentioning it."

"As you may also remember, she donated her body to science upon her death. Her remains were sent to Tulane University for study."

"And?"

Max exhaled heavily. "And her body was stolen from Tulane's cadaver lab before an autopsy could be performed upon it."

"What?" she exclaimed. "When?"

"Day before yesterday. Soon after my buddy started making inquiries about her death. Bastien thinks that his questions sent up a red flag and provoked the theft of her remains."

She sensed that Max had yet to drop the bomb that had made him reluctant to launch into this conversation. "And?" she prompted.

"We need to find her body. And figure why someone didn't want it examined."

"How do you propose to find her body?" But as soon as the words came out of her mouth, she knew the answer. She spun away from Max and then turned back to face him, accusing. "You want *me* to find her body."

His jaw muscles rippled. "Can you do it?"

"How. Dare. You."

Max was confused. He had not expected Lissa to react with such anger to his request. He'd genuinely thought she'd be pleased that he would give her and her weird abilities the benefit of the doubt. But instead, she'd reacted as though he'd asked her to drown kittens and puppies.

"Help me out here, Lissa. Why are you upset that I'm showing some faith in your psychic abilities?" he asked.

"I'm not a trained monkey performing for your entertainment," she ground out.

"I never thought so—"

"You people are all the same. You poo-poo my abilities until your precious facts and science fail you. And then you run to me and beg me to pull a magic rabbit out of my hat. And as soon as I do, you go right back to calling me crazy and stupid for daring to suggest that the supernatural exists."

She whirled around in a circle as if looking for an escape, then stopped, facing him once more. "I didn't ask for this…gift." She spit out the word as if it was a curse in her mouth.

"I don't want to be like this. I hate talking to dead people. I'm horrified by the sights I see, the terrible feelings I'm forced to experience, the awful memories I have to relive."

He hadn't thought about it in those terms before.

An alarming thought occurred to him. "How old were you when you started having visions and hearing dead people?"

"Three or so. I started to understand what was going on by the time I was about seven. I worked my first case for the FBI when I was nine."

He swore under his breath. "You were a baby. And you had to see all that stuff." He'd been several years older than that when his father made him start hunting, but at least he'd been killing game animals and not seeing dead humans. And he knew how traumatized he'd been by it all in spite of having his father explain why it was important to know how to kill. Lissa'd had nothing. No one to understand her gift and help her see it as a gift, not a curse.

"I'm so sorry—" he started.

"Save it. I don't want your sympathy. Get me out of here," she demanded. He detected a note of panic underneath her angry words. It reflexively made him look around for a threat. Of course. His father's stuff. Was she picking up psychic vibes from his old man? If so, he could entirely understand her desire to get the hell out of there.

He pocketed the sheet of paper with the names on it and led her out of the mazelike storage facility. They got in the truck, and he pointed it toward New Orleans. Lissa simmered beside him, and instinct warned him to leave that pot alone until she'd calmed down more.

They'd made it back to the outskirts of the city when Lissa burst out, "I had it almost stopped. But then you had to come along and tear the lid off my damned power."

He glanced over at her. "What are you talking about?"

"Whenever I'm around you, my talents go crazy."

"Are you saying it's my fault that you're psychic?"

"I told you that violence triggers my visions. Since I've met you, I've been able to see and hear things I've never had the skill to perceive before. It's got to be you. You're the prince of villainy, too."

"Because I'm violent." His emotions were flattening out. He was dropping into the cold, hard place his father had spent all those years pounding into him.

"Yes."

"I won't apologize for being who I am," he stated icily.

"I'm not asking you to," she snapped.

"It damned well sounds like you are."

"Don't put words in my mouth!" she exclaimed.

"I am who I am." And he was feeling colder and harder by the second. "I never asked you to reach out to me for help or go to bed with me. You chose me of your own free will."

"What was I thinking?" she replied sarcastically. "You're the absolute last man I should be with. You bring out everything I despise in myself."

The words cut through the layers of ice encasing him and eviscerated his heart like an arc welder, slicing it into neat little shreds of agony. Silent now, he guided the truck to the front of her shop.

She reached for the door handle, and he said emotionlessly, "I apologize for making you uncomfortable. I won't bother you any further with my violent and unwelcome presence."

A sound suspiciously like a sob escaped her as she slipped out of the truck and made her way to the front door of the shop. She fumbled at the latch and then disappeared into the dark. Into her magical, mystical world that had no place for him in it.

An urge to cry—or kill someone—swept over him. Cursing foully, he drove away into the night.

Chapter 12

Lissa didn't know how long she cried. Long enough that the city went to sleep as much as it ever did around her and the night became deep and quiet outside. Her eyes burned and felt puffy, and she was wrung out emotionally. As if her own pain wasn't enough to deal with, she'd been slammed by a massive wave of grief and rage from Max as he pulled away from the shop.

The fight had been building for a while. They were just too different. He pushed her triggers, and she pushed his. He unleashed in her too much power for her to control, and she saw too many of the secrets he was unwilling to share with anyone else.

Now that it had come out into the open, though, she had expected it to be easier to deal with. A clean break. But this was anything but clean. Her feelings for him were messy and persistent, not diminishing a bit in the face of her anger and frustration.

Truth be told, she wasn't angry at him for asking her to find Callista's body. She was angry that he'd denied the existence of her gift until it was convenient for him for it to exist.

She'd really thought he was different. That he could wrap his mind around her strange talent. She'd almost had herself convinced that maybe, just maybe, she deserved the same measure of happiness as anyone else.

But no. Life had reared up and smacked her in the face. Harder than ever. Her father was not only a violent criminal but apparently a spy to boot. She had tainted blood, and she would never outrun it.

She looked around her half-destroyed apartment. This was her life. A demolished mess. She could fight against it. She could put up drywall and paint it up all pretty, but it would still be a patch-up job.

Max had come along and made her kitchen perfect, and she'd been lulled into believing he could put her whole life back together. But it had been only a cruel joke, a glimpse of the life she could have had before it was yanked out of her grasp. That beautiful, gleaming kitchen was a taunt left behind to torture her.

She wasn't tired, and she couldn't stand looking at Max's perfect kitchen anymore. She headed downstairs for a change of scenery.

Despair waited for her down here, too. This was all her life was destined to be. Knickknacks and baubles contained in a wrought iron guarded box. How had Callista put up with living here for all those years? Hadn't she ever felt claustrophobic? Trapped?

Her aunt was having more adventures now that she was dead than she'd ever had while alive. Who would steal Callista's body, anyway? And why? As she considered the questions, familiar pressure began to build in the back of her mind. A spirit wanted to speak with her.

She tried ignoring it. When that failed, she pushed back, refusing to listen to the whispers tickling her ears. She railed and raged against it, but still the pressure remained, a persistent discomfort in her skull.

Fine.

She'd lost the man of her dreams. Her secret was out. She'd completely blown her attempt to start a new life. If a dead person was so hot and bothered to talk to her, she'd let the blasted spirit talk.

Angrily, she walked around the store in search of a focus item for this particular spirit. She didn't normally need a physical object to make contact, but she was too agitated to concentrate properly tonight.

Lissa stopped in front of the cash register. Frowned. Following the nudges of the spirit, she moved around behind the counter. Reached up...

Ahh. The glass case holding her aunt Callista's most prized possession, an antique porcelain doll with real human hair and eyelashes. The doll was dressed beautifully in all the frills and ruffles of a pampered Victorian child. Lissa lifted her carefully out of the case, surprised at how large and heavy the doll turned out to be. She carried the doll to the middle of the store.

"Callista?" she asked aloud. For who else could the spirit be to have led her to this doll?

Power surged through her. She'd forgotten how gifted her aunt had been. Even in death, the woman's spirit was formidable. Images flashed through Lissa's head almost too quickly to process.

She'd expected images of where her aunt's body was or maybe even how Callista had died. But these images were of children playing together. One of the children in particular grew from a young girl into a beautiful young woman as Lissa looked on.

She knew that girl from somewhere…it was the red-haired girl from the night of Peter Menchekov's party!

A new face exploded into Lissa's mind with the force of a gunshot. A young man. Good-looking in a dark, dangerous way. Wavy chocolate-colored hair and eyes blacker than midnight. He was still lean with youth, but on his way to filling out into a big, powerful man. He wore a tuxedo with all the flair of James Bond.

He smiled at the red-haired girl and held out his arm to her, and the spirit inside Lissa's head let out a scream so bloodcurdling and loud that Lissa dropped the doll.

She watched as the doll fell to the floor in slow motion, doing a half somersault to land on her heavy porcelain head. It shattered into hundreds of pieces that flew out in all directions as Lissa squawked in dismay. The doll's dress flew up over her ruined head and her sawdust-filled body thumped to the floor.

Something black fell out of the doll's petticoats. A glass lens stared up at Lissa like a monolithic eye, and she stared back at it, unable to comprehend what she was looking at. A tiny red light blinked steadily beside the lens.

And then it hit her all in a rush.

One of the surveillance cameras.

And it was recording, hence the blinking red light. It was looking right at her, and she was looking back at it.

Whoever was watching that feed knew that she knew she was being recorded.

Frantically, she stomped on the surveillance camera, smashing it beneath her foot. But she was too late.

They knew. They'd be coming for her. She bolted for the front door and out into the night.

Her other vision still in place, she looked up and down the street and reeled at the ghostly figures drifting up and down it. Dressed in the clothing of many time periods, they passed through one another obliviously. It was beyond creepy.

Since when did she see ghosts? Oh, she talked to them from time to time and got flashes of their memories, but this—this was new. She was losing her mind.

No time to figure it out. Bad guys were coming for her. She felt them jumping into a black SUV and careening toward her.

She dashed away from the store, dodging ghosts until she remembered they were ghosts and just blasted through them in her headlong flight for her life. *Oh, God. Where to go? Where to hide?*

Max considered opening a bottle of vodka and drinking until he passed out or found the bottom of the bottle, but he was too angry for that. He was angry at Lissa for the accusations she'd flung at him, and he was angry at himself for her accusations being true.

He stalked around his house, which normally soothed him, but tonight he saw her everywhere he looked. That bottle of vodka was starting to sound better.

His cell phone rang, and his heart leaped. Was it her? No such luck. "What do you want, Bastien?"

"This is an official call, Max. Where are you right now?"

He frowned. "I'm home. Why?"

"Where have you been for the past couple of hours?"

"I'd rather not say. What the hell's going on?"

"The warehouse Julio G. and his crew are known to operate out of is on fire. Initial reports indicate that many of the guys in his gang were trapped inside and are thought to have perished."

Max swore under his breath. So that had been the hellish glow on the horizon when they'd approached the city. "And you're calling me in an official capacity to ask if I have an alibi."

"That's correct."

"I do. I spent the evening with Lissa in a location that will have security film proof of our arrival and departure times. I would rather not say where that location is."

"All right, man. Make sure those security tapes don't get erased. You may need them later. Your name's come up in more than one conversation around the police department tonight."

"Thanks for the heads-up. I'll make the call now."

"One last thing," Bastien added. "Any progress on finding Callista Clearmont's body?"

He clenched his jaw, and he actually had to work at releasing it. "I'm working on it. You'll be the first to know when I locate her remains."

"Don't mess with the body if you find it. Let a medical examiner secure her remains and create a clean chain of evidence, eh?"

Max muttered something affirmative and hung up the phone thoughtfully. Someone at the police department had launched an attack against him. Who and why?

The obvious answer was the Russian mob.

Were he and Lissa getting too close to something that someone didn't want them to find?

The two of them must be on the right track regarding the identity of her father or the identity of the commander in chief of the Russian crime syndicate. He pulled the notebook paper out of his pocket and stared at the list of names he'd made earlier. If only he had Lissa's abilities. Maybe he could look at this list and have one of the names glow or something.

What must it be like to have an ability like hers? It would be nice to get freebie hints at life. But he'd observed that she didn't control when the hints came or didn't come. That would be frustrating to him. He would hate having to wait around for lightning to strike, never knowing when or if it would.

Goodness knew he didn't envy Lissa having to deal with people's reactions to her gift. Hell, he loved the woman and he'd reacted terribly—

Whoa. Wait. What?

Well, that was a hell of an irony. It took getting dumped by the woman to realize he had feelings for her. Impotent fury at his father bubbled up in his gut. The man had made him so hard, so impervious to emotions and feelings that he'd *fallen in love* and not even known it.

No wonder Lissa had dumped him.

Swearing, he headed for that bottle of vodka, but he was interrupted again by a ringing phone. He put down the unopened bottle of vodka and fished out his phone. Bastien. Again. "What do you want?" he snapped.

"We've got a problem." Bastien was breathing hard as if he was running. "The panic button at your girlfriend's shop was just hit."

"How the hell do you know that?"

"I had the police dispatchers put a note on her phone number to contact me if there was a report from her shop." An engine revved in the background of Bastien's voice.

Max's first impulse was to sprint for Lola, too. But then he remembered she'd dumped him and likely wouldn't appreciate his help. Instead he said grimly, "Let me know that she's okay, will you?"

"You're not going over there?" Bastien blurted.

"She told me to kiss off earlier tonight."

"And you give a crap about that if she's in danger?"

Aw, hell. Bastien was right. "Quit being my damned conscience for me. I'm on my way," he bit out. He'd have gone anyway. Bastien just forced him to admit it faster. He made a mental note to thank the bastard when this was all over and Lissa was safe.

Lissa crouched in an alley, shivering, her other vision clearer and realer than eyesight, as the power rolled over her. *Too much.* She couldn't contain it anymore. It felt as if every bit of the power she'd held back for all these months had come rushing in all at once. Her senses, her mind, were overwhelmed. She couldn't take it all in.

They were almost there. The men in the black vehicle with death on their minds and in their hands. She felt oiled steel in her palms. Heavy. Cold. Solid. Locked and loaded. They knew she'd found the camera. Orders had come down. Eliminate her and her visions.

Too much knowledge. Too much power.

She pressed the heels of her hands against her temples, pressing back against the threatening explosion of her brain from her skull. She was losing her mind. *Must run. Must hide.* And yet her limbs refused to move. Refused all commands. She huddled deeper in the shadow of a stack of metal trash cans as it began to rain.

* * *

Max leaped out of Lola in an alley around the corner from the shop, barely registering the spitting rain. He lifted the hatch and yanked out a bullet-resistant vest. He slammed it on, and the extra ammo clips in the pockets banged reassuringly into his ribs. He jammed a pistol into the sewn-in holster at the back of his waistband and another into the ankle holster he quickly strapped to his leg.

He picked up a light assault weapon and slung its carry strap over his shoulder, swinging the rifle up into firing position. He advanced around the corner toward the shop.

"You moving?" a voice murmured quietly in his ear. He and Bastien had wired up and set up a discreet radio frequency for themselves while they'd been driving over there like bats out of hell.

"Affirmative. One black SUV in front of the shop," Max said into his throat mike. He studied the vehicle through the thermal imaging feature of his nightscope and added, "Nobody inside the vehicle."

"Back door is standing open," Bastien reported in turn. "No movement out here in the alley."

Max aimed his high-tech scope at the wall of Lissa's shop. "I'm not painting any heat signatures on the ground floor." He moved across the street from the shop so he could point his sight up at the second floor over the shop. "No heat sigs upstairs."

"Ground floor clear," Bastien reported.

Max slowly and quietly opened the SUV's passenger door. He reached across the interior and grabbed a handful of wires from under the steering wheel column. He gave a good yank. "Vehicle is disabled," he breathed into his throat mike.

"Upstairs clear," Bastien reported.

"There's a basement. Single room, straight entry, no obstructions. Large crates around the walls that a man could hide behind," Max replied.

"I'm on it."

It was good working with a former SEAL.

"Basement's clear. I'm heading back up to the ground floor." A pause. "There's something in here you should see."

Max used his key to let himself into the shop. Apparently, the bad guys had entered and exited through the back door tonight. Bastien was crouching in the middle of the shop, looking at something on the floor. Max spotted broken pieces of what looked like a dinner plate all around his friend. And then he spied what held Bastien's interest. Something black and electronic looking.

"Any idea what it is?" Bastien asked.

"Surveillance camera," he bit out.

"It's been smashed."

Max's mind leaped into overdrive. Lissa had found one of the cameras. It had fallen—he looked at the flattened bit of electronics—no. Lissa had stomped on it. She would know that men would come in response to her finding and destroying it. She ran the last time they had come. She would run again.

Given that the SUV was still out front, the men who'd come hadn't found her yet. Which meant she was all alone, no doubt scared out of her mind, while armed hostiles hunted her.

"She ran, Bass. She's out there while a truckload of men hunt her down." He swore luridly.

"Focus, Max. Where would she go?"

"She would just run to begin with."

"Okay. That places her a couple of blocks away from here before she slows to get her bearings. Where would she go from there? Where would she feel safe?"

His surveillance blind. Would she go back there?

"I have an idea."

They left the shop, some fifty feet apart but moving in tandem. They crossed the street and headed down the alley, covering each other's movements. While Bastien guarded the alley, Max climbed the stairs quickly and let himself into the blind.

"Lissa? Are you here? It's me. Max."

Silence. He cleared the place anyway, hoping against hope that she was too scared to identify herself to him.

"Not here," he reported.

"Movement," Bastien breathed from below. Max raced on silent feet for the door, easing it open a crack to see outside. The SEAL would be frozen beneath him in the deep shadows cast by the iron staircase. He did the same in the doorway, peering out through the low-light feature of his gun sight. The alleyway leaped into lime-green relief.

A man came around the corner, a weapon similar to Max's held to his eye in a firing position. The barrel of the weapon swung left and right as the guy cleared the alley. The hostile must have spotted Bastien, for all of a sudden, the barrel swung hard right.

Two spits of noise and a brief flash of light announced that Bastien had fired at the guy. Hell of a good sound suppressor his friend had on his weapon. The hostile dropped to the ground.

Max raced outside and down the stairs, his assault rifle swinging in an arc in front of him.

"Behind those trash cans." Bastien's rifle barrel pointed at a stack of rusty trash cans.

Max advanced slowly. He spotted a bright green figure crouched in between several of the cans. Too small for a typical hired mercenary. No sign of weapons in the silhouette. A homeless person, maybe?

He moved around the end of the barrels, prepared for anything. Except the sight that greeted him. Lissa. Curled in a little ball, hugging her knees. She didn't even seem aware of his presence.

"Lissa," he murmured as he knelt down beside her. "Are you okay?"

She shook her head, her curls wild around her face, her eyes staring at something invisible to him. He held his arms out to her carefully. She looked like a feral creature that would bolt at the first sign of a grab at her.

She did bolt, but forward, directly into his arms. He pulled her against him, absorbing her trembling as he held on to her fiercely. "I've got you, baby. You're safe now."

"Um, not exactly," Bastien responded in his ear. "There are more hostiles out here. We need to get her out of here."

"Upstairs to the blind?" Max suggested.

"For now. I'll come around in my truck and pick you two up. If you're right about who's trying to kill her, we've got to get her out of town and call ourselves in some cavalry."

Max led Lissa up the stairs. She went without resistance and without saying a word. Which worried him.

He eased the door shut and turned to face her. She

was soaking wet and her hair hung in black spirals around her face. "Talk to me, Lissa."

"They came for me. Cloaked in death."

"But you ran. You got away from them. And now I'm here. Bastien and I will keep you safe."

"A face. I saw a man. And then the screaming…" She trailed off, her face screwed up against some inner pain that looked like too much for her to bear.

He felt so damned helpless. If he didn't know better, he'd say she was in the middle of some sort of psychotic break with reality. But he did know better. The visions had her in their grip and weren't letting go.

"Lissa, I need you to come back to me. In a few minutes, you and I are going to leave here. I'll need you to follow my instructions. Can you push the visions back?"

She looked up at him as if searching for the sound of his voice.

"I'm right here."

Her gaze lost its momentary clarity.

Dammit. He swept her into his arms and kissed her. Her lips were ice-cold; her entire body shivered against his. But he ignored all that, focusing on the woman he loved. In spite of his desperation, he forced himself to be gentle with her, to coax her mouth open rather than forcing it.

As soon as her lips parted on a little gasp, as if she'd just registered being kissed by him, his tongue swept into her mouth, demanding her attention and her response. All of a sudden, she unfroze. She surged against him, her arms going around his neck, her lithe body moving sinuously against his. And she was kissing him back, inhaling his heat and strength as if she couldn't get enough of him.

"Welcome back," he murmured against her lips.

"Never let me go," she gasped.

"Never." At least not metaphorically. Not until she made him. And maybe not even then. He'd lost her once. He didn't intend to lose her again.

The kiss threatened to become naked, sweaty sex as her hands thrust under his vest and shirt to his bare flesh. But when she reached for his belt buckle, he reluctantly had to let her go and reach for her fingers. "Hold that thought, darling. First we have to get you out of town."

"Out of town?" she echoed, lifting her head to stare up at him in the dark.

"Those men who came for you after you found the camera. They won't stop until they find you. We have to get you someplace safe until we sort this out."

Bastien spoke up just then. "I'm en route to your position. I'll be there in sixty seconds."

"We're ready to move," Max replied. He led her over to the door and spoke quickly while she was still lucid. "We're going to run down the steps and jump into Bastien's truck. I'll go first, and I need you to stay right on my heels, so close you think you might trip me. Can you do that?"

"Of course."

He grinned down at her. There she was. His fireball was back. "On my mark. Three. Two. One." He twisted the doorknob and leaped out the door. "Go."

The maneuver went exactly as planned except for the man who raced around the corner at the far end of the alley, no doubt drawn by the sound of Bastien's truck.

Max took aim and double-tapped two rounds into the running man's torso. The guy staggered but didn't go down. Must be wearing a bullet-resistant vest, too, dammit. The guy's gun swung up into firing position as Max took aim again, this time at his head. Two quick squeezes of his right index finger and the hostile was down. This time for good.

"Ohmigod," Lissa cried from behind him.

Max reached the bottom of the stairs and threw open the truck door. She dived in and he lunged in after her. Bastien turned hard, rolling him on top of Lissa. From his prone position, Max awkwardly reached for the handle and yanked the door shut.

The truck straightened and flew down the street as he sat upright. Lissa started to do the same, but he barked, "Stay down, baby." He stroked her wet hair back from her face to soften the harshness of his instruction.

Bastien drove like a man possessed, and Max recognized the tactic. The SEAL was checking to see if anyone was attempting to follow them. Max watched out the rear window tensely, but no other vehicle behind them was driving like a bat out of hell. The truck accelerated and cornered about as aggressively as Lola.

"What have you got under the hood of this beast?" Max asked.

"A few little modifications out of my bag of magic tricks," the Cajun answered, grinning as he threw the vehicle around a corner and shot forward.

"You got a well-armed cavalry in that bag of tricks, too?"

"I just might, bro."

Lord, he hoped so. They were going to need a miracle to survive a professional hit team. And he ought to know.

Bastien shot up a ramp onto a highway before taking

his foot off the accelerator and slowing to normal speed. "You can sit up now," the former SEAL announced to Lissa.

"What was all of that swerving around and tire screeching about?" she demanded.

"It's called offensive driving," Bastien replied casually.

"Offensive, indeed," she muttered. "I feel bruised from head to foot. And cold."

Max held an arm out to her. "Can I interest you in some free body heat?"

She wasted no time cuddling up against him.

"What happened after I left you?" Max asked her. "Walk me through it."

"Umm, I cried for a while. And then I had this—" She broke off and glanced at Bastien warily.

Sensing where she wanted to go with the conversation, Max told her, "You can speak freely in front of him. Not only is he a Cajun and superstitious—he also knows how to keep his mouth shut."

She nodded resolutely. "I had a vision."

Bastien's head swung toward her sharply, but he didn't comment. Max said encouragingly, "Tell me about it."

"First, I went looking for a focus item. I could tell it was going to be a big vision, and I wanted help capturing it. The spirit led me to an old doll that belonged to Aunt Callista. I took it out of the case and carried it to the middle of the shop."

"And then?" he prompted when she ground to a halt.

She continued reluctantly. "Normally, I would see where a body is or get a flash of memory of the spirit's death. But not tonight. I got this whole flood of old im-

ages. They came from a girl's childhood and then jumped
to when she became a young woman."

"Do you know the girl?"

She shook her head. "I've seen her before. At the
Menchekov mansion."

"When were you *there*?" Bastion demanded. "We've
been trying to nail that guy for years."

"Remind me to give you my file on him. It'll put
him away for life," Max replied absently. Then to Lissa,
"The red-haired girl you told me about the night of the
party?"

"Yes."

"Go on."

"I saw a young man. Handsome. A little older than
her. And no sooner had I seen his face than this horrible, piercing scream exploded in my head."

Something eager leaped in Max's gut. Was this *the*
face? Had she spotted the man he'd been looking for
all this time?

She continued, "I dropped the doll. It hit the floor
and broke, and one of the surveillance cameras fell out.
It was looking right up at me, and a little red light was
blinking on its side. I panicked and stepped on it." Lissa
took a deep breath, and he squeezed her gently with a
steadying arm. "I felt them coming, Max. I hit the panic
button on the alarm, and then I ran."

He expected her to stop there, but she didn't.

"There were so many ghosts on the street. They were
walking through each other. It was awful. This town is
so freaking haunted."

Bastien chuckled at that.

"So you ducked into the alley and hid until we found

you. Did you see any of the men chasing you?" Max asked.

"No. I asked the ghosts to lead them away from me. I don't know if they did or not, but no one came into that alley until you guys."

"How long you been seein' ghosts, *chère*?" Bastien asked, his Cajun accent thick enough to cut with a knife.

"I only started seeing them tonight. But I've been hearing them all my life," she replied cautiously. "Do you think I'm crazy?"

"Nah. My *grand-mère* talked to de spirits all de time. She knew stuff, she did."

They fell silent after that as Bastien guided the truck out of Orleans Parish and deep into bayou country. Lissa dozed while Max kept an eye out behind them for tails. It appeared they'd made a clean getaway from the city and the armed men roaming it.

Bastien asked quietly, "Does she really have the gift?"

"If you're referring to psychic abilities, all the evidence I've seen says that she does."

"You okay with that?"

That was, indeed, the question of the hour. "Where are we going?"

"To my people. You two will be safe with them while you figure out what to do next."

"I dunno. The guy she pissed off has a pretty long reach."

Bastien shrugged. "My people are better. I guarantee it."

Max was inclined to believe him.

They drove a while more in silence, and then Bastien asked in full police officer mode, "Who were those men back in the Quarter?"

"They work for the head of the Louisiana Bratya."

"How'd she get tangled up with that bunch?"

"You're aware that I've been infiltrating a criminal organization for the past couple of years, right?"

"Yeah, Max. And you've given us some good busts out of it."

"It's the Bratya I've been infiltrating."

"Day-umm, boy. They're a nasty bunch."

"Yes. They are. And I think they're even nastier than anyone in law enforcement realizes. I'm convinced that the leader of the entire outfit is a Russian spy using the mob to finance his espionage activities."

Bastien swore. "You got proof?"

"I'm getting there."

"What have you got so far?"

He considered the man beside him. A former navy SEAL, Bastien had helped his sister and her fiancé out of a bad jam, discovering who Max was in the process. And in the ensuing year, the guy hadn't breathed a word of Max's covert activities to a soul. If he was going to trust anyone, this man was the one he would choose.

"My father was a Russian spy."

The truck swerved slightly, then righted itself.

Max continued grimly. "The US government is aware of this. They are also aware that he attempted to recruit me to follow in his footsteps."

"Dude, you talkin' classified stuff." Bastien gestured with his chin toward Lissa, who was dozing on his shoulder.

"She knows everything." He added ruefully, "And

anything I haven't told her, she's probably already picked out of my head, anyway."

"She's that good?"

"She's better, man." And as he said the words, he realized he was proud of her talent. Not that he had any right to be after the crappy way he'd acted about it with her, doubting her and all but calling her a charlatan.

"How deep into the Bratya have you gotten?"

"Upper management. I work for Peter Menchekov."

Bastien whistled between his teeth.

"With Lissa's help, I'm closing in on the identity of the ringleader. I've got it down to a half-dozen names."

"When we get where we're going, you should send that list to Jennie."

"I'm planning to."

They turned off the highway and onto a decent road that quickly turned into a narrow road overhung by massive cypress trees. At any second, Max expected them to drive off the narrow strip of land into the swamp glinting blackly on either side of them.

"Where are we going?" Max repeated.

"To get you that cavalry you asked for."

Cavalry indeed. Hopefully, the modern kind with tanks and big-ass guns.

Chapter 13

Lissa listened to the men talking quietly over her head as she pretended to be asleep. Max must really trust Bastien to be revealing so much. Heck, the only reason she knew anything about Max's covert activities was because he couldn't keep it secret from her if he tried.

She could imagine how much it must stink to be in a relationship with her and feel naked and exposed all the time. Especially for a man like Max, who lived for secrecy. But there wasn't a thing she could do about it.

The truck stopped, and Bastien cut the engine. She opened her eyes to look outside. And gasped. All she could see in any direction was water. Black, oily swamp water. Gnarled roots stuck up out of the water like the crests of hideous monsters, and broad-leafed kudzu vines hung over everything in a choking blanket. It was scary as hell.

"We're here," Bastien announced cheerfully.

The ground was spongy and moist beneath her feet. Eeyew. She followed the two men onto a short wooden dock with a flat-bottomed, metal-hulled boat moored to it. The guys threw back the tarp covering it, and Bastien unlocked a chain securing boat and motor.

"We're going into the swamp in that?" she asked reluctantly.

Bastien grinned at her. "She be a fine vessel. Faster than the truck by a long shot."

"Saints preserve us all," she muttered as Max helped her into the boat.

Bastien took the tiller, and she was startled to see him pull on some sort of bulky goggles. Max donned some and then passed a pair to her. Confused, she pulled the apparatus over her eyes. Max fiddled with the side of the gadget, and the swamp came into green relief around her.

The motor rumbled to life, sending vibrations through the boat. They eased away from the dock into the night. They must have traveled for an hour, down open causeways, skirting the edge of a big lake and then winding deep into a maze of islets covered in thick undergrowth. How Bastien wasn't completely lost, she couldn't fathom.

Eventually, she couldn't resist asking, "How do you know where you're going?"

The cop answered, grinning below his goggles, "This be home sweet home to me, *chère*."

Sheesh. He sounded as though he actually was fond of this wild tangle of vegetation and water.

"It's not far now," he warned Max. He cut the big engine and switched to a smaller electric motor that he dropped behind the boat.

"Do we need to be quiet?" she breathed.

Bastien laughed heartily. "Hell to the no. You sneak up on my people, they shoot you dead. I just went to the fishing motor 'cause the water be too shallow for Big Bertha."

Max responded in disgust, "No need to terrify the lady any more than she already is."

"Aw, c'mon, bro. I was just playin' around a little."

"Don't scare Lissa." Max's voice was flat and without inflection.

Bastien chuckled. "Power down, dude. I'll quit messin' with your lady."

Max's lady? She liked the sound of that. "Does whoever we're meeting actually live out here?"

"Lots of people live out here. The ones we're going to see use this area to do some training."

Max made a sound of satisfaction. What was that about? She asked, "What kind of training?"

"The kind you shouldn't ask too many questions about."

"I expect that you and I are going to have to sign a big pile of federal nondisclosure agreements when we get back to civilization," Max added.

"No lie, dat," Bastien responded. He cut the motor. "Okay, boys and girls. We're here."

Here was the end of a long dock winding away in the darkness.

"This looks like something out of a horror movie," she commented as Max helped her up onto the dock overhung by huge old cypress boughs. The two men tied off the boat, and then Bastien led the way forward with one last warning. "Keep your hands away from your bodies and in plain sight until we've made contact and they've cleared us in."

"Where the heck are you taking us? Some sort of armed compound of crazies?" she asked.

Max chuckled behind her. "I suspect that's closer to the truth than you might guess."

"Sure 'nuff, sweet stuff. They all crazy out heah."

"Hey now."

Lissa jumped as a deep male voice came out of the trees somewhere ahead of her.

"Speak for yourself, Catfish." A man materialized out of the night wearing camo pants and a black T-shirt. He slung a big, scary-looking rifle-thingie over his shoulder as he moved toward them.

"What brings you out here in our neck of the woods, LeBlanc?"

"Hollywood!" Bastien exclaimed. The two men traded hugs and back thumps with one another.

The newcomer, a muscular dark-haired man, startled her by holding a hand out to Max. "Glad to see you're still in one piece, Kuznetsov. Your sister doesn't think you're reporting in often enough. She was about to send me out to check on you."

Max rolled his eyes. "I've been busy."

"Who's your friend?"

"This is Lissa Clearmont. Lissa, this is Ashe Konig, my future brother-in-law. Assuming he ever gets off his butt and makes an honest woman out of my sister."

Ashe laughed in protest. "Dude. We've been a little busy out here, too. Gimme a break. And Hank's not complaining."

Max explained, "Hank is my sister. Her real name is a big, long Russian mouthful, and she usually just goes by her nickname."

Lissa got a burst of impressions of a skinny blonde

girl, all knees and elbows, sticking her tongue out at Max as he teased her by calling her Hank. "You stuck her with that moniker, didn't you?" she accused.

Max swore under his breath. "I can't hide a thing from you, can I?"

"Sorry."

"I admit it. I was a rotten brother."

Another swarm of images leaped into her head of him arguing with Hank, insisting that she stay in college while he dropped out of school instead to care for their ailing mother. "You made her stay in school and sacrificed your education for hers."

Max muttered, "You can stop picking stuff out of my brain anytime now."

Right. He liked his secrets. "I'm sorry," she apologized again. "I can't help it. The images just come to me. Maybe if you weren't touching me…"

His arm tightened slightly around her. Willing to risk her seeing his innermost secrets, was he? Her heart beat a little more hopefully.

"C'mon up to the house," Ashe said. "Everyone should be up by now."

"It's the middle of the night," Lissa protested. "We don't mean to impose—"

Bastien cut her off, laughing. "Sure we do. I got a project for ya'll."

"Does it involving shooting people and blowing stuff up?" Ashe asked hopefully.

"Sure does," Bastien replied jovially.

"Awesome."

The dock turned into a boardwalk under a long alley of huge trees. She spied a sprawling home in front of them, pale and ghostly. It was a beautiful plantation-

style home built on tall stilts. A graceful staircase led
to a covered porch encircling the structure.

Dormers in the roof announced that there was a second floor, which meant the place was larger than it
looked. As they drew near, she saw that the structure
was immaculately restored.

"The old place is looking good," Bastien commented.

Ashe grinned over his shoulder at them. "Turns out
it's good exercise to restore antebellum homes. And
we've got plenty of cheap labor around here."

Bastien and Max grinned at some private joke among
the men.

For her part, she frowned at an image of several
women scraping paint in blistering sunshine. "What
is this place?" she demanded. "Why are women doing
such hard work?"

Ashe's eyebrows shot up. "Come in and I'll introduce you to the ladies. You'll understand why then."

She reached out to grasp the wood stair rail and
reeled. She was vaguely aware of Max's arm support-
ing her as she stared at pirates and slaves, smugglers
and prostitutes. Prosperous times and poor ones, hur-
ricanes, feuds and…a recent violent encounter.

She muttered, lost in the thrall of a man and a woman
fighting off several male intruders. "How long ago was
the gun battle?"

An arm guided her inside a big kitchen. The door
closed and the vision faded, closed out of the house.

She blinked and realized that Bastien and Ashe were
staring at her, along with a half-dozen men and women
seated at a big table. One of the women rushed forward,
and Max released her to hug the woman tightly. That
must be his sister. The unfortunately named Hank. Lissa

saw the resemblance in their fair coloring, height and general perfection.

She glanced around at the silent, fit women observing her alertly. No surprise, a rush of images burst into her head. She gasped aloud.

"What?" Ashe asked sharply. He and everyone else in the room went onto full alert.

Of course they did. "You're all soldiers," she stated in wonder. "Especially…oh, my. It's about time they had women SEALs."

The atmosphere in the room went from pleasant to deadly in a nanosecond. "Who's your friend, Max?" Ashe asked gently. Hostility dripped in his voice, and Lissa shuddered.

"She's psychic. I swear I didn't say a word to her about any of you. She just knows things. There's no keeping a secret around her." He added that last wry observation with a touch of bitterness.

Lissa squirmed as every eye in the room turned on her.

"What brings you out here in the middle of the night?" Ashe asked Bastien.

"The Russian mob is trying to kill Lissa and sent a hit squad after her. I was wondering how ya'll would feel about running a little bait-and-kill op."

A bait and what?

"How bad do they want to kill her?" one of the women asked.

Bastien grinned. "They sent four men to her shop. Body armor and assault rifles. I'm thinking twice that number out here."

"Hold on," Lissa interrupted. "There's no need for a gunfight on my account."

"Yes. There is," Max replied flatly. "These are not good men, Lissa. They're violent criminals. Murderers. They smuggle drugs and weapons—hell, they ran a sex trafficking ring until Ashe and Hank broke it up last year. They don't deserve your sympathy. They deserve to die."

She might have protested that no one deserved to die, but a wave of agreement flowed from the other people in the room. These were warriors, in the business of ridding the world of violent criminals. They were violent so other people did not have to be. *Well, okay, then.*

"I'm the bait, aren't I?" she accused no one in particular.

Bastien shrugged.

"There's one thing I have to do before you can use me to kill anyone."

Max looked down at her in surprise. "What's that?"

"I have to find my aunt."

"The dead one?" Bastien blurted. Everyone jolted at that.

"She's close. I can feel her."

"How close?" Max asked. No one else seemed to know how to proceed with this strange conversation but him.

"Within, say, twenty miles."

"Can you tell a direction?"

She closed her eyes and focused on the flood of power from earlier. She pointed to what she thought was the northeast. "That way. In a building. A town of some kind."

"Lamarr City is the only town that way within twenty miles," Bastien remarked.

"Would somebody please clue me in here?" Ashe asked.

Max quickly filled in the group on her aunt's suspicious death and the disappearance of Callista's body.

Hank asked, "If you're sure the Bratya killed her, why does finding her body matter?"

Lissa shook her head. "I don't know. But Callista wants to show me something."

Everyone but Max flinched at that. Apparently, he'd gotten used to her brand of weird. But these people looked at her as if she needed a white jacket and a nice man with a syringe of tranquilizers.

"Everybody gear up," Ashe ordered.

Lissa looked around in surprise as the room emptied. "Where did they all go?"

"You heard Ashe. To get their gear," Max answered.

"Why?" she asked blankly.

"We're leaving for Lamarr City."

"Now?"

He grinned down at her. "Welcome to working with SEALs. They don't mess around. They get stuff done."

"It's the middle of the night," she protested.

"Exactly. Darkness puts them at an advantage over potential hostiles."

Everyone adjourned to a big room off the main hall, and a stream of night vision goggles, clips of ammunition, radios, microphones and who knew what else was passed around and donned by men and women alike. In short order, they were armed for World War Three. The group piled into a sleek cigarette boat parked in a boathouse next to the dock and roared off into the night before Lissa hardly knew what was happening.

They clambered ashore a little while later and climbed into a pair of Land Rovers. As they headed north and east, Max asked her, "So how does this corpse-hunting thing work?"

"We get close to where I've sensed a body, and then I'll zero in on it." The Land Rovers pulled into a small town, quiet and deserted at this time of night. She got out and closed her eyes, taking a deep breath.

Nothing. She swore silently. They were all staring at her, expecting her to pull a rabbit out of her hat. Of all times for her gift to fail and make her look colossally stupid...

She reached out blindly for Max's hand. And no sooner had she touched him than a wave of power washed over her. *Ahh, yes.* There she was. Aunt Callista's energy was weak but clear, off to Lissa's right. And close. Very close.

Lissa took off walking, her eyes still closed. Max steadied her when she stumbled, steering her around unseen obstacles as Lissa closed in on the energy source. She stopped, practically on top of the signal.

A faint chuckle came from beside her, and she opened her eyes. They stood in front of a funeral home.

"What better place to hide a body?" she murmured.

They moved quietly around the back of the building, and one of the women went to work on the door lock. A click, a nod and everyone but Max and her raced inside.

"Where'd they go?" she whispered.

"Looking for the alarm to disarm it before it goes off," Max breathed.

A quiet female voice came from the darkness inside. "Clear."

Max ushered her in. "Any idea where in here to look for your aunt?"

"That way." She moved off down a hall to her left.

No surprise, she stopped in front of a set of double doors that led to a morgue-like room. Four refrigerator-style doors lined one wall.

Lissa didn't hesitate. She went to the last one on the end and pointed at it. The SEALs must have finished clearing the building because most of them piled into the embalming room, minus two who were no doubt standing lookout.

Max opened the refrigerator door and pulled out a stainless steel table with a body bag on it. She girded herself and nodded as he unzipped the bag to reveal her aunt's remains. Lissa was grateful for the darkness, because it hid whatever shade of dead her aunt's corpse might be. She bit back a sob at the sight of the familiar face and long white hair splaying around it.

Were you murdered, Auntie Cal?

No speeches were forthcoming, but a series of fuzzy visual images and impressions of feeling flooded through her. Anger. Fear. Outrage at realizing she'd been…poisoned, maybe? Snippets of an argument came to Lissa. Something about Callista telling the police of the dead drops in her store.

Huh. Was that why her aunt had been killed? Had the mob thought she'd betrayed them?

Lissa relayed her impressions and conclusions to the others, and Max inhaled sharply beside her. "I'm the reason she was killed. God, I'm so sorry, Lissa."

His surveillance setup across the street from the shop. The mob must have found out about it and assumed that Callista had betrayed them to the police. The Bratya had no idea it was one of their own doing the surveillance on the shop.

She was too numb at the moment to know how to feel about that revelation.

"Can she tell us any more about who killed her or how?" Max asked gently.

Lissa closed her eyes, grimaced and reached out to lay her palm on her aunt's ice-cold forehead. Her aunt's spirit was faint but present. She preferred to be at the shop in New Orleans and not in this strange, cold place she didn't know.

Lissa sent out comforting vibes and silently coaxed the spirit to tell her who'd killed her. But that was clearly not what her aunt's spirit was fretting over. Confused, Lissa trailed her fingers down her aunt's cheek to her shoulder and then curled around behind the bones there.

She looked up at Max. "Help me lift her."

Frowning, he turned the body on its side. Lissa pointed. "There. That."

Ashe shined a flashlight on something faintly visible on her aunt's shoulder blade. "A tattoo," he announced.

Max bent down to examine the tiny drawing that was maybe an inch across. "A heart. With two sets of initials. *C* and *L*. And two Russian letters. A *yu* and a *peh*."

And just like that, Lissa felt a faint sigh of relief on her cheek. The spirit's work was done. She could move on to her rest, now. The presence began to slip away.

All of a sudden, Max dug in his back pants pocket and pulled out a piece of notebook paper. He stabbed at a name with his finger. "Yuri Petrov. That must have been her lover. Which leaves the other five men on this list as the possible spy/ringleader."

Lissa held out her hand. "May I see that?"

Max passed her the paper. She glanced through the names, although she couldn't read them. They were all written in Cyrillic. "Callista," she murmured urgently. "I need one more thing from you before you go. Which one of these men is my father?"

Deep resistance pulsed into her.

"Please. I have to know," she said forcefully. "For the man I love. You owe me."

If souls could swear under their nonbreath, Callista's did then.

"This one, Max," Lissa declared, pointing at the one that glowed faintly on the paper.

"Markus Petrov? Yuri's brother?" Max slapped his palm against his forehead. "Of course. His *brother*! Callista meant it literally. Her lover called the rapist his brother. I thought he meant it in the sense of being comrades. Brothers in arms."

"Are we supposed to know what you're talking about?" Bastien asked cautiously.

"Lissa and her aunt just gave us the identity of the ringleader of the Bratya. The Russian spy."

"A spy?" Ashe exclaimed.

"Long story," Max bit out. "I need to talk to Jennie Finch. Now that we know who to target, maybe she can drill down into Petrov's life and find more evidence on him."

"Dude," Bastien said regretfully. "We don't have *any* evidence. We just have Lissa pointing at a name on a piece of paper."

Max opened his mouth to defend her—which was sweet of him—but she placed a restraining hand on his arm. "I've got this," she said.

"Did I or did I not find my aunt's body?" she asked Bastien.

"You did."

"And did I or did I not know your friends were SEALs without being told?"

Bastien huffed.

"I'm not asking you to believe in psychic powers. But I am asking you to allow for the possibility that, somehow, I know things from time to time."

One of the lookouts swept into the room. "Right now I'm asking you all to leave the building quickly by the back door. Police car just parked down the street. Local cop is making a foot patrol of the area."

"ETA?" Ashe asked.

"Two minutes."

In well under half that time, the group had put Callista's body back where they found it, exited the funeral home and run across the parking lot to hide in the shadows.

Bastien whispered to Ashe, "If he checks the engines of the vehicles, they'll still be warm."

"He'll have to call it in. He's not miked up, so he'll have to go back to his squad car. We'll egress then."

Ashe called it correctly. The cop felt the hoods of the cars, then moved off at a brisk pace toward his squad car. She and the others piled in the Land Rovers and went cross-country into the brush behind the funeral home parking lot until they hit another street. They were just driving docilely away from Lamarr City when a deputy sheriff's car flew past them, light bar flashing, ignoring them.

Lissa let out what felt like her first breath since they'd

stepped into the funeral home. "Now what?" she asked no one in particular.

Max answered her grimly. "Now we use you as bait to draw out Petrov and his flunkies, and we take them down."

Chapter 14

Max's plan sounded so easy to Lissa. But when the SEAL team went back to their hideout and started preparing to lure in the hit squad and take it out, the reality was a hundred times scarier.

The big problem was that, with a relatively small team, they would not be able to guard every approach to the island. The good news was the SEALs used the island for training and had all crawled over every inch of it.

There was a lengthy conference call with a SEAL operations center of some kind that included the famous Jennie Finch and the team's boss, a man named Commander Perriman. He seemed to think that this whole plan would make a dandy training exercise. If this was just training for these people, she'd hate to see what they considered a real job.

Bastien set the bait by calling back into his precinct and asking for a couple of days off to deal with the crazy girlfriend of an acquaintance who'd gotten herself in some trouble. Lissa was dismayed that Bastien assumed word would spread quickly to mob informants on the force.

After the call, Bastien left his cell phone turned on. Apparently, the mobsters trying to kill her would have no trouble locating his mobile signal and coming straight to it. Which made her feel even more naked and vulnerable than ever.

Max was silent through most of the planning. She hoped he was just letting the SEALs do their thing. But her gut told her he was conflicted about the whole plan. Was that what he was worried about? Blowing his two-year investigation when he was getting so close to identifying his target?

Whenever she probed his mind for an answer, she hit a wall of icy control. He was intentionally trying to block her out of his mind. She sensed that she could blast through the wall if she wanted to. But Max would never forgive her if she did. He was already deeply uncomfortable with her ability to suss out his secrets.

The bad guys would arrive as early as that night, or it might be days before they came for her. The SEALs seemed unconcerned either way, but she wasn't sure her nerves could stand a lengthy wait for all hell to break loose.

After the evening meal, everyone drifted off to their rooms, abandoning her and Max at the kitchen table. The good humor evaporated, leaving behind simmering tension.

"Talk to me, Max. What are you hiding from me?"

He looked up at her grimly. "You know I'm hiding something?"

"Hey. It's an improvement. You can shield a little bit from me. That's what you wanted, isn't it? To keep me out of your life and out of your secrets?"

"I never wanted you out of my life."

"How did you plan to make me part of your life and not share your secrets with me?"

He frowned at her as if he didn't understand.

"Think about it, Max. Serious relationships are based on trust. On knowing each other. People may keep small secrets from one another, but the big stuff—they share that with their loved ones."

He huffed in what might be frustration, or maybe disagreement.

She continued battering at his misguided beliefs. "You know my deepest, darkest secret, and I'm still here. I didn't run away and ditch you because you know I hear dead people. And I didn't run away when I found out your family was spies. It's obvious that you're some sort of spy, too, but I'm still here."

That made him shove back hard from the table and stare at her intensely.

"Oh, come on. That didn't even take woo-woo powers to figure out. You dropped my mugger like he was a rank amateur. And you and I both know he wasn't. You recognized that bug I found in the shop. Your surveillance setup. The way you knew how to ditch our tails at the auction house. Who but a soldier, cop or spy would know how to do all that stuff? And you're not a soldier or a cop."

He shoved an angry hand through his hair, denial written all over his face.

"For goodness' sake, Max, you're hunting a spy. Who but another spy would do that?"

He swore under his breath and charged out the back door, disappearing into the gathering twilight. She let him go. It hurt like hell to watch him walk out on her like that. But she couldn't force him to let her into his life. He would either accept her into his secret world or he would walk away and never look back. Her heart warned her that the latter was the likely outcome.

Had she lost him before she'd ever really had him? If only he would trust her even a little. Maybe if he got his obsession with finding the leader of the Bratya—

She had an idea. She picked up the handset phone that Ashe had used earlier to call the SEAL operations center, hit the redial button and crossed her fingers that this would work.

"Team Ops. Go ahead." It was Jennie Finch. Just the person she wanted to talk to.

"Hi, Jennie. This is Lissa Clearmont in Louisiana."

"What's up?"

"I need your help. That list of names that Max sent you. The five Russian ones? Have you found anything on them?"

"Not yet. Since we talked, I've been doing the paperwork to request satellite overview of your location. I'll look into Petrov later this evening, assuming no new crises develop."

"Can you get me a picture of him when he was in his early to mid-twenties?"

"I expect I could with a bit of digging. Why?"

"I saw a…picture…of the man Max is hunting when he was young. If I could see a photo of Petrov at that age, I'll be able to tell Max if he's chasing down the right target."

"Will do. I'm sure there's a driver's license picture or yearbook photo of the guy lying around somewhere."

"He's got a brother, Yuri Petrov. Make sure you get a picture of the correct Petrov. I gather Markus is extremely secretive and may be trying to hide behind his brother's identity."

Jennie chuckled. "Good to know. The more secretive they are, the more I enjoy exposing them."

"I think I like you, Jennie Finch."

"Keep your head down and don't worry. The Misfits are as good as they get."

"The Misfits?"

"FITS. Females in the SEALs. It's a classified program to train women SEALs. That's the group you're hanging out with. They call themselves the Misfits as a play on that acronym. All three women operators with you are pretty much done with their training and are full-fledged SEALs. Commander Perriman's getting ready to send the whole team, men and women, out in the field any day. So you're in good hands." The analyst added, "I'll be in touch as soon as I find your picture."

Lissa disconnected the call. And now the waiting began.

"Incoming," a voice said urgently over the microphone in Max's ear. He lurched to full consciousness in the porch swing he'd been dozing in.

Well, that hadn't taken long. The mob's hit squad was already here? A scant twelve hours after Bastien had dropped the bait. The NOPD must be more deeply infiltrated than anyone had guessed. Either that, or the mob had intentionally placed one of their own close to Bastien as soon as Max had reached out to the former SEAL.

Chagrin rolled through Max, along with a stern reminder to himself not to underestimate the Bratva. Much of its senior leadership was former KGB and FSB agents, and they were as highly trained as any espionage operators on earth.

Jennie spoke again. "I only have spotty coverage because cloud cover's rolling in fast. But two high-speed boats are approximately three miles from your position and headed your way."

Ashe replied, "ETA?"

"They were moving at a high rate of speed but appear to have cut engines. They appear to be doing recon of the area. Sorry I can't see more."

"No sweat. Thanks for the heads-up."

The radios went silent. Nothing had substantially changed. They still didn't know when or from what direction the attack would come. All that had changed was the tension level in and around the house. Everyone was on high alert now.

Lissa would probably be freaking out. He checked an urge to go to her and comfort her. But then her earlier words floated through his head. Was he wrong to hold himself apart from her? Were his feelings and secrets really so special that she didn't deserve to know them?

Problem was, everything she said went directly against a lifetime's worth of training, first from his father and then from the CIA.

He headed inside in search of her. After all, it made operational sense to keep the bait from panicking. He was surprised to find her awake in the front parlor, sitting in the dark. "You okay?" he asked.

"Actually, yes. I've been listening to the house. It has some good stories to tell."

"I think Ford owns this place. He could probably tell you the history of it."

"Ford, who's in love with Trina?"

"The same."

"They're a cute couple."

He snorted. "I doubt they'd appreciate being called cute."

"Still."

Silence fell between them.

"What's the news?" she asked.

"Two boats full of bad guys are in the area but not moving in. They're probably trying to do some recon on the island before they blast ashore. They know you, me and Bastien are here, but they'll want to know we're here alone."

"Will they back off when they see a SEAL team?" she asked hopefully.

"Nobody on earth hides better than the SEALs. And remember, we want the Bratya's boys to come ashore."

"Speak for yourself," she muttered.

"The mob won't leave us alone until they're more afraid of what'll happen to them if they don't stop."

"Personally, I like the idea of identifying the leader and arresting him."

He paced a lap around the spacious room before replying, "An arrest won't stop the mob. If you cut off the head, another man steps into place. We have to scare the hell out of the entire organization. Make them unwilling to tangle with you and me ever again."

"Your cover will be blown."

He paused in front of the sofa she huddled on. "Sweetheart, it's already blown. I was done as soon as Bastien let the mob know I ran with you rather than turn you over to them. I'll never find out who killed my mother."

"What if the leader of the gang is the one who killed her? If we get him, we get justice for your mom."

That sent him pacing again. It was several minutes before he stopped circling the room to stare at her hard, wishing there were more than faint starlight to see her by. Her words had a ring of truth to them. "Dammit, now you've got me listening to gut feelings," he complained.

"You told me people in your line of work learn to trust their instincts. What's wrong with that?"

"We listen to them to know when someone is following us or lurking around a corner. That's a far cry from listening to intuitions that someone did something evil twenty years ago."

"How is it different?" she asked reasonably. "One is a small act of intuition, and one is a larger act of intuition. They're the same act, though."

He had no answer for that. His father had sworn by listening to his gut. Hell, the SEALs ringing the house swore by it. Were they all doing what Lissa did to a smaller degree?

"How soon will the bad guys come for me?" she asked.

He was relieved to hear her sound relatively calm when asking that question. "No telling. We're losing satellite coverage as the front moves in. It's going to boil down to old-fashioned eyeballing the approaches to know when they make their move."

"I'm scared."

"That's a sensible way to be feeling. Don't fight it. Just let it pass through you, and then let go of it."

"Easy for you to say," she grumbled.

He sat down beside her, too tense to do more than perch on the edge of the sofa. "Take comfort in knowing I'm not scared and neither are any of our friends outside. They live for this kind of stuff."

"You're all crazy. I'm the only sane one here."

That made him laugh. "Truer words were never spoken."

She asked, "What happens when this is all over? Assuming this goes well."

For just an instant, he let down his wall of control. "Once you're safe—" He broke off the thought, unwilling to voice it. He could hardly bear to think of it. Once she was safe, he had to get her as far away from the mob as he could, and then he had to stay away from her forever. For her safety.

"Oh, no you don't!" she declared forcefully. "You're not going anywhere without me!"

Damn her uncanny ability to read his thoughts! "Lissa. It's for the best. Until the entire Bratya organization is dismantled, you won't be safe."

"You'll get the bastard eventually," she declared. "But with me at your side and not halfway across the country."

"I have to know you're safe before I can continue my operation."

"I'm safer with you."

He wasn't going to have this argument again. "I'm going to go check on the others. They'll want to move you to the hiding place as soon as they spot our visitors arriving."

* * *

Lissa watched Max's shadow sadly as he retreated from the room. So much pain in him. If only he would let her help him bear the burden. He didn't need to be so alone. She knew what it was like to live in utter isolation from her fellow man, and it hurt at a soul-deep level.

Perhaps a half hour passed. The air outside was heavy with unshed rain, and flashes of lightning were indistinct in the sky, not quite seen or heard. The wait was oppressive, and she grew too restless to sit still anymore. She paced the long central hallway of the house until it became too confining, and then she went out onto the porch to do laps around the sprawling house.

Max arrived on the front steps as she completed her second circuit. "Trina said you looked antsy and sent me in to check on you."

"Any idea when the bad guys are going to get here?"

"You tell me." He made the comment flippantly, but a note of serious inquiry underscored it.

She frowned. "Do you happen to have anything that belonged to one of the men coming for me?"

"No. Sorry."

"Can you describe them to me in detail?"

"Sure."

She sat down on the porch swing and he sat on the top porch step, leaning back against the railing. A frisson of disappointment that he didn't sit with her coursed through her.

"I can't touch you right now. It'll distract me too much, and I need to keep my head in the game," he commented ruefully.

Huh. Did he realize he'd just picked up on her thought? She listened as he described the men who would be coming for her—their training, the types of weapons and equipment they would likely be carrying. She closed her eyes and let his words paint a picture in her mind. Gradually, her would-be killers took shape. She didn't see faces or details, but their intense, malevolent energy rippled across her skin. They were still at the moment. All concentrating on something together. Maybe a map or a photograph.

But as she felt them more clearly, she felt them split up. She murmured, "They've broken into four groups of two men each."

Max swore quietly. "That was what we were afraid of. Too many points of attack to defend them all." He relayed her impression over his radio and then listened for a moment. "Roger that," he replied.

"They want me to mike you up and get you in your body armor. This situation could get very dynamic very fast."

"Meaning the bullets will start flying soon?"

"Something like that." He hustled her inside and into a black vest. The thing must weigh close to twenty pounds.

"I thought Kevlar was lighter than this," she said.

"It is. The ceramic chest plate is what makes it heavy." He knocked on her vest with his knuckles and hit something hard.

She stood patiently while he strapped a choker around her throat. "This is a voice-activated microphone," he explained. "Once this switch here is flipped, just talk or whisper and the microphone will pick up and automatically transmit everything you say."

"That could be dangerous," she quipped.

Max smiled down at her and fitted a rubber-sheathed

earbud into her ear. "You'll be able to hear everything the team says on this. Follow any directions you hear quickly and without question. This will be a fluid situation, and the SEALs may need to adapt very fast."

"Is that fancy talk for this is going to be a tough fight to win?"

"Just do what they tell you to. For the most part, they'll need you to stay out of sight and keep your head down. The SEALs will do the rest. They should be able to pick off most of the bad guys before anyone knows what hit them."

A voice said abruptly in her earpiece, "I have movement twelve hundred yards out. Get Lissa to the foxhole now."

"Roger," Max replied. "Leaving the house now." He took her by the arm and hustled her down the front steps toward a thicket at the far end of the front yard. Some sort of hiding place had been prepared for her in the bushes on the assumption that the hit squad would target the house as the obvious place to protect Lissa.

They reached the heavy wall of undergrowth and he carefully lifted a mass of brambles aside. "You'll have to crawl."

She thanked Max's sister silently for the virtual bath in bug spray Hank had given her earlier. Now the leather work gloves Max had made her don made sense, too. She crawled on her hands and knees without any serious injury to a shallow depression in the ground. It was lined with green leaves and reasonably comfortable.

Max stretched out beside her in the foxhole.

"Now what?" she whispered.

"Now we wait for the fireworks to begin."

She gathered from the chatter of the SEAL team that

they were in positions all around the island. The plan was to converge on the bad guys wherever they ultimately came ashore. There was a fair bit of discussion of how to control fields of fire if Lissa's prediction of four separate landing teams came to pass.

Most of the technical language of known and unknown corridors and pie wedge angles made no sense to her, but Max seemed to approve of whatever he was hearing. The chatter wound down, and her defenders settled into waiting silence once more.

Another ten minutes or so passed. Finally she asked Max, "How come the bad guys haven't landed yet?"

"They're watching the island for any signs of movement to get an idea of what they're walking into. They're not in any hurry."

"Will they use heat-seeking goggles like we have?"

"Most likely." He added in light humor, "But they don't have the cool bodysuits the SEALs have."

"What's so cool about them?"

"They block heat signatures from escaping."

"How?"

"Classified technology."

She did her best to stay calm and alert, ready to react to whatever she was told to do. But then she felt a disturbance in the energies swirling around her. "Max, someone's coming."

"The hit squad is on the move?"

"No. A big boat or something is headed this way. It has a bunch of people on it."

"As in reinforcements?"

"As in an army."

"You hear that, Ashe?" Max asked tersely.

"Yup. Can she pick up a head count or direction of approach?"

The SEAL named Ford interrupted. "I've got movement at 090 degrees. My pair is backing off."

Trina piped up. "Mine, too. The bass boat is backing off. Turning around."

Ashe spoke quickly. "Okay, so the four teams were doing reconnaissance. They'll back off and brief a larger strike force. Max, does it sound logical that they'd come in hot?"

"It's their style," Max replied tersely. "Particularly if they think they have a numerical edge." Which, of course, they did.

She gathered that coming in hot referred to charging in guns blazing, without any attempt at stealth, relying on brute force and overwhelming numbers to win the day.

"We need a direction of approach," Ashe said urgently. "If they have one large vessel, they'll have to come ashore at a single beachhead. We'll have to mass our firepower to hold off the assault."

She was no military expert, but even she knew that this was not good. The SEALs were widely spaced all over the island and it would take time for them to converge to defend against a major attack. In the meantime, whichever SEAL took the brunt of the initial push was going to be in deep trouble.

She turned off her throat mike. "This isn't worth it, Max. Let me surrender to these guys and save all of you."

"Negative," he replied sharply.

She noted that he'd pulled the assault weapon off his shoulder and had it lying ready beside him. The plan hadn't included him participating in the firefight. He was supposed to worry only about protecting Lissa in the unlikely event that an assassin managed to slip past the SEALs. Apparently, that eventuality was looking a lot more likely now.

He reached down to his ankle and passed her a pistol. He asked her quietly, "Ever handle a gun before?"

"No."

"Too bad. Put your thumb in this groove here. Keep your finger off the trigger until you plan to shoot. Prop your arms out in front of you straight, like so." He positioned her body correctly and showed her how to look down the short barrel and sight the weapon. But then he said wryly, "Don't shoot until your target is within a dozen feet, though. Less chance of you missing that way. And whatever you do, don't close your eyes when you shoot. You have to look at your target."

He knew her too well. She could see herself squeezing her eyes shut and firing blindly in panic.

"The gun will jump like crazy in your hands and be loud as hell. Ignore all that and just concentrate on firing your next round. One shot at a time. Got it?"

"Don't tell me any more. I won't remember it."

"Right. Just one more thing." He reached over and flipped a little switch on the side of the heavy pistol. "Safety's off now. Your weapon is live."

She gulped as he switched on her throat mike again.

About a minute later, a wave of violent intent rolled over her, crushing all the air out of her lungs. She whispered urgently, "They're coming."

Chapter 15

How she knew the assault force was making its move, Max didn't know. But neither did he question it.

Ashe announced, "Look sharp, everyone." Which was probably as close to an endorsement of her skill as a SEAL would ever give a psychic.

If only they knew the direction the attack was coming from. This had way too much potential to turn into a bloodbath. Lissa fairly hummed with tension beside him. He took several slow, calming breaths, but violence was close to the surface in him tonight, ready to explode at the slightest movement. No one was hurting her on his watch.

"If only I could see them," she breathed.

She'd said before that violence triggered her visions. He sure as hell was feeling violent right now. Adrenaline roared through his veins, and the hunter within him ached for something to kill. He reached across his weapon to her and laid his palm on her cheek. "Find them, Lissa," he murmured.

Lissa glanced over at him, startled, but then her eyes glazed over with another vision. It took her a few seconds, but then she said, "The dock. They're landing at the dock so they can run down it and come ashore fast."

"Got that, Ashe?" Max bit out.

"Roger."

He waited for the team leader to pull his operators off the north end of the island and send them to the dock in the south, but Ashe was silent.

"She's not wrong, Ashe," Max urged the SEAL.

"You willing to bet your lives on it?" Ashe growled.

He didn't hesitate. "Yes."

"Okay. Go, Ford. Brand and Jackie, you, too." Ashe's voice sounded as though he was doing something strenuous while he gave the orders, like maybe sprinting at a dead run with sixty pounds of gear, gun and ammo.

Max caught a glimpse of a figure running south through the trees. God, they were taking a huge chance. The whole north side of the island was wide-open now, completely undefended. If Lissa was wrong, the hit squad could waltz right up the driveway and mow her down without having to duck a single bullet. Never in his entire life had he felt so naked and vulnerable.

A light hand touched the side of his neck. "It'll be okay, Max. I've seen it."

She might catch glimpses of possible futures, but the hard work still had to be done to make them happen. And this fight was far from over.

A patter that sounded like hail on a glass window made him start. Gunfire. It had begun.

He was impressed at the lack of conversation among the SEALs as they went about their business. What few orders became necessary were spoken in calm tones.

And then he heard a more ominous sound. The distinctive scream of man-portable missile fire. *Holy crap.* The fight had just gotten real. Fast.

Ashe ordered his team to pull back under the withering fire to less exposed positions.

Another barrage of gunfire exploded. Within it, he heard individual loud shots every thirty seconds or so. That would be Ford and Trina, the two snipers, working with their big sniper rigs. He expected that each sharp report of sound announced a kill. He'd seen SEAL snipers at work before, and at the close range they were firing from tonight, neither Ford nor Trina would miss.

"Fall back to Position Charlie," Ashe ordered tersely.

Ashe was starting to sound a wee bit tense. And there was only one more fallback position before the house. He started to seriously contemplate moving Lissa farther north, away from the firefight that could spill onto the lawn just in front of them at any moment.

"Fall back to Delta," Ashe ordered.

Oh, man. It had taken less than a minute for the Russians to flush the SEALs out of Position Charlie.

"Want me to pull back Lissa?" he dared to distract Ashe by asking.

"Yes. Go." Ashe was obviously under enough pressure not to be able to say any more.

Max gestured Lissa to her feet and pointed into the heavy underbrush at their backs. He didn't like having to send her first, but he needed to stay between her and the bulk of the firefight, which meant he would bring up the rear behind her. He mouthed, "Gun up. Be quiet."

She nodded. Her eyes looked twice their normal size. No help for it.

They moved out slowly. The undergrowth was all but impassable, and each step was a struggle. He did his best to pull the brambles and saw grass back into position behind them to slow down their pursuers, and he prayed that it would be enough.

"Fall back to the house," Ashe ordered. "Arm the minefield."

Max swore under his breath. The SEAL team was having to resort to blowing land mines?

He started counting seconds in his head as he and Lissa continued their painfully slow retreat.

Kaboom.

Dammit. Under a minute until the Russians had made it to the backyard. There wasn't a whole hell of a lot of island left behind them to retreat to.

Without warning, Lissa squeaked behind him. Or at least she started to. He whipped around as the sound cut off abruptly enough to send him into full kill mode. A black shadow had Lissa in its grip, hand over her mouth, using her body as a human shield.

He took an aggressive step toward the attacker until the man muttered, "Easy, bro. It's me. Bastien."

He exhaled hard. He'd almost killed the cop.

Bastien mouthed, "Follow me."

The path that Bastien had used to approach them was relatively clear. All too soon, though, the cop halted. Black water yawned before them.

"Now what?" Lissa wailed in a bare whisper.

"Into the water," Bastien answered grimly.

"Oh, God," Lissa breathed.

Personally, he shared the sentiment. But he responded,

"SEALs are most at home in water. We're going into their best hunting ground, baby. It'll be okay."

"But...alligators," she whispered as they waded out into the cold water.

"More afraid of you than you are of them," Bastien replied in a voice so low it would only carry a few feet.

When they were chest deep, Bastien paused to smear something black all over both of their faces. "Camo grease," the former SEAL explained. "Your weapons will still work wet," he added.

They hid behind a fallen tree, and Lissa felt little bits of bark and dirt sticking to her face.

Bastien transmitted over the team frequency, "We're at Location X-Ray. Have fun, boys and girls."

"What does that mean?" she asked him off radio.

"Now that the only moving targets on the island are bad guys, the SEAL team will cut loose." And no sooner had the words left his mouth than a barrage of gunfire exploded in front of them. It was continuous and deafening and sounded like hell on earth. Before long the sounds of men shouting in Russian could be heard. They sounded panicked and disorganized.

Lissa jolted as several men she didn't recognize came into sight along the shore and commenced camouflaging themselves and setting an ambush with big, scary-looking rifles. They looked like the sniper rifles Ford and Trina had been carrying earlier.

Max and Bastien traded wolfish smiles beside her. They let the men get entirely set and still, and then Max and Bastien eased out of the water far enough to brace their weapons on the big log in front of them. A nod between the two men and they opened fire on the unprotected backs of the hidden Russian snipers.

She flinched violently at the noise and speed with which the Russians were killed. Bastien went ashore to check the slumped bodies, presumably for pulses, and then he disappeared into the trees.

The gunfire wound down, and Max cautiously led her toward the shore, as well. They were maybe waist deep when something that felt like a fist grabbed her ankle and yanked her under the water violently.

It was black and cold and she couldn't breathe and the thing that had grabbed her was holding her under. She thrashed around in panic. Her lungs burned and her body screamed for her to breathe. She was going to drown!

Her arm banged into something that felt like the vests the SEALs wore. Shock and comprehension roared through her. This wasn't an alligator. It was a *man*. The bastard must be using scuba gear.

Lights danced before her eyes, and her grip on consciousness was slipping fast. She fumbled at her hip, and her fist closed on the metal grip of the pistol. She yanked it out. Using the fist around her ankle as a guide, she pointed the weapon and pulled the trigger. Bastien said it would work wet. Hopefully it would work submerged.

The gun jerked in her hand and she all but lost her grip on it. She fired again. It was going to be a miracle if she didn't shoot her foot off. She fired a third time, her self-control at refusing to breathe in water all but gone.

The fist abruptly released her ankle. She flailed around a moment more until her foot hit squishy mud. The bottom. She pushed off it hard and burst up to the surface with a mighty gasp.

"Max!" she cried.

He was nowhere in sight. Had there been another assassin lurking under the water who'd gotten him?

A dark-faced man burst up to the surface like she just had, gasping for air. She started to swing her pistol in his direction, but then she caught a glimpse of pale hair. Familiar cheekbones under black greasepaint. Frantic eyes.

She surged forward, impeded by the water.

He did the same, wrapping her tightly in his arms when he finally got to her. "Thank God, Lissa. I thought I'd lost you."

"A man. Grabbed my ankle. Pulled me under." She panted, still trying to catch her breath.

"Let's get you out of the water," They swim-waded ashore and lay down beside the corpses of their would-be killers. Body warmth still emanated from the one pressed against her back.

"Are you sure they're dead?" she whispered to Max.

"Oh, yeah. Bastien would have seen to it if they weren't already dead when he came ashore."

"So many people dead. Why? I'm not worth all this carnage."

"It's not about you. It's about the spy protecting his identity at all costs. He'll throw everyone he's got under the bus to save himself. It's classic spy behavior."

"Then why didn't you just hand me over to the Russians to save yourself?"

He stared down at her for a long moment. "Because I love you."

"You waited until I'm soaking wet, covered in swamp filth and black grease, shivering cold and stinking to high heaven to say that?" she groused. "You couldn't have picked a slightly more romantic moment to have announced it?"

He grinned down at her, equally wet, filthy, shivering and stinky. "There's no time like the present. Besides, if I love you in spite of all that, you know I really mean it."

She rolled on her side and threw her arms around him. "I love you back, you crazy, wonderful man."

"Who's calling whom crazy?" he murmured against her lips. "I thought you were supposed to be the crazy one."

"Which makes you even crazier for loving me."

He kissed her with a reverence that all but made her sob. She broke it off to ask, "Are you sure about this? You know I'm going to figure out all of your secrets."

"I don't have any left. Other than the fact that I'll never be a good enough man to deserve you."

"Oh, Max. You've been good enough for me ever since the night you saved me from that mugger. Everything else you've done for me has been frosting on the cake."

He stared down at her in the darkness. "Are you sure about that?"

"Dead sure."

He smiled a little. "Either a deeply unfortunate or exactly appropriate choice of words."

"I choose the latter. Now stop overthinking this and kiss me."

Chapter 16

It took the SEALs, and the FBI team they called in, most of the night to clear the island, gather bodies and haul away the survivors. Max and Lissa were whisked off the island under a tarp in the bottom of a speedboat and then hidden in a hotel well away from the aftermath of the gun battle.

At about sunrise, Lissa's cell phone rang. Startled, she answered it eagerly. "Jennie, thank God. Maybe you can tell us. Is everyone on the island okay? The FBI won't tell us a thing."

"Any number of Russians on the island are not okay. But all of our friends are fine. A few minor injuries here and there. Nothing to write home about."

Lissa relayed the news to Max, who gave a big sigh of relief. "So what can I do for you, Jennie?" she asked.

"It's what I can do for you. I found a picture of

Markus Petrov. I'm going to send it to you now. Lemme know if he's our guy."

In a second, Lissa's phone dinged to indicate an incoming text. She pulled up the picture and gasped. She put the phone back to her ear. "That's him!"

"Great. Then I'll start digging on him and see what I can uncover."

She and Max took turns in the shower, no doubt to the vast relief of the FBI agents tasked with guarding their stinky persons. They both made written statements about the previous night's events and took naps. And then Max insisted on being allowed to return to the island. Lissa concurred. She owed Bastien and his friends huge thanks for their help.

An hour later, Max helped her climb onto the island's dock, and she stared in shock at the burned-out hull of a big cabin cruiser half sank in the bayou a dozen yards away. The SEALs had done a real number on it. Color her impressed.

She and Max had to step aside as two men wearing FBI jackets carried a body bag past. A dozen body bags lay on the ground along the boardwalk to the house. Max whistled low. "Petrov really wants you silenced in a big way. It looks like he sent his entire cavalry after you."

"Yeah, well, now that we know who he is, I'll be a lot less important to him."

"Assuming Jennie and the gang at SEAL ops can find evidence to link him to crimes and/or espionage."

"They'll get him," Lissa declared confidently.

"Until then, you and I are laying low far, far away from here."

"Mmm. That sounds nice." She tucked her arm in his and they approached the house together.

His sister, Hank, called out as they climbed the back steps. "Hey, it's the lovebirds!"

Max gave her a relieved hug and slapped backs with the men while Lissa hugged the women.

A new athletic, good-looking man came into the kitchen, and Ashe said formally, "Max, Lissa, this is Commander Cole Perriman. He got here a few hours ago."

"Hell of a hornet's nest you two kicked," the commander said. "Well done."

Max laughed. "The congratulations go to your team. They were amazing in the face of overwhelming numbers and force."

Perriman shrugged. "Just another day at the office for my people."

The man actually sounded as if he meant it. *Scary.*

"So, Max. I have a proposition for you. How would you like to train my team of misfits in undercover operations? Anyone who can survive two years inside the Russian mob sure as hell knows what he's doing in undercover work. We'll be relocating the team to a new classified location now that this facility's secrecy is pretty well blown. Lissa can come along. We'll provide protection for her while Markov is investigated and taken down, and you can train my people."

Her heart expanded when Max glanced at her before answering. "What do you think, Lissa?"

"Being anywhere with you sounds pretty close to perfect to me."

Max swept her into his arms in front of everybody and laid a big, sexy kiss on her right there. But as soon as their lips touched, the kitchen and everyone in it disappeared. Instead, they were surrounded by a bunch of children—their grandchildren, she realized in shock. Love, family and laughter filled the space around them. Years of joy stretched out behind and ahead of them in an unbroken chain. Whole. Complete.

They were going to be just fine. Forever.

Max announced wryly, "I saw that."

She jerked away to stare up at him in shock.

"Grandkids? Really?" he grumbled. "Do we have to have so many of them?"

"Oh, yes. Piles of them." She whispered against his mouth, "I love you, Max."

"I love you, too."

* * * * *

HER SECRET SPY by Cindy Dees

If you love Cindy Dees, be sure to pick up her other stories:

UNDERCOVER WITH A SEAL
HIGH-STAKES PLAYBOY
HIGH-STAKES BACHELOR
A BILLIONAIRE'S REDEMPTION

Available now from Harlequin Romantic Suspense!

REQUEST YOUR FREE BOOKS!
2 FREE NOVELS PLUS 2 FREE GIFTS!

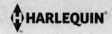

ROMANTIC suspense

Sparked by danger, fueled by passion

YES! Please send me 2 FREE Harlequin® Romantic Suspense novels and my 2 FREE gifts (gifts are worth about $10). After receiving them, if I don't wish to receive any more books, I can return the shipping statement marked "cancel." If I don't cancel, I will receive 4 brand-new novels every month and be billed just $4.74 per book in the U.S. or $5.49 per book in Canada. That's a savings of at least 12% off the cover price! It's quite a bargain! Shipping and handling is just 50¢ per book in the U.S. and 75¢ per book in Canada.* I understand that accepting the 2 free books and gifts places me under no obligation to buy anything. I can always return a shipment and cancel at any time. Even if I never buy another book, the two free books and gifts are mine to keep forever.

240/340 HDN GH3P

Name _____ (PLEASE PRINT) _____

Address _____ Apt. #_____

City _____ State/Prov. _____ Zip/Postal Code _____

Signature (if under 18, a parent or guardian must sign)

Mail to the **Reader Service:**
IN U.S.A.: P.O. Box 1867, Buffalo, NY 14240-1867
IN CANADA: P.O. Box 609, Fort Erie, Ontario L2A 5X3

**Want to try two free books from another line?
Call 1-800-873-8635 or visit www.ReaderService.com.**

* Terms and prices subject to change without notice. Prices do not include applicable taxes. Sales tax applicable in N.Y. Canadian residents will be charged applicable taxes. Offer not valid in Quebec. This offer is limited to one order per household. Not valid for current subscribers to Harlequin Romantic Suspense books. All orders subject to credit approval. Credit or debit balances in a customer's account(s) may be offset by any other outstanding balance owed by or to the customer. Please allow 4 to 6 weeks for delivery. Offer available while quantities last.

Your Privacy—The Reader Service is committed to protecting your privacy. Our Privacy Policy is available online at www.ReaderService.com or upon request from the Reader Service.

We make a portion of our mailing list available to reputable third parties that offer products we believe may interest you. If you prefer that we not exchange your name with third parties, or if you wish to clarify or modify your communication preferences, please visit us at www.ReaderService.com/consumerschoice or write to us at Reader Service Preference Service, P.O. Box 9062, Buffalo, NY 14240-9062. Include your complete name and address.

HRS15

SPECIAL EXCERPT FROM

HARLEQUIN®

ROMANTIC suspense

Rookie cop Annabel Colton is hot on the heels of a serial killer. But when she meets the suspect's brother, sexy cowboy Jesse Willard, he soon becomes her number one person of romantic interest!

Read on for a sneak preview of
COLTON'S TEXAS STAKEOUT,
the latest chapter of the thrilling series
***THE COLTONS OF TEXAS**.*

He could see Annabel wanted to ask him more. She might be a police officer, but she had questions like a detective. "You can't blame yourself for the decisions your mother made. I used to think I must have done something to make Matthew Colton unhappy at home. I tried to connect my actions as a child to his actions as an adult. They aren't related. Whatever you did when you were a boy and however that affects Regina, that's hers to deal with."

He liked what she was saying. Logically, he understood that he couldn't have done anything different to help Regina, but emotionally, it was hard to let go of the past. "Thanks for saying that." It unburdened his soul, though not entirely. Nothing could fully absolve him of the guilt he carried.

"Sure." She tossed the bread she'd been using in the trash and then walked slowly to the front door, grabbing her coffee-stained pants. She spun on her toes to face him. "I still owe you a cup of coffee."

He had long forgiven her, but he wouldn't turn down the opportunity to see her again. "Maybe next time I'm in town, I'll stop by the precinct and see if you're available."

"I'd like that."

He crossed to the door. He had manners; he would open it for her. Annabel was living up to that first impression he'd had of her. She was gorgeous, obviously, but she was thoughtful and classy and smart. How was this woman not already taken? Maybe she was as messed up as he was in relationships. Devastating childhoods left their mark, and that mark was often ugly and deep.

Their hands brushed, and electricity snapped between them. The air around them heated and sparked. She backed up against the door.

Her palms were flat against the door and her mouth was tipped up invitingly. He set his hand on her chin, lightly, testing her reaction. He was aching to kiss her, and his palms itched to touch her. Did she want this, too?

Don't miss
COLTON'S TEXAS STAKEOUT by C.J. Miller,
available April 2016 wherever
Harlequin® Romantic Suspense
books and ebooks are sold.

www.Harlequin.com

THE WORLD IS BETTER WITH

Romance

Harlequin has everything from contemporary, passionate and heartwarming to suspenseful and inspirational stories.

Whatever your mood, we have a romance just for you!

Connect with us to find your next great read, special offers and more.

f /HarlequinBooks

🐦 @HarlequinBooks

www.HarlequinBlog.com

www.Harlequin.com/Newsletters

◆ HARLEQUIN®

A *Romance* FOR EVERY MOOD™

www.Harlequin.com